AS SWEET AS HONEY

ANNA KLEIN

BONNETPUNK PRESS

ISBN 978-0-473-48507-8

❀ Created with Vellum

ACKNOWLEDGMENTS

The very first version of this book was written for NaNoWriMo 2015, and I'd like to thank everyone that supported me during that time, especially my writing group that endured long beyond the end of that frantic November: Alina, Amy, Che, Michelle, Natalie and Sierra. You all kept me going! Thank you to my beta readers, and to Ellen and Emma B your thoughtful feedback. Thank you Moo for the last minute advice; Vanya for your expertise in the world of aerial silks; and Prema for inspiring me and boosting me.

Thank you to team at Hot Tree Editing for their fantastic work in seeing this project through the editing and proofreading stages!

A special thank you to the SPA Girls: Shar, Trudy, Wendy and Cheryl, for their fantastic workshop and ongoing encouragement and support. It was instrumental in getting this book out there.

To my Mum, Dad, Judit, Nick

and always, to Tigger

1
___

The café had the longest line Chelsea Lambert had ever seen. She stared at it in disbelief. It was hard to believe the universe wasn't conspiring to get her fired. It had been the worst morning of Chelsea's life. Her alarm had not gone off, she had spilled breakfast down her skirt, ripped her hose, and then locked her handbag in her house, necessitating jimmying open a loose window and shimmying through to retrieve it. She still had hope that she would catch the next bus and avoid a cataclysmic confrontation with her boss, Helen the Patron Saint of Corporate Perfection. Shifting her weight from foot to foot, the nagging voice of adulthood whispered in her ear. *Leave the coffee, Chelsea. Just go wait at the bus stop. You can't risk this.* As much as she hated her job, she needed it.

Dammit, it wasn't fair. What was the point of living if she couldn't have a measly coffee on the worst morning of her life?

Chelsea looked around the café to distract herself from her worries, her eyes settling on a tall, attractive man in a crisp dark suit, reading the newspaper by the standing counter and checking a sleek silver phone occasionally. His profile was striking with a narrow, angular jaw and pronounced cheekbones. His hair was a pale blond and severely cut. As he turned to collect his coffee order, Chelsea saw he was wearing a cerulean shirt, and she couldn't help but smile. It was rare to see a man of obvious means eschew the fashion for bland shirts.

Chelsea checked the time on her phone as the line shuffled forwards another inch. It was now ten minutes until her bus was expected to arrive. There was almost no chance of making it to the front of the line, let alone being served her coffee. The staff looked run off their feet, and she really couldn't risk missing this bus. Shifting her weight impatiently in the queue, she glanced towards the standing counter again. The attractive man in the suit had gone, along with his coffee, but his expensive silver mobile phone remained peeking out from under the newspaper he had been reading.

Damn, he's going to miss that. She glanced at the unmoving queue and decided to abandon her hope of coffee in favour of a good deed.

Stepping out of the queue, she grabbed the phone from under the newspaper, and after making sure the man was definitely not in the store, she approached the counter.

"Excuse me," Chelsea tried. The harassed-looking barista didn't even look up.

"Get in line, ma'am," she said, before the noise of the coffee bean grinder drowned out all further possibility of conversation.

Fine, I'll just return the phone to the attractive suit myself. Phone in hand, she bounded out the door, slowing down when she felt her ankle wobble unsteadily in the bright green heels. *Bad choice of shoes this morning, like so many other things.*

Outside the café, she scanned the street. Auckland's central city fringe neighbourhood was busy on a weekday morning. Chelsea searched for the attractive suit in a crowd of mothers walking children to school, university students shambling in packs, and dozens of other men in suits. Her heart pounded as she hurried towards her bus stop, still keeping an eye on the crowd for the mystery man.

I really thought this would be easier. How far could he have gone? He was just here.

She checked the time. Five minutes until her bus.

There. Across the road. She looked at the time again, then the distance, then the traffic, deciding that she had no time to try and reach the crossing. *Now or never.* She stepped out onto the road, ducking between cars that dribbled along at the rush-hour crawl and reaching the other side of the road with nary a scratch nor a wobble of her ankle.

"Excuse me! Excuse me, mister!" she shouted, as the attractive suit reached for the door of the car. He paused, throwing a half-interested glance at the street. "Over here! Hey! You, the tailored suit with the coffee! Yes, you!" she shouted as he finally saw her barrelling towards him, confusion reigning on his face until he saw the phone she was brandishing.

"You left it behind in the café," she said as she finally reached him, puffing. Half the street had paused to stare at her. Chelsea tried to appear nonchalant.

"Thanks," the suit said, taking the proffered phone and looking at her intently. He spoke with an American accent. "Thank you very much. I don't know what I'd do without this." He slipped it into the interior pocket of his jacket.

"I know, right. I'd go crazy without my phone. I swear I

keep half my brain in there," Chelsea said with a slightly too loud laugh that was brought on by adrenaline and embarrassment and the attractive man in front of her. "I'm only kidding. It's more like most of my brain."

The attractive suit looked on in confusion, a small line creasing between his brows. Chelsea felt herself colour in embarrassment. Maybe this was a bad idea.

Ya think?

"Is there anything I can—" the suit began, but Chelsea cut him off.

"No, no, don't even worry. Happy to help. I have to dash. I have a bus to catch!" She shook the hand that he had started to offer, then turned to cross the road again. She paused, waiting for a safe moment, only to see her bus pulled in at the stop.

Panic flooded her, overriding any sense, and seeing a gap, she leapt forwards. This time she was not so lucky. A green light ahead suddenly freed up the traffic, and it was moving fast, impatient morning drivers offering no quarter.

"Please, wait!" Chelsea shouted, running as fast as she could in her bright green heels, waving her arm in a desperate bid to catch the attention of the bus driver. She was caught between lanes of traffic.

You are the queen of bad decisions, Chels, her inner voice chided.

"Wait!" she shouted again, to no avail. The bus was closing its doors. She plunged back into traffic again, lungs burning. Her left ankle wobbled as the heel hit a dip in the ground. She gritted her teeth and willed it to hold, pushing herself faster towards the bus.

Around her, horns blared. Then her ankle wobbled again. She heard a sickening crack as her ankle went out from under her, and the next thing Chelsea knew, she was looking up at the sky, pain blossoming through her.

2

———

"Good God, are you all right?" The attractive suit appeared above her. "Can you sit up?"

The bus! Chelsea suddenly sat bolt upright on the pavement where she'd landed, just in time to see her bus turn the corner down the road, taking with it any hope of getting to work on time. She let out a strangled, anguished wail.

The attractive suit paled. "I'm going to call an ambulance. What's the emergency number here? Is it 911?"

"Don't bother. It's not that. It's..."

He paused his dialling, looking intently at her as though he didn't quite believe she was as uninjured as she claimed. Chelsea's heart pounded wildly from multiple adrenaline surges, fear, pain, and clawing despair.

"I'm going to be late, and I'm going to be fired, and I'm going to become homeless and have to sleep under a bridge, or worse, go back to my aunt," she found herself blurting out, her voice quivering, and her vision blurry from tears. She wished the earth would swallow her up whole so she wouldn't have to deal with the embarrassing fact that she was sitting on the pavement on a busy Wednesday morning, crying like an upset toddler. The worst was still to come. She still had to get to the office and face Helen.

"I'm sure it won't come to all that," the attractive suit said, crouching down beside her.

"You don't understand." Oh, if only she'd double-checked her alarm. If only she'd worn sensible shoes. If she hadn't locked her handbag inside. Hadn't gone for coffee. Hadn't returned the suit's phone. She felt the awful crushing knowledge that she had no one to blame but herself.

Definitely the queen of bad decisions.

"I hear that a lot, and while I'm sure you're right, I'm also sure we can fix this," the suit said. His voice was calm and unperturbed, and something about his unshakeable composure sank into Chelsea. She looked at him hopefully. "Why don't I drive you to work. It's the least I can do to repay you for returning my phone to me."

"You don't know where I'm going. I work across town, in Botany. It'll take at least half an hour to get there."

"I'm heading that way myself. Please let me help. It's only fair." He stood up and offered Chelsea a hand, a gold-looking watch sliding down his wrist.

Chelsea finally glanced down and was enormously relieved to see her ankle in one piece and that it was the heel of her shoe that had broken in her sprint. She looked up at him; his expression was earnest, calm, and slightly impatient all at once. His eyes were a striking blue, brought out by the brilliant hue of his unusually colourful shirt. Chelsea guessed him for maybe his late thirties.

She relented. "All right. Thank you," she said as he helped her back across the road to his waiting car. "It'd be just my luck to get kidnapped and murdered. Though with the luck I'm having, I shouldn't be surprised."

He looked up from opening the car door, clearly startled. "Why on earth would you be kidnapped and murdered?"

"Oh." Chelsea faltered, wishing desperately that she didn't say every thought that went through her head. The attractive suit was looking at her with mild concern. "You know, bad morning. Missed my bus. Nearly broke my neck. Nearly run over. Didn't get a coffee. Getting into a car with a strange man seems like tempting fate."

His expression relaxed, and the corners of his mouth crinkled slightly in the hint of a smile.

"I suppose I understand the concern, but you don't need to worry," he assured her, opening the rear passenger door for her. "Of course, that's just what a murderer would say," he added after Chelsea had climbed in.

She laughed in surprise and sank into the leather seat, noting the car was just as expensive as everything else about the man. Intently checking her ankle for damage, she didn't notice until the car started that he had slid into the rear passenger seat beside her from the roadside door. Her confusion must have shown clearly in her face, as he gestured towards the barrier between the front and back seats.

"Lance will be driving us," he explained.

Chelsea smiled weakly, but in her mind, she was reeling with astonishment. How rich was this guy? Maybe that wasn't a gold-looking watch on his wrist. *I should have just left his phone where it was. He can afford to replace it, but I can't afford to lose my job.*

They sat in silence for a few minutes, Chelsea acutely aware of the fresh, masculine scent of his cologne, an all-pervasive scent in the confines of the car.

"Thanks for giving me a lift," Chelsea said, breaking the

silence. "I'm probably still fired, but I appreciate you helping me out. I'm sorry for the murderer comments."

The attractive suit waved his hand, a gesture of effortlessness. "*De nada*," he said. "Tell me. Why is it you're so sure you're going to be fired?"

Chelsea paused rubbing her sore ankle and sighed. It was tempting to unload, but she knew she had a problem with oversharing, and more than once she had regretted shooting her mouth off. Then she shrugged. He *had* asked.

"I work as a receptionist at Honey. It's one of those websites that calls itself a dating website, but it's just for older men with stacks of cash to pick up young, stupid women. Well, maybe not stupid," she amended. "They know what the score is. They're in the market for a sugar daddy. They're the sort of girls who eat nothing but a few leaves of lettuce and spend their lives vaporising body hair with lasers. All so they can be more appealing to these greying wallets, you know what I mean? Sometimes I feel like I got hired because all their previous receptionists used the job to pick up rich men when they came in for consultations on their profiles. No chance of me doing that, not with how I look, so they hired me."

The attractive suit was staring at her, expression unreadable, one eyebrow slightly raised. "I see. And why is it that you work there, since the entire enterprise is nothing short of odious to you?"

"I'm an artist," Chelsea explained. "A sculptor. I make all sort of art—big, colourful, tactile art. I need materials, time, and a place to live. You know. Helps me avoid some family problems too." She looked down at her broken shoe. *Come on, Chels, no one needs to hear about your family angst. Back it up.* "Anyway, as a receptionist, I get to sit down all day, and the hours are fixed. Money's better too, by a long way. I just have to hang up my morals and good taste at the door."

He inclined his head. "Something tells me you haven't been able to do that," he said, the faintest shadow of a smile, the first she had seen from him, tugging the corner of his lips.

"Not so much," Chelsea said, slumping into the plush leather seat and looking out the window. "It's my own fault. I don't have anyone else to blame. I should just shut up, smile, and do my job. But I don't."

"I can only imagine what havoc you can wreak. Tell me no one was fool enough to give you the admin passwords to the dating website," the attractive suit said. The amusement in his eyes encouraged Chelsea. He seemed to be enjoying her tale.

"No, nothing like that. But I can never dress quite right. They all wear black and white and look so posh I just want to puke. I say silly things and make jokes, and I'm really bad at hiding what I think. People say I have a very animated face."

"I must invite you to one of my poker nights, then," the suit said dryly.

"So, on account of my generally insubordinate demeanour and inability to kiss up to the clients, I'm on my last warning," Chelsea carried on. "And today's a big day. A really important, lecherous moneybag is visiting today. All the other websites in the business want him, but he's looking at ours. All the girls are busy shaving their everything in preparation, and I'm honestly surprised my boss didn't just replace me with a supermodel temp for the day. Maybe she's expecting me to fail. One more toe or comment out of line, and I'm fired. And everything went wrong today.

I look like a wreck, and I won't be there to fawn over Moneybags when he sleazes in. It's a disaster."

"I can see why you don't fit in," the suit said. "I don't think you should let it bother you. I'm sure you're the most interesting person there."

"Yeah, well, too interesting. And about to become the most interesting person not there." Chelsea felt like crying again. While the suit's humour was welcome, all she could think of was her dire situation if her job was gone. She kicked herself internally, repeatedly and hard. "I'm sorry," she said, blinking back tears. "I shouldn't have babbled on like that. This is one of those things I'm told not to do."

He waved his hand, the same effortless gesture, as if he were completely unperturbed. Chelsea felt a pang of jealousy. How nice it must be to be able to hand wave everything.

"Your company is not an imposition," he said, "no matter what your bosses tell you."

"Easy to say. I'll bet you've never been out of place. You're the sort of person who sets the tone, not breaks it."

There was a long moment of silence.

"I suppose that's fair. I haven't been out of place for some time, but I'll wager there isn't a person on this planet who is a complete stranger to the feeling. Usually I don't encounter it as much of a problem," he acquiesced with another understated incline of his head, a quiet amusement that suffused his eyes, and the faint tilt of his lips. "But you'd be surprised the occasions on which I can be made to feel out of place."

"I'm Chelsea, by the way. Chelsea Lambert," she said, sticking her hand out.

"Very formal," he commented as he reached out to shake her hand. The familiar tingle of a blush spread across

Chelsea's cheeks as she realised again how attractive the suit was. She glanced out the window.

"Oh God," she said, sitting bolt upright and dropping the suit's hand. "That's my building. I have to go." She grabbed her lime green shoes in one hand, hoisted her handbag on her shoulder, and fumbled with the door latch.

"Wait—"

"No time!" Chelsea said, her heart pounding furiously, mostly—she was sure—due to the impending confrontation and imminent dismissal. "Thanks for the lift! Really appreciate it!" Taking advantage of the car being stopped at an intersection, she opened the door and tumbled out into the lanes of mostly stopped traffic.

"For God's sake!" she heard him shout from behind her, but the rest was cut off as she slammed the door and wove between the cars, serenaded by a cacophony of horns she felt she really didn't deserve.

I don't have time to fall for rich, attractive strangers. That's exactly the sort of thing I'm against, she told herself as she limped barefoot along the footpath and into the marble-tiled elevator hall of her building. Stepping into an elevator, she took a deep breath. Nothing else for it. The drive with the attractive suit, who never introduced himself, had pleasantly distracted her from reality. Now she had to face the music. Face unemployment and the end of her independence. Face Helen the Immaculate.

3

———

As Chelsea tumbled out of the car, Neil O'Connell could barely move before she was ducking and weaving through passing traffic and vanishing from sight into a building.

Neil slowly lowered himself back into his seat. He felt as though he'd been through a hurricane. A kaleidoscopic, charming hurricane, yet nevertheless leaving him breathless and a little battered.

He'd seen her in the coffee shop; her purple-and-green outfit stood out, as did her blonde hair with vivid pink streaks through it, and the large peacock earrings. She was a flash of bright colour drawing attention with her existence. He hadn't thought he would see her for more than a glance at the café, so when she appeared at his car to return his misplaced cell phone, he had been surprised, yet pleased. Kindness from strangers was not something he expected. He had learned that kindness was in short demand where money was concerned.

There was no way he could walk away from the look of plain devastation upon her face as she sat on the pavement, her ankle blossoming into a livid bruise, and offering her a lift to her destination seemed the easiest way to assuage her distress. He may not be one to expect kindness from strangers, but it was something he tried to practice. If he were completely honest with himself, he was fascinated by her, and any extension of time in her company was welcome.

However, he still wasn't sure whether he regretted their conversation or not, even as Lance parked the car in his allotted visitor space. Her frank assessment of her job and the sorts of people it brought her into contact with, along with her open condemnation of the whole enterprise, had put him on the back foot. It was lucky she needed only the lightest of prompts to speak, and he hadn't had to figure out how to respond to anything she had said. He was amused, yes, but largely at the surrealism of the situation. He still didn't know how he felt, nor how exactly to deal with the awkward conversation that was now unavoidable in his immediate future.

Neil stepped out of the elevator on the eleventh floor and pushed open the glass door emblazoned with the logo of Honey. As he walked into the reception area, he saw Chelsea again—bedraggled, barefoot, her broken shoe clutched in her hand. Her hose had ripped, and her knee was bleeding freely, a lazy trickle of blood making a steady march towards the gold carpet. Her dishevelled hair and the small rips and tears on her outfit from the fall she had suffered on the road were more obvious when compared to the magazine-perfect woman who towered over her.

"...making a mockery of me, after I warned you yesterday. Yet you seem unable to take this seriously enough to make it here in one piece and on time," said the tall, thin woman, all sharp angles and pointed chin. Trendy black clothes hugged her figure. She had the permanently emaciated build of a professional ballerina, or runway model. "Do you think I enjoy having these conversations with you? Your job is not hard, Chelsea. All I asked of you today was to be on time and to look presentable. How can an adult of your age not manage that?"

They hadn't noticed him enter the reception area. Neil saw Chelsea shrink into herself as though she wanted to vanish. Her audacious, irrepressible spirit had disappeared.

The choice hung in the air before him, to save her or to destroy her.

Oh, what the hell. Neil cleared his throat as he strode towards the pair.

"Ms Blake, I presume," he said to the tall, angular woman and extended his hand. Out of the corner of his eye, he saw Chelsea stare at him in confusion. He kept his gaze fixed on Helen Blake, with his best corporate smile.

"Mr O'Connell!" Helen said, moving forwards to meet him. "Welcome, we have been—"

"Expecting me, yes. I am, of course, very sorry I am late. Ms Lambert reached out to me ahead of this morning's meeting. She thought an informal introduction might be worthwhile before our scheduled consultation."

Uncertainty flashed through Helen's eyes, and her gaze darted between Chelsea and Neil. Chelsea's expression was rapidly giving way to dawning comprehension, as evidenced by the sudden and dramatic change in her pallor.

Neil dragged Ms Blake's attention back to himself, adding, "I am now more certain than ever that Honey is the right service for me. Ms Lambert painted an excellent picture of the people, and I feel much more at ease. She is clearly someone who takes excellent initiative. I feel quite badly for the fall she had. She was trying to keep pace with me, and I was rather thoughtlessly striding ahead."

"Of... of course," Ms Blake stammered after a long pause. "I am... constantly surprised by Chelsea and her... initiative. Yes. How wonderful. Would you... would you just step this way, Mr O'Connell?"

Chelsea was looking at him in horror, her deathly pale pallor changing now to a deep shade of scarlet and her mouth open. Embarrassment rolled off her in waves. She had been right in the car when she had said she had an expressive face. Neil could easily see the war being played out between livid anger and gratitude.

Neil didn't look at her as he walked past her to a well-appointed consultation room, taking with him the formidable figure of Helen Blake, leaving Chelsea Lambert standing alone in the reception area, still wringing her broken shoe in her hands.

***

Greying wallets... lecherous moneybag... I won't be there to fawn over Moneybags when he sleazes in...

What else had she said? Chelsea racked her brain trying to remember which of her enormous collection of tawdry epithets she had applied to the anonymous rich client who had, in fact, turned out to be the audience to her rant.

Helen's wrath was as bad as she had expected when she finally threw herself through reception's doors. Chelsea had forsaken all hope of trying to win a reprieve and was weathering the storm as best she could until it was time to pack her things in a box and limp home. When the attractive suit —Neil O'Connell, successful multi-millionaire CEO of somewhere or other—had walked into the reception, she was first confused.

Then he had addressed Helen.

Chelsea slowly limped into the luxurious bathrooms and dumped her handbag on the counter. She needed to comb her hair, touch up her make-up, and try to make her knees stop bleeding.

She needed the earth to swallow her whole.

She had been obnoxious in the car, about Honey, about their clients, about the work. About him—though how could she have known he was the client? Sure, he couldn't have been more obviously rich if he'd had neon dollar signs swirling around him, but he had been kind and funny and incredibly hot. What was he doing coming to a place like this? He shouldn't have any trouble finding women to date the normal way.

Oh, what do you know, Chelsea? You had one conversation with him. He's probably a total creep. She tugged a brush through her hair, then began to scrub her face with cold water, trying to wash the embarrassment away.

That's right, Chelsea, most total creeps will lie for you to save your job right after you mouth off at them.

There it was: more than the feeling she had been tricked —*why didn't he say anything in the car?*—and the feeling of humiliation—*oh God, why did I say those things?*—tearing her up inside was the unwanted gratitude she felt for the complete fabrication he had invented on the spot to pull her back from the brink of unemployment.

What was she supposed to say when he came out of that meeting? "Thank you"? "I'm sorry"?

Chelsea left the bathroom, her appearance as repaired as it could be with what she had in her handbag. After taping her knee up with supplies from a first aid kit in the kitchen, she returned to her post at reception and mustered every ounce of professionalism she had within her, hoping desperately that the pounding of her heart wasn't audible in the meeting room.

Forty agonising minutes later, she heard the door open and the soft, warm rises and falls of Helen's voice carrying down the corridor towards her. Her fingers faltered in their typing as she heard Neil's voice, and she forced herself to keep her eyes on the screen.

She heard Neil bid farewell to Helen and felt rather than saw his presence. He evidently didn't want to leave without saying something.

Chelsea looked up. His face was solemn and unreadable.

"Thank you, Ms Lambert. It was an exceptional experience to make your acquaintance."

Chelsea could feel Helen hovering nearby, probably craning her already elongated neck towards them. She mustered her chirpiest smile.

"I'm glad I was able to make your introduction to Honey so memorable. Do let us know if there is anything more we can do for you."

"I most assuredly will," he said softly. Chelsea couldn't breathe as embarrassment and something else wrapped around her chest and caught in her throat. He looked as though he wanted to say more. Then, abruptly, he turned and walked through the glass doors. Chelsea didn't dare breathe until she heard the elevator doors close.

"What are you playing at, Chelsea?" Helen demanded, stalking across the floor towards her. "What's this nonsense about reaching out ahead of the meeting? Looking like a wreck?"

"Mr O'Connell explained it all pretty well, I thought. You told me to make more of an effort. That he was important. I thought I would make myself an asset for once." Helen stared at her in silence. The word "seething" sprang to Chelsea's mind. "Did he sign up?" she asked, trying to keep her voice conversational.

"Yes," Helen all but spat. "Our most premium plan too."

"Wonderful," Chelsea said, even as her stomach did an unexpected sick little somersault. She pictured Neil with a half-dozen leggy models hanging off his every word. "That's a great outcome for Honey. Shall I start processing his paperwork? Or would you like to fire me after all?" She held out her hand. Helen continued to stare at her with hostility for a few moments longer before finally slapping the folder into her hand.

"Fine. You can stay. You're still on your last warning, however, so just try to get through the day without... something else." Helen sighed almost tiredly, turned on her heel, and returned to her office. Chelsea jealously noted her heels were taller than hers, and Helen never once wobbled. Corporate perfection.

Chelsea sank into her chair, suddenly shaking all over. Still hired. That was a good thing. New client for Honey. That was a good thing. Attractive suit didn't seem to hold a grudge. That was a good thing.

Yet Chelsea couldn't explain the bitter tendril of disappointment that wormed its way through her as she began typing up Neil O'Connell's profile.

4

____

THE DAY, CHELSEA CONCLUDED, HAD BECOME THE LONGEST day in existence. She sighed as she looked at the time on her computer monitor. There were still twenty long minutes to go until she could pack everything up and hobble home from this train wreck of a day. Her knees were throbbing, and her ankle wasn't exactly feeling peachy either. She wanted a hot shower and hot food. Helen hadn't bothered her again after that morning. Chelsea wasn't sure how long Helen would be able to keep up the silent treatment, or what had spurred it—was she afraid that Mr Moneybags McLiar was keeping tabs on Chelsea?—but she was prepared to take it as a gift.

Chelsea was bored. She had long ago finished typing up and creating Neil O'Connell's online dating profile. She had it proofread and had run it past the designer. As of an hour ago, it was online, ready to be seen by Honey's hordes, with their long legs, blonde hair, and scary-looking salads that wouldn't fill up a goat, much less a whole human being. Chelsea's IT access allowed her to see the interest Neil's profile was generating, and the answer was _considerable._

There was no reason it should bother her. But it did. Chelsea didn't know why she was being so prickly over Neil, or why she had been watching the website statistics, seeing the hits roll in on his page.

"Probably because he was such a jerk this morning," she muttered under her breath in the utterly silent reception. *Yeah, what a jerk*, a little voice in her mind whispered, *tricking Helen into not firing you. What a scoundrel.*

Oh, shut up, Chelsea snapped internally at herself. He had lied to her. He let her carry on in the car, bagging him like that, without the common decency of heading her off at the pass and explaining who he was. Chelsea still burned with embarrassment when she thought about it.

I can't believe I thought he was attractive. I'm sure I must have been imagining things.

To prove to herself how ugly Neil O'Connell was, she loaded up his profile page and was greeted by a professional, smiling photo of the fiend who had saved her job.

When the telephone rang, Chelsea jumped slightly.

"Welcome to Honey. This is Chelsea speaking. How may I help you?" she chirped into the phone, doing her best to sound attractive and seductive.

"Chelsea, it's your aunt."

Chelsea's stomach sank. This day was actually going to be the worst day of her life. It was as if the universe had looked upon her humiliations and thought, *No, not enough.*

"Chelsea, are you there?"

"Yes, Aunt Esme, I am," Chelsea said, dropping her assumed tone. There was no escape from her now.

"You could sound happier to hear from me, but I guess I should be used to this sort of thing from you." Esme's voice was resigned and ever-so-slightly aggrieved. Chelsea tried not to sigh.

"I'm sorry, Aunt Esme, but I'm at work. This isn't a great time for me to talk." Her eyes flicked to the clock. The excuse would hold water for the next seventeen minutes she had left of her workday.

"Yes, I understand anything is better than talking to me, even that job you hate," Esme said with a sigh. "Your mother would be so disappointed if she were here. As it happens, this is a business call. Do you suppose you can spare the time?"

Chelsea's fist clenched briefly around the telephone receiver. No matter how often Esme used her deceased sister as an emotional bargaining chip, it hurt.

"What can Honey help you with?" Chelsea repeated, trying to sound patient and accommodating. "I thought you were very happy with Uncle Luke."

"Try to be sensible, Chelsea," her aunt warned. "I am of course not calling about myself. I am calling about Mikaela. I'm getting very concerned about her. With her looks and personality, it's dreadfully worrying that she can't hang on to a man at her age." Mikaela was two years younger than Chelsea. She did not miss the obvious dig. "And then I thought to myself, who do I know that has access to eligible men of means who are looking for an excellent girlfriend? Why, my dear niece!" She paused triumphantly.

"Mikaela can sign up for Honey's services just like anyone can," Chelsea replied after a few moments of awkward silence. "I don't see how you need me for this." It had been a few years since she'd seen her cousin, but from memory, Mikaela paid the sort of attention to fashion and grooming that it took to do well with Honey's users.

"Yes, she can, but you see, there is a role you can play here. My dear Mikaela is shy and needs help. It would be such a relief if she found someone steady and financially stable. Her father and I are struggling. Truth be told, Vicky's care and medical bills really put a strain on us all those years ago, and we're still recovering. And since you've chosen to go your own way and not join us at the family business, well, we're having to pay extra for staff to cover that, which is *fine*, but you see how life is hard for us with the decisions you've made." Chelsea could visualise Esme shaking her head and looking disappointed. "It would be a real shame to have to sell off Vicky's artwork. I would really hate it to come to that."

Guilt and fear gripped Chelsea's stomach. "Fine, Aunt Esme, fine. I understand. What would you like me to do for Mikaela personally?" She glanced at the clock—seven more minutes.

"Fast-track her into your website thing. Make her the most desirable woman on your lists. It shouldn't be hard, I expect, and then I expect you to do whatever's in your power to make sure she ends up with a decent catch. And after everything we've done for you and Vicky over the years, I don't think Mikaela needs to worry about costs and things, do you?"

"I can't just give—" Chelsea drew in a deep breath and returned to her assumed reception voice as Helen strode past with her bag and coat, heading home for the day. "Absolutely. The registration process can be completed online, or we can schedule an appointment and a photo-shoot here at our premises next week. Which would you prefer, ma'am?" Chelsea finished her speech, flashing a winning smile at Helen.

"Next week is not good enough."

"We're booked until then," Chelsea replied, looking at their calendar. She could feel her aunt's disappointment and passive-aggressive resentment radiating down the phone line. "You could send her to my house Thursday evening, and I'll sort it all out with her."

"You can be so resourceful if you put your mind to it, when you're not fussing around with paint and garbage."

"Artist, Aunt Esme. I'm an artist."

"If you say so," she replied delicately. "Mikaela will be in touch tomorrow. Well, it's been nice to chat. Don't leave it so long next time." She hung up before Chelsea could say a word.

Shaking slightly, Chelsea hung up her phone and buried her face in her hands. Esme had always had some strange ideas, but using Chelsea as a pimp for her daughter was a new level even for her. She sure hoped Mikaela was actually interested in finding a rich husband.

The clock was two minutes shy of five. She turned her computer off and began to lock up the office. It was finally time to go home and hide under a blanket.

Today really was the worst.

5

"No way!" Kim exclaimed.

Chelsea's best friends sat around a small table at a crowded bar, listening to her recount the whole horrible story of the previous day.

"He lied for you, just like that? Even after all those things you said?" Delta said, mouth hanging open. "You have some serious luck, Chels!"

"Are you kidding me? I almost died on the spot when I realised who he was!" Chelsea said, drinking from one of the colourful cocktails sitting on the table. "Why is it the earth never swallows me up when I need it to?"

"Because then who would entertain us so wonderfully," Tony said.

Chelsea swatted at him in mock outrage. "I'm glad I have you three to keep me sane."

"She's drunk already. She's going to start telling us how she loves us." Delta groaned. "So, is that it? Is that the last time you saw the attractive suit? He vanished into your perfect boss's web for catching rich men, never to be seen again?"

"Did she devour him, do you think?" Tony wondered, sucking an olive off a toothpick.

"No, he made it out." Chelsea paused, unsure what to say about their final conversation. "He said it was exceptional to meet me."

"That means he thinks you're crazy," Kim told her. Tony nodded in agreement. Chelsea wanted to agree, but there was something about the way he'd said it that made it feel cheap for her friends to be picking it apart.

"And then I got a call from my aunt who wants me to marry my cousin off to a rich man, or else," Chelsea said, changing the topic and telling them about her conversation with Esme.

"You so need to stop taking calls from your aunt, Chels." Delta shook her head. "You can't keep letting her blackmail you like this."

"I can't do that, Delta. She was there for Mum when she was dying. I owe her a lot." Chelsea looked down at her empty cocktail glass.

"Gratitude is one thing, but being held to ransom over your dead mum is another." Delta didn't even try to hide her disgust.

"She's family, so I can't get rid of her. And I can't afford to buy Mum's art off her yet, and I don't want to lose them, so here I am." Chelsea shrugged. "But hey, maybe if I can find Mikaela that rich husband..."

"It won't be that hard. You say she's pretty. Just throw her in front of some old rich dudes and you're home free," Kim said.

"It's not that easy. Being a sugar baby is an art form in itself," Delta said sagely. "I've been there. Let me know if you need advice."

"Speaking of art!" Tony said, slapping his hand on the

table and springing to his feet. "It's time to get our little star to the opening! Before she runs away in terror."

Chelsea covered her face, hiding behind her hands. "I'm scared!"

"We know, sweets. That's why you called us." Delta patted her arm. "We've seen your pieces, and they look great, and the gallery was pleased to have them. Think of it like this: the more time you spend doing this kind of thing, the greater the chance of making it big and you getting to chuck your notice at Helen and her harem of gold diggers and honey traps. It'd make your aunt sick with jealousy too."

"Onwards to artistic greatness, I guess," Chelsea said. Her friends cheered. "You guys are the best, you know that?"

"We just know a good thing when we see it. When you make it big, don't think we won't be riding on your coat-tails and mooching off you," Tony reassured her. "You're gonna be our sugar mama."

Chelsea allowed herself to be piloted down the road to the waiting car. Tony slid behind the wheel, and once the three women piled in, he slid into traffic.

Chelsea tried to breathe. The noise of her friends talking and the radio in the background melded into an indistinguishable babble of cheerful noise. Soon, even that too faded to nothing in the face of her screaming panic at the thought of the exhibition, the gallery, and people looking at her art. It wasn't the first time Chelsea's work had been in an exhibition, but nothing fuelled her insecurity quite so much as the thought of being judged by others, by outsiders, by people who might hate it.

"Chin up, Chels. You're going to a gallery, not your execution," Kim said, driving her elbow into Chelsea's side. Chelsea smiled weakly. Delta gave her a hug from the other side.

"Don't worry, sweets. It'll be fine once you're there; you know it will."

"You need to learn to trust us. We wouldn't let you exhibit anything that was total crap," Tony chimed in from the driver seat.

They pulled up near the gallery, on a dark, steep street thrown into shadow by towering trees and ferns that created a living archway even in the suburban area. The suburb of Titirangi was half wild, living amidst the bush at the foot of the untameable Waitakere Ranges. Its people were creative, flamboyant, lovers of all things verdant and living. They adored the unusual and the artistic. Which was how Chelsea ended up in one of their offbeat galleries.

Before heading in, they let her check her hair and make-up. Chelsea chose to wear a vibrant fuchsia dress with dashes of silver and a large fascinator in the shape of a flamingo. Her dress was an artful patchwork, sweeping out into a flared skirt, and her jacket was dazzling with sequins. She looked like either a fantastical, whimsical creature, or, as Helen had put it on seeing Chelsea run out the door in the outfit, a ridiculous spectacle. Chelsea eyed the flamingo headpiece in the mirror. She went with fantastical.

The gallery wasn't enormous. The entrance foyer, where they were displaying the photography prints, was already busy with people. The vibe was pleasant; the attendees seemed excited about the art. Chelsea could see it wasn't all just friends and family of the artists exhibiting. Art lovers and art collectors had a certain air about them, and they too were here in force.

"Chelsea, darling!" Marian Vines, the organiser of the exhibition, called out, materialising out of the crowd. She was short, even shorter than Chelsea, and in her sixties. She smiled warmly at Chelsea and hugged her. "I'm so pleased you're here. I've been looking for you!"

"I'm not that late, am I?" Chelsea asked, mystified. It was hardly like these things ran to a strict timetable.

"No, no, I just have fantastic news for you!" Marian looked like she was bubbling with delight. "Chelsea, two of your pieces have already been purchased!"

Tony, Kim, and Delta whooped in delight, clapping Chelsea on the shoulder. Chelsea herself could only stare at the diminutive woman, her mouth gaping inelegantly.

"Are you sure?" she finally managed to ask, as disbelief warred with elation in every cell of her body.

"No mistake! A gentleman was very taken with them and purchased them not long after we opened. I think he's still here if you'd like to be introduced."

"I don't think that's a great idea. I don't need to do that," Chelsea said, panicking at the thought. "I'm really pleased someone liked them enough. Just... wow, I'm floored."

Marian beamed at her. "I knew they were great pieces, Chelsea." With a pat on her arm, she disappeared to greet someone else. Chelsea couldn't believe it. Someone bought her art? Two pieces? Within an hour of the opening? Madness.

"There really must be some mistake," Chelsea said.

"Let's go look, you great dolt," Delta said, grabbing Chelsea's sequin-covered arm and navigating her into one of the interior rooms. The gallery was a beautifully renovated nineteenth-century villa. The rooms had high ceilings and hardwood floors with mouldings along the upper skirting. The elegant bay windows were currently black, reflecting the lights and movements from within the room. They moved through the crowd of art and people, and the forceful push of Chelsea's friends got them into the room with the sculptures and other multimedia pieces. Chelsea saw that two of her pieces were indeed marked as sold.

"Get in there, Chels. We'll take your picture next to it. Look at you, hot stuff!"

"I just can't believe it. Who on earth would buy my stuff?"

"If you'd let Marian introduce you like she wanted, you'd know," Kim said pragmatically. Then, as if summoned, they heard Marian's voice near them.

"Yes, yes, here she is. She's being a bit shy, but I know she won't mind me introducing you. After all, you seem to be a fan." Marian moved through the crowds with ease. Chelsea's body barely had time to fill with panic at the prospect of being introduced to a buyer before she was able to catch a glimpse of the individual in question: a tall man in an immaculate suit.

6

"You," Chelsea said, the single word catching in her throat. Marian didn't seem to notice.

"Chelsea, this is Neil O'Connell. He's recently moved to New Zealand from the United States. Mr O'Connell, this is the wonderful artist."

"I've had the pleasure of Chelsea's acquaintance before," Neil said, his face almost unreadable. "I'm thoroughly delighted with everything I've seen here tonight. The pictures on your website do not do your work justice."

"I'll leave you two to it!" Marian said before catching another passer-by on the arm and steering them away with smiles and conversation. Some small part of Chelsea's brain that wasn't preoccupied with Neil O'Connell thought that if Marian Vines were any better at vanishing from tight confines, she'd have to change her name to Houdini.

"What are you doing here?" Chelsea demanded, returning to the attractive suit-wearing problem before her. "How did you find out about this?"

"Chels, is this the suit?" Kim asked. Her three friends

each took half a step towards her, closing ranks and staring with thinly veiled suspicion at Neil.

"The suit?" Neil inquired, his expression unchanged.

"Yeah, *the suit*. We've heard all about you, buddy," Tony said.

"I'm surprised and pleased I made enough of an impact to be mentioned," Neil said, a hint of amusement on his face.

"What are you doing here?" Chelsea repeated. "I mean it. What are you doing here? You didn't just wander in off the street."

"No, I didn't. I found your website, and it told me about this exhibition. I wanted to come see your work in person."

"Are you trying to buy my affection or something?" Chelsea asked. "Do you think that's how this works? You save my job and throw some money at my art, and then I... what? I owe you my time?"

"No," Neil replied patiently, "the way this works is I throw some money at your art, and I get to take your art home to decorate my house with. Every time I see it, it will make me smile because it is beautiful, and it will remind me of the adventure yesterday morning." Neil shrugged and looked coolly at her. "I was, however, hoping you would be here tonight, because I did want to see you again. I want to..." He stopped talking and glanced at the three friends arrayed behind her.

Chelsea kept her eyes firmly on Neil, a steely look of utter inflexibility. Inside, however, she was wobbling a little. Against her better judgement, it was flattering that he'd come out all this way to look at her art.

Oh, come off it, another voice in her head said. *You're being naive, Chels. He'll think you owe him. That's how these guys all work.*

"Do you think we could talk privately?" Neil asked.

"No. I'm not going off alone with you. Do I look stupid? You can say whatever it is in front of my friends," Chelsea said firmly.

Neil's face was unreadable, his eyes sweeping over the faces of her friends—Chelsea resisted the nearly over-whelming itch to turn around—and his mouth tightened to a thin line.

"I have no intention of committing any atrocities upon your person either in the garden of this gallery or any other place on earth," he said quietly. He looked at her friends again. "Fine. Ms Lambert, I bought five pieces in addition to the two of yours. I did not buy the other two you have on display because I did not like them. One is too dark, and the other I thought was abstract to the point of lunacy. Were I trying entirely to simply buy your interest, I would have bought all four as well as placed several favourable reviews in whatever periodicals I could pay my way into."

"Christ, Chels," Kim muttered in Chelsea's ear. "He's brutal."

"I would like to take you out to dinner, or a movie, or a coffee, or a walk along the beach on a Saturday afternoon, because I find your company makes me smile. And I would like to see if your vitriolic honesty grows more appealing or simply tiresome with extended exposure."

Chelsea blinked. "My *what* honesty."

"He's not wrong, Chels. You do just say whatever pops into your head," Delta said. Chelsea glanced sideways. Her friend was failing to hide a smirk.

"Quit it, Delta. You're meant to be on my side." Chelsea turned back to Neil. "You can't buy me. Your money doesn't get you anything with me. You don't scare me. You don't wow me. I don't owe you anything."

"No, you don't," Neil replied. He looked at her for a long

moment. Chelsea stared back, outwardly defiant, but internally wondering what the hell was going on. "I'm sorry. It seems my presence here has upset you. I have crossed the boundary between romantic spontaneity, and, what's the word? Oh yes, 'creepstalk.'"

He smiled at Chelsea, a small, thin smile, that bare lift of the edges of his lips, as if they were sharing a secret. Chelsea wondered if this small quirk was his real smile, then berated herself for letting him lead her on.

"Well, yes. I'm not interested in creepstalks," she said somewhat lamely. Neil didn't even glance at her assembled companions; his crystal blue gaze fell on Chelsea.

"You have my apologies for overstepping my bounds. You don't need to worry; I won't follow you up again. If you would like to try to meet on your terms, I will leave the getting in touch within your power." He turned and began to move through the crowd.

"How do I?" The question was out of Chelsea's mouth before she realised what she was saying. She blushed down to the roots of her magenta-tinted hair.

Neil paused and half turned. "I'm sure you can find me," he said before continuing to walk out of the gallery.

Chelsea and her friends stood in shocked silence for a few moments before Tony let out a low whistle.

"Whoa, Chels, it looks like you've... piqued his curiosity."

"He's got a whole website of interested women to pursue. He hasn't got any reason to be turning up here and trying to buy me," Chelsea replied, her face flaming. "He looked me up on the internet! Isn't that creepy?"

"Nope," Kim said. "That doesn't really get a creep card. Every one of us would have done the same. It's not stalking if you're looking up someone you just met. That's just research. It's the rules of the internet age."

"You could be in there, Chels, rubbing shoulders, or much more interesting things, with a rich man," Tony said, grinning.

"Mm-hmm, you could see just how attractive Mr Attractive Suit was without it!" Delta teased.

"Come off it," Chelsea said. "You don't get it. I see what the women these guys go for look like. They're taller, skinnier, blonder, and much better at kissing ass than I am. It's a whole... lifestyle, you know? They spend all their time prepping for being a girlfriend to one of these men. I don't have time for that. When would I do my art?" She shook her head. "You'll see. He'll meet the Honey girls, and he'll forget all about me." She ignored the disbelieving looks on her friends' faces. Just because they had fallen for his line didn't mean she had to.

7

Neil pushed through the gallery crowds, the press of people suddenly too intense. It was too hot in the gallery, there was no air, and the crowd was too noisy. Neil moved faster, wanting to escape the room and his terrible mistake.

Outside, the night air was cool and earthy, echoing with soft trills and hoots, a soothing chorus that he had never heard until he set foot into this country. Tall trees and bushy ferns crowded around him, soaring up and making dramatic silhouettes against the dark sky. It felt peaceful and relaxing. He released a deep breath, letting his heart slow in time with the echoing hoots. He glanced back briefly at the gallery, the noise within muffled behind walls of colonial wood and glass. He realised he was quite content out here in the New Zealand night, ensconced in darkness and primordial ferns.

His driver, summoned with a message from his phone, arrived not long after. Neil spent the long drive across Auckland brooding quietly to himself over his actions and questioning himself. Why was he even interested in her?

Arriving home, Neil found his lounge occupied by a

younger man with floppy blond hair and a designer shirt. He was sprawled luxuriously on Neil's expansive white couch, flicking through channels on the TV, even as he had his laptop and his tablet open on the coffee table.

"Eddie. How was your flight?" Neil asked, reaching out to shake his younger brother's hand. Eddie grinned, sprang off the couch, and pulled Neil into an enormous bear hug.

"Great, great. You could fly through the apocalypse in business class. When they roll out Wi-Fi and cellular connection on all flights, I may never actually get off a plane," Eddie replied. "So, New Zealand. This is the tropical island you're hiding out on."

Neil winced. "Yes."

"I thought there'd be more palm trees, more charming markets, more flower necklaces, and less... less bad traffic and provincial city centres." He waved his hand towards the extravagant windows through which the Auckland skyline was in full view. "It's a cute skyline, you have to admit."

"Thank you for the observations, Eddie, but I think you have New Zealand confused with Fiji. It's very nice here. Everyone is very relaxed, and I still have plenty of scope for my business."

"Anyway," Eddie continued as though Neil hadn't spoken, "you're home early. I thought you had a date."

"I was at an art gallery," Neil said. "It wasn't a date."

Eddie squinted at him. "Why on earth didn't you take someone? Chicks love that kind of sophisticated stuff. You don't even have to pretend you know stuff, just ask them for their opinions."

"Unlike you, I don't consider an evening without a woman an evening wasted, Eddie," Neil replied dryly. Shrugging out of his jacket, he cast it across the back of the single-seater before sinking into a chair opposite his brother. He shut his eyes tiredly. "I finally did as you suggested. I signed up for one of those websites. The woman I spoke to seemed confident that I will be attractive to their female users."

"You *did*? And the devil goes ice skating after all. Now look, your love life will be revolutionised. Trust me." Eddie grinned. "You're never going to end up with your heart broken again. These ladies don't care about wanting your heart, or giving you theirs. They care about power, success, and your ability to buy them expensive things and get them into exclusive places."

Neil glanced away. He could feel his younger brother's shrewd gaze on him. "I have doubts about using this site. The consultant felt nothing short of a vampire, eyeing me up for how much money she could suck out of me."

"You're so squeamish and old-fashioned, brother," Eddie said. "You're in New Zealand, you're a free man, and you can't even stomach the idea of going out with a woman because of *her*. Right?" Eddie didn't pause to let Neil answer. "So this is perfect. You're rich and you're mature. It's a straight-up deal. They're not looking for love, marriage, and the baby's carriage. You want company; they want exactly your sort of company. It's clear cut. You're not going to be trapped."

"You forgot money," Neil said.

"What about money?" Eddie asked, exasperated.

"They want money."

"Goddammit, Neil, they're after gifts and a bit of financial lubrication in their social lives. They're not prostitutes."

Eddie sighed when Neil looked at the ceiling. "I'll get us some beers," he said, and left the room.

What his brother said made sense, Neil knew that. It still felt odd to be looking for a relationship, but he was getting lonely. He and Eddie had talked about it before, the nature of the modern world and the women who sought particularly advantageous relationships. Clear roles and set expectations were what Neil craved in all his social contracts. Mysteries and vagaries unsettled him, and, as Eddie kept reminding him, he tended to throw money at problems anyway, so why not throw money at this?

Something inside him twisted.

"I've never seen beers like this before," Eddie announced, walking back into the room.

"They're local beers," Neil told him, sitting up and taking an open bottle. Eddie made a face. "I forgot you like everything to look the same no matter where you are in the world. I think differences are what make things interesting."

"I just like to know what I'm getting."

"We have these conversations, and I have no idea how I got the reputation of being the conservative brother and you being the adventurous brother."

Eddie looked hurt. "I'm not *not* adventurous just because I like to know what to expect with my beer."

They sipped their drinks in silence for a few minutes. Neil never felt a hundred percent comfortable with their designations. Eddie was younger, louder, and seemingly the more reckless of the two. He wore his shirt slightly unbuttoned, and his hair was darker and without the scattering of grey that had afflicted Neil since his midtwenties. Neil knew he always looked older than he was, and because he was quiet, people equated that with a stolidity that he didn't feel he deserved. After all, he was the one here in New Zealand at the bottom of the world. It was only across the ocean from California, but it might as well have been on a different planet.

Eddie liked things the way he'd always done them. He

didn't like risk. He liked things the way he expected them. Neil liked challenge. He liked surprises. He liked homes and art and beers that were unconventional. Dare he say it, he even liked unconventional...

"I did meet a woman," Neil told Eddie after a moment.

Eddie lit up. "Great! Let's see her profile." He made a grabbing motion towards Neil's tablet. "Who is she?"

"She's the receptionist at Honey."

"God*dammit*, Neil. I didn't know you were so lonely you were going to fall for the first woman you saw when you walked through the door."

"It doesn't really matter. I tried asking her out, and she pretty solidly told me to go jump. She thinks I'm some old rich guy who thinks his money can buy women."

"Why the hell would she think that?"

"Probably because she met me using a website for rich old guys who want to buy girlfriends with money," Neil replied dryly. He surrendered the tablet to his brother, who pulled the Honey site up on the big-screen TV.

"Touché. Look, I think this is a good thing. It reminded you how much you don't want to be hurt again. You don't need someone like her. See here, your profile, you've got a dozen messages already. Let's go through them. Let's go look at some profiles and find you some nice women to meet. I'm not messing you around; they're nice women. They'll be so happy for your company."

"This feels sleazy," Neil said as Eddie began to scroll through profiles, commenting. "Like shopping online. For women."

"Don't be such a stick in the mud. This isn't forever. You just need something while you're here, until you feel better and you can come back home."

Neil watched the profiles flick by. He knew his face was

neutral, a polite look of unreadable blankness. Inside, he felt tired and hurt and raw. He regretted what he'd done, pursuing Chelsea like that. How arrogant and entitled he must have seemed!

He was under no illusions. He knew he'd never hear from her again, and if he played his cards right, he'd never even have to set foot in the Honey offices again. He was sorry he'd never get to know her, never get to explain himself, but ultimately, she didn't owe him anything. Not time, not a chance to explain. He knew Eddie would disagree, but then, he and his brother were very different men. At least he had her art to look forward to.

He allowed Eddie to compile a shortlist of women for him before retreating from his own living room. All of the women Eddie had found were attractive, intelligent, and probably more open to his company than Chelsea was. He shut off the device without writing a single message. He made no judgement on the users of the site, the men or the women. But he wasn't ready to join them.

8

WHEN MIKAELA ARRIVED, CHELSEA KNEW SHE WAS RIGHT AND that her cousin fit right in with the Honey girls. She was taller than Chelsea, even more so with fashionable strappy heels and the above-knee skirt that made her legs look longer. She was beautifully tanned and toned, with immaculate make-up and perfect blonde hair. She had given Chelsea a hug when she arrived, so Chelsea surmised she had better social skills than Aunt Esme.

She could not for the life of her fathom why Mikaela needed help getting a boyfriend until they sat down to write the profile, at which point her cousin's complete lack of interest in the enterprise became apparent. Every answer longer than a single word was like pulling teeth.

Halfway through the profile, Chelsea finally became exasperated.

"What's wrong, Mikaela? Your mum said you wanted this."

"Yeah. I promised her I'd give it a go. Mostly, I just wanted to get her off my back. She thinks I'm going to end up an old maid."

"Do you want to stop?"

"No, it's fine," Mikaela said with a long sigh. "Probably an easy way out of the whole dating thing, right? Just keep dating rich guys until one of them wants to marry me, and then I'm done."

Chelsea looked up from the laptop. Mikaela was prowling around her living room, picking up knick-knacks and staring at the colourful prints on the walls.

"What are you doing?" Chelsea asked.

"Is this your whole place?" Mikaela asked, ignoring Chelsea's question. Chelsea felt her cheeks colour. *Guess the apple didn't fall too far from the tree.*

"I have a bedroom and a bathroom too," she said.

"Through there?" Mikaela said, striding over to the door.

"Yes. Don't go in!" Chelsea all but threw the laptop down on the coffee table and went after her. Her bedroom was a riot of colour, and the floor was ankle deep in clothes. Mikaela had waded in and was holding up a pink shirt that looked large next to her rail-like frame.

"Is this yours? Are these all your clothes?"

"Yes, but can you put it down? I'm just... sorting things out. Stop snooping, Mikaela."

Mikaela didn't seem to be listening. She was looking towards the bay window that faced out to an overgrown back yard. "Do you live here by yourself? How much do you pay for a place like this?"

This was beyond humiliating. It reminded her of when they were children and Mikaela had boasted about how much better she had things than Chelsea. How her toys were better. How her house was better. How her mummy was better.

"Yeah, Mikaela, I live alone in a small place. I'm lonely and poor and a failure. You can report that back to Aunt

Esme, all right. Can we please just finish the profile?" Chelsea felt like she was going to cry.

Mikaela looked around the room and then at Chelsea. Seeing the look on her face, Mikaela shrugged and draped the top on the bed.

"I didn't mean it like that." She walked back out of the bedroom, gracefully picking her way across the clothing-strewn floor. Chelsea, face flaming, shut the door behind her. "How much more is there to do on this profile?"

"We're about halfway through."

"I don't have time for this anymore. I have to go. Look, just make it up. Whatever these guys want to hear, write that. I'll just roll with it. You have enough photos?" Chelsea nodded. "If you need anything else, just pull it from my social media. I hereby give you permission, yada yada." Mikaela scooped up her bag from the couch. "And this social mixer is... tomorrow night? Just email me the details. I'll be there."

She checked her phone and winced. "I am so late. Thanks, Chelsea. See you tomorrow." The door rattled as she pulled it shut behind her.

Chelsea let out a long breath. Nobody could make her feel inferior the way Aunt Esme could, but Mikaela was a close second. She went back to the couch and picked up the laptop. Her cousin's semi-completed profile gazed at her. It was tempting to fill it in with things that would make life difficult for Mikaela. She giggled briefly at the thought of some date questioning her on her doctorate in Australian fungi or WWII-era fighter planes, but she pushed the childish urge away. Mikaela might not be so interested, but Aunt Esme was not going to let a little thing like Mikaela being half-hearted stop her from blaming Chelsea for the lack of a millionaire son-in-law.

Involuntarily, Chelsea found herself thinking of Neil the Suit. She wondered if he would come to the Honey social mixer. She didn't know what would be worse—if he did and she had to face him again, or if he didn't and Helen found out it was because she yelled at him in an art gallery.

Come to think of it, he was almost certainly on the list of new clients she'd have to call tomorrow to remind about the event. Something to look forward to during another joyous day at the office.

9

Neil was distracted from his work. His central Auckland office had an unobstructed view of the sparkling Waitemata Harbour with its cerulean seas, complemented nicely by the baby blue of the pristine sky. It had been grey and raining two hours earlier. But, as he was learning from his Auckland staff, that was Auckland. The harbour bridge, an eight-lane bridge that provided the only means of crossing the harbour that bisected the city, shone in the sunlight, glittering as the sun hit the many cars moving across it. The harbour bridge was never still, except at rush hour.

It was those cerulean seas that had captivated his attention. The intensity and brightness of colour brought Chelsea to his mind. It was some combination of the colour, vibrancy, sparkle, and a realness so brutal it seemed almost fake.

He startled when the phone rang. He picked it up without even checking the number, swivelling his chair back to continue looking at the view.

"Neil O'Connell."

"Hi, Neil. It's Chelsea Lambert from Honey." Neil froze slightly. Chelsea had blurted out these words in a tremendous rush. "Hello?"

Neil realised he hadn't spoken. "Yes, I'm here. How may I help you?"

"I'm calling to remind you about our Honey social mixer tonight. It's a fantastic opportunity for the website users to meet each other in an informal setting. There'll be food, music, and excellent drinks in one of the hottest bars in Auckland. Honey would be delighted to have you along." Her voice sounded uncertain, as if she weren't at all sure about the invitation she was extending. Neil stayed silent for a few moments as he thought about it. Eddie would certainly be angry with him if he didn't go. On the other hand, he might see Chelsea, who had made it abundantly clear she did not wish to see him.

"All things considered, I think it might be best if I gave the event a miss, wouldn't you say?" Neil said, turning away from the window.

"It's up to you, Mr O'Connell," Chelsea said hesitantly. "I would really hate it if you didn't come just because of what I said."

"I realise this is a perfunctory call being made because of your job requirements. You would feel intensely uncomfortable if I did attend. And I would not like that. So, thank you, but I shall have to decline." Neil moved to end the call.

"Wait!" Chelsea's voice stayed him. "I wanted to say I'm sorry. Honestly. Sorry for yelling at you at the gallery the other day. I mean, I'm probably sorry."

"Probably sorry?" Neil repeated, managing to keep the amusement out of his voice.

"Yeah. If you're not a creep, then I'm sorry. Which you probably aren't, so I'm more than probably sorry. Dammit," she said. "Please come tonight. It will be a nice night. I won't yell at all. I've made a complete hash of everything, and you've been nothing but kind. Please come along tonight, and I'll get you a drink and you can see that literally everybody else who is associated with this company is a sane, regular human being and not like me at all."

"That's a shame. I find whatever you are most entertaining to be around," Neil said. "Very well. How can I refuse an invitation like that? I will be there tonight."

"Great. Great. It's all in your inbox. As soon as I send it. Right." A moment's pause. "See you tonight."

Neil listened to the soft click as she hung up her office phone. Her awkwardness was plain, but she seemed to genuinely want him at the event. Perhaps her boss had put the hard word on her about his presence, but he imagined that would have invoked her hard-to-disguise ire instead of the sheepish, back-footed conciliatory attempt he'd just experienced.

Why had he agreed to go? Despite Eddie's attempts, he still had no real interest in Honey. He had just wanted to make her sound less anxious.

He wanted to see her again.

Neil turned back to the window. While he was on the phone, some clouds had rolled in from the west, and there was a dark shadow over the harbour, the water dark blue and slightly choppy. He watched as the winds carried it away and restored the clear skies. Mercurial, like Chelsea?

Like him?

"I have to admit, Chelsea, you always do a marvellous job on these functions," Helen said as she looked around the lively bar Chelsea had hired for the occasion. Chelsea glanced up at her, towering nearly a foot over her in a combination of generous genes and killer heels. Helen managed a smile. "But what did we do to earn the honour of your actual presence at the event?"

"I'm trying to be a better employee," Chelsea lied.

Helen gave a doubtful little sniff. "Well, enjoy your handiwork. These evenings are almost always a hit." With that, Helen turned and made for the bar. Chelsea almost followed her, but instead, she squared her shoulders and moved back to her post by the door, where she was greeting guests and giving them gift bags.

The bar Chelsea had chosen for the event was located in the heart of central Auckland, in the extremely hip waterfront promenade that had a few short years ago been nothing but run-down offices and a tangle of graffiti-ridden shipping containers. The urban renewal project had spread across it like some sort of hipster transformation spell. Fashionable eateries and bars had taken the place of detritus, of which this bar was one. The walls were bare brickwork, and the lighting was warm spotlights criss-crossing the large room from exposed beams across the ceiling. Plants hung in partial barrels. The stools were made from old bicycles, and all the other furniture from wooden pallets.

Somewhere on the internet, the entire bar was photographed and tagged as upcycled. Chelsea liked it. It was modern, open, light, and just what the lonely hearts liked. There was nothing sleazy or seedy about the place. And the drinks were superb.

She normally didn't attend these monthly mixers, even though it was her job to organise them, but tonight she wanted to be here to make sure she helped Mikaela find someone. She was mortified at the prospect of seeing Neil again, but the thought of Aunt Esme's relentless guilt trips about her mother if she didn't help Mikaela was even worse. In a tea-length, sweetheart-neckline dress that was so crimson it hurt, Chelsea stood next to the door with fake cheer.

The guests arrived in groups; apparently nobody was confident enough to come on their own. Twos and threes of European women with lightened hair and tanned skin, dresses fitting their bodies, and make-up just enough to look expensive. Asian women with sleek black hair stood together, heads bent together, taking photos of their groups with glittering gold smartphones. There were Indian women, Pacific Island women, and others. The whole cultural spectrum of Auckland was represented in immaculately presented women angling for a rich boyfriend.

The men arrived in smaller groups, more pairs, a few friends out for a night. They were older than the women, and the air of casual wealth hung off them like a cologne. They all blurred together, the beautiful women and dapper men, and Chelsea didn't even realise she was handing Neil his gift bag until he looked her directly in the eyes and said, "Hello, Chelsea." She almost dropped the bag.

"Nice to see you!" she said with a professional smile plastered to her face as she all but shoved the bag at him. Her hand brushed his, and the room suddenly got very warm. "Everyone gets a free drink. Have a wonderful night!" She kept smiling. She felt like an idiot. He was staring at her.

"It's nice to see you again too. I'll try not to do anything tonight that will cause you to shout at me," he said at last and moved into the crowded bar.

Chelsea fought the urge to make a rude gesture at his

back. *Why does he make me feel three feet tall and gawky? I hate him. I hate him.*

The trickle of people arriving slowed. Chelsea was about to start worrying about Mikaela when she walked in alone, looking gorgeous in a little black dress.

"I thought you weren't going to make it," Chelsea said.

Her cousin shrugged. "Like Mum was going to give me a break if I didn't come here." Her eyes wandered over the sea of people, lingering over a large group of women laughing together and comparing cocktails. If Chelsea didn't know better, she'd have said Mikaela looked afraid.

"Don't worry about them," Chelsea told her, following her gaze. "You're as good as any of the competition."

Mikaela laughed at this, and whatever painful thought had gripped her was dispelled.

"You'll warn me if any of the men are real creeps, right?" she asked.

Chelsea nodded. "Cross my heart and hope to die."

Mikaela gripped her hand briefly. "Thanks," she said, then headed to the bar.

Chelsea watched her and wondered how much of this was Mikaela's idea and how much was Aunt Esme's. Maybe she shouldn't be pushing Mikaela. She looked over to where her cousin went. She was now by the bar, flirting up a storm with a pair of businessmen. She was clearly doing just fine.

Whatever was going on with Mikaela, it was hers to deal with. Chelsea went to get her own drink and stay out of the way of the flirting would-be Romeos.

As she sat near the wall with her wine, she had to admit, the whole thing was not as revolting as she had imagined. In her mind, these mixers had become an unholy meat market, but in truth, Chelsea saw it was nothing more than what it said on the box: a social. People were talking animatedly.

Everyone's touching was flirtatious but tasteful. Her ideas of rampant pawing and bidding wars were mercifully incorrect. She even found herself in several conversations, where the only hint of what was going on was the intent way the men would watch what she said, looking for an opening to make an invitation.

"Look," she found herself saying with a laugh, "I'm the staff. You can't date me."

"More's the pity," said the handsome Japanese man who had tried to invite her to an art museum in Tokyo. "I would have loved to hear your thoughts on the new installation."

"Have you met Aisha and Jasmine?" Chelsea replied, directing him towards two new website users who had just returned from the bar with colourful cocktails. As the art enthusiast introduced himself to the two women, Chelsea slipped into the crowd and found herself face-to-face with Neil.

"It's a great museum," Neil said by way of greeting. "I think you would have enjoyed it." Chelsea made a face. Neil's lip twitched slightly.

"I don't think it would go quite the way he wants it to," Chelsea said. "I'd be stuck in Japan, at the mercy of a man who wants to use art to get into my pants." She looked at Neil and winced. "I didn't mean it like that. There will be women here who will be happy to be the companion he wants. But not me."

"It seems your acid wit is a regular feature of your company," Neil said, drinking from a bottle of the bar's in-house craft beer.

"How's your evening? Met anyone you'd like to date?" Chelsea said, ignoring his barb.

"I've had a pleasant time in conversation, but only one person I'd like to date."

"What did she say?" Chelsea asked.

"She said no."

"She sounds a bit daft," Chelsea said. Neil simply looked at her. Chelsea suddenly felt herself go the colour of her dress. "Oh. I just meant, if you're in the market for a millionaire, you're one of the better catches."

"That is perhaps the nicest thing you've said about me," Neil said.

"Excuse me, my cousin is calling me," Chelsea half lied and fled into the crowd in the direction of Mikaela. She found her at the far side of the room in a darkened corner near the bathrooms, hastily ending a call as Chelsea arrived.

"Who was that? Esme checking up on you?"

"Something like that," Mikaela said, looking unhappy.

"So...," Chelsea prompted hopefully. Mikaela just looked at her. "Have you found anyone to go on a date with?"

"Yeah, there's a guy, but he's not interested." Mikaela shrugged.

"Which guy? I'm sure I can make him see reason."

"That guy you were just talking to."

Disbelief blossomed inside Chelsea.

"The Japanese guy?" she said hopefully.

Mikaela shook her head. "No, the blond guy." She looked at her nails. "I should get going."

"Give me five minutes. Don't go anywhere, okay?" Chelsea didn't wait for agreement before plunging back into the crowd and pushing her way back through to Neil.

"My cousin said she meet you," Chelsea said to Neil. He followed the line of her pointing.

"Mikaela Peters." He nodded. "I didn't realise she was your cousin."

"I think she'd be great for you. She's... just great. I think you should go out with her. She really fancies you."

Neil peered at Chelsea. "I'm not certain I agree."

"Look at her! She's gorgeous and low-key and easy-going. Not at all like me."

"I would say that last point is more of a detraction than you think."

"Look—" Chelsea took a deep breath. She had a wild idea. "Let's make a deal. If you go on three dates with her, I'll go on three dates with you. You get to see us both in a romantic context, and I am certain that you'll find Mikaela much more suited to you."

Her heart pounded as she watched his unreadable face. She wasn't even sure if she wanted him to say yes or no.

"You want me to try dating both you and your cousin," he repeated, the smallest thread of surprise in his voice.

"Yeah. You can see how annoying I am in the long term, and that someone like Mikaela is so much easier to deal with."

"All right," Neil said after a moment's further consideration. He inclined his head. "We have a deal. Pending your cousin's agreement to her share of the dates, of course."

Chelsea let out a breath of either relief or heightened trepidation, she wasn't sure.

"Great. That's so great. You won't regret it. I mean, you'll regret the dates with me because we just absolutely won't get on, but Mikaela, she's really great. You'll see." She practically bounced on her heels. "What did you have in mind for our first date?"

"I was going to leave that up to you," Neil said with an understated shrug.

"You're not just going to pick something?"

"I'm certain you would feel more comfortable on all counts if you were to arrange the date. You feel threatened and uncomfortable when you are off balance, and I'd hate for our date to be an unfair representation of our 'getting on' because you don't like the restaurant."

"I hadn't thought of it like that." Chelsea racked her brain. "My friend Delta is performing tomorrow night. Would you like to come along to that? It's a bit small and independent, but it'll be fun."

"Small, independent, but fun. Just like you," Neil said with a warm edge to his voice that Chelsea was beginning to suspect indicated humour. "May I pick you up, or would you like to meet there?"

"I'll meet you there," Chelsea said, immediately uncomfortable at the thought of his fancy car coming anywhere near her shabby little villa.

"I expected that would be more to your taste," Neil said. "Why don't you email me with the details for tomorrow, and I'll go and ask your cousin out." With another nod, he moved away from her through the crowd towards Mikaela.

Chelsea remained standing where she'd been, her heart pounding wildly. What the hell had she suggested? What the hell had she agreed to? Her feelings were a tumultuous mix of relief and excitement and fear. She'd gotten her cousin a date with a millionaire like her aunt wanted. Now all she had to do was get through three dates of her own with him. And that thought terrified her. Or was she excited? She didn't want to actually date Neil "the Suit" O'Connell, did she? Why was he still so damn nice to her?

She finished her wine in a hurry and went to tell Helen she was heading home before some other man tried to pick her up. She never would have figured she'd get this much interest from the male Honey clientele. Clearly, she was getting too good at blending in.

10

CHELSEA CONTINUED TO QUESTION HER SANITY FROM THE moment she'd arranged the date to the moment she arrived at their meeting point. What if they just didn't get on? Her friends' patience levels were worn thin, and in the end, they told her that was simply the risk of dating.

They did, however, question her choice of date venue.

"It's not that I don't love you for coming, Chels," Delta said when Chelsea told her she'd be bringing her date to the performance. "It's just I think it's an unusual date, especially for someone as straight-laced as your suit is."

"I want to see how he reacts. I'm not going to pretend to be anyone I'm not, and I'm not actually trying to win him over," Chelsea replied with a shrug. "And he's not *my* suit."

Her fierce cleaving to her individuality would have been a better idea, she reflected, had she the confidence to back it. After all, Delta was right. It was an unusual choice, and Neil looked terribly conservative. On the bright side, maybe he would admit they were wrong for each other and she'd be off the hook for the other two dates she had promised.

Come the evening, Chelsea felt great in her cerulean

outfit with sweeping sleeves and little diamante dragonflies sewn onto the neck and shoulders of her top. Her skirt skimmed the tops of her knees, and she loved catching the shimmer of her glittery stockings in the street lights as she waited. She wore tall heels again, strappy black shoes that added what she felt were much-needed inches to her height. Overall, she felt fantastic, even as she nervously awaited her date, shifting from foot to foot in the cooling evening breeze.

His car appeared on the road in front of her, and Neil gracefully climbed out onto the pavement. He was much taller than her; she'd forgotten that. His short blond hair, with its incognito collection of silver, was neatly combed back, and his casual-cut suit was impeccably tailored. She forgot to breathe for a single second, her heart catching on something, as she regarded how very good-looking he was.

"You look lovely," he said by way of greeting.

"Thanks," Chelsea said, finding her voice. "You look pretty good yourself. Do you ever wear anything other than a suit?"

Neil gave her his small smile. "Very rarely. There are so few events where a suit is inappropriate."

Chelsea made a face. "Don't you find it gets a bit stuffy? Like you're in a uniform or something?"

"And the interrogation begins already," Neil said with a slightly wider smile that lasted a few seconds before fading. God, but he was hard to read. "Not all of us can dress as though we were hummingbirds." He gestured at the street as his car drove away. "Will you lead the way?"

"Hummingbird?" Chelsea repeated, then shook her head. "It's this way." She guided him down the pavement, moving quickly, but Neil still had to adjust his large stride to suit her much smaller one.

"What is the performance we're seeing?" Neil asked as they strolled down the road. "You've been quite mysterious."

"Have I?" More like nervous after what Delta said. "It's... a slightly unusual performance. Delta is a silks performer." She braced and waited for the reaction.

"A silks performer."

"Yes. You know. Aerial silks. It's a performance art. Like acrobatics. Like Cirque du Soleil."

"I'm intrigued," Neil said, his voice unreadable again. "I've never seen one."

"There's going to be all kinds of acts. Even pole performers. It's different from a strip club, all right? It's not sleazy. It's a performance art. So don't go tucking money into their knickers or anything."

She caught his reproving look. "You really do believe I'm an incorrigible sleaze, don't you?"

Embarrassment flooded Chelsea.

"Look," Neil said, lightly putting his hand on her arm. Chelsea stopped walking and looked up at him. He seemed serious, but around the edges of his eyes and mouth there was something like pain. "This isn't going to work at all if you're going to start the night feeling angry at me for something I haven't done. You said you wanted to show me what you were like, to give me a proper chance to see what we could be like. I don't know why you feel so intimidated. I don't need to know, either," he said when Chelsea began to open her mouth. "You don't owe me explanations. You don't owe me this date. If you've changed your mind, I'll leave right now."

He looked intently at her. His face and voice seemed utterly sincere. Chelsea shook her head.

"I'd like to stay," he continued softly. "I'd like to have our three dates. But I'd only like to stay if you could let me actually make an impression on you, rather than spend my night fighting your strange preconceptions about what I must be like. It's not fair to call me here and treat me as 'the suit.'"

Oh God, is that really what I'm doing? She was aware his hand was still sitting lightly on her upper arm.

"Am I really doing that?" she asked.

"Believe me, it's not flattering to have your date tell you to not put money in a performer's underwear because she assumed that was your default behaviour."

"You're right." The words came out of Chelsea with difficulty. "I'm sorry. It wasn't fair. I won't behave like that for the rest of the night."

"If I act like a pretentious, sleazy man with more dollars than sense, then you have full rein to give me another tongue lashing. But please do not start by assuming that's how I will act."

Chelsea nodded. "All right."

Neil smiled at her. "You still want to take me? To the show, I mean," he added hastily.

"Yeah," Chelsea said, nodding. They strolled down the inner-city street, lit by harsh neon and fluorescent lights and the orange-and-red glow of cars sitting in traffic queues alongside them. She led him down a steep, narrow street, drawing farther away from the arterial route where they had met. Here, the buildings were older, the shadows were longer, and Chelsea unthinkingly picked up her pace when she saw a man with a large beard and a black beanie pull away from the shadows of a wall and amble after them.

"I'm sorry it's not a very nice area of town," she said to Neil as they walked past a group of shadowed youths who were drinking beer out of bottles in an alleyway, laughing between themselves. "It's an indie performance, so you get whatever venue you can, you know? The bar is pretty nice. We just have to get through this bit."

"It's fine. My travel insurance has a kidnap clause," Neil said, glancing down at her. Chelsea wondered if the lip quirk meant it was a joke or that he found the situation humorous.

"I don't think we'll get kidnapped. Even getting robbed is unlikely. It's just a bit of a rough neighbourhood." Chelsea stopped walking and put a hand on Neil's arm. "We're here," she said, indicating a set of stairs heading down below a shadowy Italian restaurant. The doorway had a sign declaring it to be Lamplight Club, with a picture of an old-fashioned lamp post.

Chelsea looked over her shoulder, but the man in the beanie she thought might be following them was gone. She sighed with relief and all but bounded down the stairs, gripping the black-lacquered rail to stop herself from tumbling straight to the bottom. Her other hand still held Neil's lower arm, pulling him after her into a dim room with moody lighting, tall tables, and spindly chairs. There was a raised stage with a runway and a sturdy metal pole at the end. Posters covered the walls. If anyone looked closely, they could see that almost nothing matched.

"Come up here. I have tickets for up front," Chelsea said. Neil blinked in the low light, taking in the surroundings. She wondered if he hated it here. Soon, they were seated at a tall table near the stage, beneath a light that moved between green and blue, bathing them in brilliant hues.

As they were seated, Neil looked expectantly at Chelsea, and she looked equally expectantly back at him. The music was loud, but not loud enough that they could get away without talking.

"Delta's going to be amazing," Chelsea blurted out. "You'll see. It takes a lot of physical strength to do silks."

"I believe you," Neil said with an upwards quirk of his lip. "I'm looking forward to it." He glanced towards the bar. "Would you like a drink?"

"All right," Chelsea said after a moment's consideration. "But I'll get the next round."

Neil infinitesimally lifted his eyebrows at her and slid off the chair before moving through the thickening crowd towards the bar, where a woman with a green Mohawk was tending.

"Hey, Chels, I see you ended up bringing the suit after all," Delta emerged from the crowd. Chelsea looked down at her friend.

"Yeah. I can't help but feel this is a disaster already. I don't know what to talk to him about."

Delta shrugged. "Just be yourself. Open your mouth. Something interesting always comes out. Ask him questions. Tell him about yourself. He's human, for all that he's a suit." Delta gave Chelsea's arm a squeeze. "I have to get backstage now. Good luck. Try to have fun."

By the time Neil arrived back with their drinks, Chelsea had brainstormed a couple of questions. She wasn't sure why she felt so off balance around him. Did his wealth really bother her that much?

"Thanks," she said, sipping her drink as Neil settled back onto the stork-legged chair. "So, how long have you been in New Zealand? Why here?"

"About four months," Neil replied. "I needed to—well, I wanted to leave California and the United States for a while. I wanted to go somewhere that was close enough that I could get back if my business affairs required me, or if my family needed me. I wanted to be somewhere that felt far away."

"Most people go to Australia. Sydney and Melbourne are popular for business people."

"New Zealand is quiet. I needed quiet." Chelsea's hurt feelings must have shown in her face, because Neil's habitually unreadable face softened a little. "I forget how easy it is to wound the New Zealand pride. I mean quiet in a good way. Have you ever been to San Francisco or Los Angeles or New York?" Chelsea shook her head. "Then you can't understand how incredibly loud it can get in your skull. It's a noise you can't get rid of. It can be invigorating, or it can be maddening. Here, I feel like I have everything within my reach, yet none of it is overwhelming. You have no idea how lucky you are to live here. New Zealand is safe. Safe and quiet." Neil smiled at her a little. "And how is your job going?"

Chelsea made a face. "Have I managed to get myself fired since you saved my job the other day, you mean?" Neil nodded with a flash of a smile. "I'm still employed, and I haven't fought at all with Helen. I've dealt with user issues and some helpdesk queries, and the social last night went very well, so Helen has hardly glared at me. Things are looking up." She pointed towards the stage. "Do you see those bits of white fabric?" Chelsea indicated upwards, and Neil followed her gaze.

"Yes?"

"Those are Delta's silks. They're really strong. She does... well, some really cool things with them. It's kind of like pole performing, except instead of a stable metal pole, you're trying to balance and counterweight and put all your weight on those things."

"I can't even imagine it." Neil kept eyeing the silks as

they were tucked out of the way. "What does the club do with them when there are no performances?"

"Nothing. They belong to Delta. They're just set up here when they're needed. It would be better if they had a dedicated performance space, but you know." Chelsea shrugged. Neil nodded understandingly.

Just then, the lights dipped and a woman stepped out. She looked like a 1950s pin-up poster, with lustrous black curls, sweeping eyelashes, and colourful tattoos. A 1950s dress swelled out in a bell shape around her lithe frame. The show was about to begin.

A catlike woman performed athletically on the pole to vibrant electronic music, impressing everyone in the room with the strength she needed to hold her body aloft at a right angle from the metal performing rod. She twirled, holding on only by the grip of her legs, her hair swirling, and her skintight outfit sparkled. She was followed by a pair of fire performers, who twirled two staves burning at both ends, then adorned their fingertips with long metal rods that burned at the end. Their dances were slow and sensual. Next there was an acrobat trio that smoothly contorted themselves through complicated moves that threw them high up towards the ceiling before gracefully descending. Around them, the lights changed moodily, and the beat of the performer's chosen song reverberated through Chelsea's chest.

The performances kept her attention, but she never lost her awareness of Neil's presence. She knew that he too was watching her; she could feel his glances when she was watching the show, and she gauged his reactions as much as he watched hers. His applause seemed genuine and enthusiastic, and more than once she caught him leaning forwards with a held breath when a particularly difficult feat was being attempted.

Delta was the final act of the first half, and Chelsea cheered as she came out on stage. As Delta walked down the runway, looking magnificent and strong in her golden skintight leotard, a stagehand passed her a long pole, with which she pulled long white swathes of material out from where they were tucked. They unfurled, and two thick hanks of silk hung on either side of her. She smiled widely at the audience, then began to wrap herself in the silks. Using her weight, gravity, and the strength of the material, she hauled herself upwards artfully, falling backwards and upside down to the thrill of the crowd, to be caught by her loops. The music was pounding and energetic. The performance was as fast as any Chelsea had seen before, but Delta remained in control of her body and its place in space. She had worked her way almost to the very top and was ensconced in what looked like too-loose knots, and Chelsea's heart pounded even though she knew it was still safe.

With a beatific smile at the crowd, Delta let her weight drop, the knots and loops tightening around her as they caught her weight... for a second. The scream of tearing silk could be heard, a pop of metal, and Chelsea saw Delta's face contort with terror as she lost control of the descent. She lunged upwards, grabbing onto the silk to stop her fall, and everyone heard her cry of pain above the music.

11

———

DELTA HUNG FROM A TANGLE OF SILKS, HER KNUCKLES turning white as she gripped the one set of silks still secured to the ceiling. She breathed through gritted teeth. Someone had turned the music off, and all that could be heard were the sounds of panicked voices, then the organiser's voice asking for calm. For a few seconds, it felt as though Chelsea had forgotten how to operate her body. Then she found her feet and ran onto the stage. Neil was on the stage beside her, calmly but urgently talking to the stagehands.

"What are you doing?" Delta shouted down to Neil.

"We're looking for a ladder backstage," Neil said, his voice steady. "There must be one, if someone got those silks up there."

"It's no use. I've broken my damn leg. I won't be able to get down," Delta shouted. Her face was turning red, and her voice was twisted with pain. Neil put his hand on Chelsea's shoulder.

"Delta, honey, we'll get you down," Chelsea tried.

"Well, it's you doing it, sweetheart, or it's gravity, and if you don't hurry, Isaac goddamn Newton's going to beat you to it." Tears were on Delta's face. "Do something!"

"Delta, I know you've done this a lot before, so I know you'll have thought about strategies for if something goes wrong." Neil's voice was completely calm. It cut through Delta's panic. "Let me worry about your leg. You just think about whatever you need to in order stay as calm as you can and to stay up until we can get you down in a controlled manner. Can you do that?"

Chelsea looked between Neil and Delta. She could see Neil's voice having an effect; her friend was calming, fighting for deep breaths. Several stagehands brought a ladder out and began the task of setting it up.

"Thank you. Secure it, please," Neil told them with authority but no harshness. He looked at Chelsea. "Could you please make sure the organiser has called an ambulance? We want it to be here as soon as possible." Chelsea nodded and hurried towards Holly, throwing glances over her shoulder at Delta as she went.

Chelsea found Holly in tears, but she calmed and leapt into action the second Chelsea delivered Neil's directives. Her task dispatched, Chelsea ran back to find that Neil was now nearly atop the ladder. The top step was still free.

"I think I know how I'm tied up," Delta told Neil. Her voice was calmer. "I just don't know how I can get down with one leg."

"Think about your good leg. Can you untangle yourself so you're still gripping the silks and manoeuvre yourself so you can set your good leg on the ladder here?"

Delta nodded, concentrating. She wiggled experimentally. Then, gritting her teeth, she loosed several loops, and her tangled harness gave way. The ripped silk floated to the floor, and Delta was sitting in a single loop, crying out as her left leg fell down unsupported. Livid bruising was already visible on her thigh muscle. She looked towards Neil for support.

"That's great. Chelsea's organised an ambulance. You'll be with them soon." Neil broke his eye contact with Delta and looked around. "Can I get one of the acrobats here, please?"

All three appeared within moments. "I need the tallest one here alongside the ladder. I'm going to pass her down as quick as we can."

The tallest acrobat stepped forwards. Chelsea noted he was still a few inches shorter than Neil. One of the others went to steady the ladder, while the third fell in next to Neil, into a spotting position.

"Chels?" Delta called.

Chelsea could see her friend's face was pale and tinged with blue around her lips. "You're going to be all right, babe. Just let Neil get you down." Chelsea filled her voice with confidence. "You can trust him." She swallowed hard. *Please don't make me regret saying that,* she thought, eyes on the back of Neil's head.

"All right. I'm coming down," Delta said, taking a deep, shuddering breath, lowering her uninjured leg and finding purchase on the ladder. Delta's confidence visibly returned once she was in motion. With her injured leg carefully slack and clear of the ladder, Neil held on to her and allowed her to shift her balance. With Neil as a support, she managed to get herself low enough that the muscular acrobat was able to scoop her into his arms, and the forgotten audience around them erupted in cheers.

Chelsea hugged Delta as best she could as the other girl cried with pain, relief, and embarrassment. "I just feel like such a tit, Chels. They must think I'm the world's worst performer. I mean, you'd think I wasn't prepared for this. I just never expected to break my leg up there. When I landed, sure, but not actually up in the air."

"You're all right, Delta. You're safe now," Chelsea repeated, clutching Delta's hand. She heard behind her Neil's calm voice dispersing the performers that huddled around them. The music came back on, and they were shepherded backstage. It felt like only seconds later that the paramedics arrived and were deftly loading Delta onto a stretcher.

"I'll come with you," Chelsea said.

Delta shook her head. "Nah. Go tell your suit thank you from me. I completely lost it up there. I couldn't think. If it wasn't for him, I think I'd have stayed up there forever. He's good people, Chels. I don't think he's a creepstalk." Her eyes fluttered slightly as the painkillers took effect. "They're gonna call my mum for me. I'll be fine. Kim will pick me up. You go. Drink some fancy champagne. Anyone that climbs up half a storey to save a screaming performer without even blinking has gotta be good people, right?"

"You just take care of yourself, Delta," Chelsea said, squeezing her friend's hand again.

With Delta taken away, Chelsea could finally hear herself think, and she realised she was shaking from the soles of her feet upwards—from cold or adrenaline or fear or all of those things. And she had no idea where Neil was.

12

———

"HERE," NEIL SAID, APPEARING BEHIND HER, DRAPING HIS jacket over her shoulders. "You look cold. Would you like to sit down before you fall?"

Chelsea gratefully sank into the seat behind her, an uncomfortable, rickety wooden thing, but it would carry her better than her legs would at that moment. Neil knelt in front of her, staying at eye level. His hands folded around hers gently. Chelsea liked their warmth.

"Delta says thanks. She says..." She tried to remember what she had said. "She says she didn't want you to think that she wasn't prepared for something like that. She said she just wasn't prepared for breaking her leg in mid-air."

Neil smiled thinly. "It's all right. I'm glad I could do something to help." He watched her apprehensively for a few moments. "Would you like to stay here for the second act?"

"The second act?" Chelsea all but squawked. "How can they even think of having a second act after what happened?"

"I convinced them to do it—no, hear me out." He

squeezed her hands reassuringly. "If we ended the show on that note, that's all they would remember. Delta would have a lot of bad publicity to cope with when she was back on her feet. There isn't a performer alive who wouldn't feel embarrassed at being caught up in the air like that. I convinced Holly to continue with the second act. They'll remember Delta's accident, but it will be just one event of many."

Chelsea couldn't believe how calm he was. How had he thought of all this so quickly?

"Have you done this sort of thing before?" she asked.

"Not this specific sort of thing, no. But human psychology is generally fairly constant. It's a gentle misdirection technique. The bar will be serving free drinks for the rest of the evening, and that will help improve people's experience of the evening too. We'll obviously need someone to come in and examine what happened with the silks, but I've talked to Holly and the owner. We'll have the relevant liability and insurance assessors come through first thing tomorrow."

"Oh. That's great." Chelsea had no idea what that had to do with anything.

"It's nothing," Neil said with a shrug. "What I'm concerned about right now is how you are doing. Would you like to go to hospital to see Delta? Would you like to stay for the show? Would you like to go home?" Neil looked at her, unreadable, unshaken, patient.

Chelsea thought about it. She had no interest in the rest of the show. When Delta said she didn't need her at the hospital, she meant it. And Chelsea couldn't imagine continuing the date even though Delta had given her blessing.

"Home. I just want to go home," Chelsea said. "I'm sorry."

"May I take you home? My car is around the corner. Please," he said, seeing she was about to protest. "I would not feel right putting you in a taxi after a scare like that. It would be heartless."

Some part of her thought about fighting, muttering about debts. A memory of what he had said about a night's worth of free drinks suddenly being provided for the remaining crowd at Lamplight Club. And then she remembered a shaking Delta eased through blind panic and out of harm's way by this man's patience, quick thinking, and kindness.

"I'd like that. Thank you."

"It would be heartless," he had said. Whatever else he was, Chelsea was sure he was not heartless.

Neil was as good as his word, and within minutes, Chelsea was once again ensconced in the back of the expensive BMW, being driven through Auckland by a well-mannered and, to all appearances, deaf driver. Beside her, Neil sat similarly quietly.

"That wasn't quite the date I had in mind," Chelsea said after a minute. "It was just meant to be a bit of fun. I promise you not everything that happens in my vicinity is a calamity."

Neil flashed a brief smile. "I had fun, up until Delta's accident."

"Thanks for helping her."

"You already said thanks. It was nothing."

"No, I said *her* thanks. Now I'm thanking you. As me. And you know it wasn't nothing. She's a performer; you can only imagine how important her limbs are to her. If you hadn't had the presence of mind to talk her down, I don't know what would have happened. Maybe the paramedics might've done it. Maybe she would have fallen if the other silk had come down. I don't know. Thanks, is all."

Chelsea stopped and looked out the window. The darkened streets of Auckland were zipping by. Neil didn't say anything, and when Chelsea looked over at him, he was watching her as apprehensively as he had been backstage.

"What's wrong? Why are you giving me that look?" she asked, confused. Neil shook his head. "Fine. How did you know what to do? You stayed so calm."

"I have got a talent for problem-solving." He smiled. "Others are musically gifted or strong or good with animals; I haven't got anything that exciting. I can problem-solve. When something goes wrong, I start unravelling it and figuring out what to do next."

"And you don't panic?"

"No. Not unless there's nothing I can do. In most situations, there is something to be done, at least a couple of steps, until I can get the experts or specialists there. For example, I couldn't fix Delta's leg. But I could at least keep her calm while she was up there. If I could get her down, that was a bonus. Mostly, I wanted to keep her calm by offering her sight of a way out. She did the work herself. When she calmed down and started moving, she knew what to do."

"But you gave her that calm, that confidence," Chelsea said.

He smiled. "It's a boring superpower."

"Is that why you're so rich? You just problem-solved being poor?"

Neil laughed. "You're really fixed on this whole wealth thing, aren't you?"

"Starving people think a lot about food," Chelsea said.

Neil grimaced. "Fair comment. My family was wealthy, so I was born into it. I made a lot off my own business decisions, ventures, and risks, but there's no denying the start-up capital from my family helped, and that I was never going to be in terribly dire straits, unless I did something inept and illegal. Which I've never had the urge to do. Problem-solving does lend itself well to business. It probably helped with the being rich, yes."

"I'm sorry for bringing it up again," Chelsea said. "I'm not going to shout, I promise."

"Thank you."

They rode in silence for a while, Chelsea lost in her own thoughts. She wanted to say they were about Delta. They were in fact about the man sitting beside her. It was hard not to focus on him while sharing the confines of the vehicle, and despite his quiet, self-contained presence, she felt drawn to him.

"Neil, can I ask you a question? Why did you... why did you save my job? After I said all those really crappy things about, well, not you, exactly, but... you know." She knew she was blushing. If Neil noticed, he pretended not to.

"To be honest, I'm not entirely sure," he said. "I was still confused about how I felt. How I felt about what you said. But even if I were not especially flattered by your descriptions of me, I didn't want to see you lose your job. It didn't take anything from me to do you a kindness."

"But why did you come to my exhibition and ask me out? You'd just signed up to the site with all those women on it. All of whom are prettier and much less annoying than I am, I might add."

Neil glanced at her, his face looking pained, before he looked away again. "Our conversations made me smile."

The car slowed to a stop. They had arrived outside Chelsea's house.

"Are you going to be all right?" Neil asked, grasping Chelsea's hand across the back seat briefly.

"I'm all right. I can't invite you in without connotations. I just want to be in my embarrassing pyjamas and watch some bad TV before calling it a night."

"I'll walk you to your door."

The house they had stopped at was a towering late nineteenth-century colonial villa, well maintained, with a deck that went around the upper storey. The hedge was ill kempt and overgrown, as was most of the yard. Chelsea led Neil around the edge of the property towards the back, past a mouldy birdbath that hadn't attracted anything but mosquito larvae for a few years, and up a small set of stone steps to her front door.

"It's a very impressive house. Are you secretly very rich and you've been testing me all this time?" Neil asked.

Chelsea laughed. Standing on the top step, she was eye level with Neil. She handed him back his jacket.

"Don't I wish. It's a converted villa. It used to be one house, but now it's a bunch of separate flats. It's pretty and gets a good bit of light, even if it is the devil to heat in the winter." Chelsea was acutely aware of Neil's body as they stood only a hand span apart. She could smell his cologne and his unfamiliar hair products that weren't purchased in New Zealand.

"Thank you for this evening." He paused, thinking his next words over. "I'm seeing Mikaela tomorrow evening, but I look forward to your call about our second date."

The mention of Mikaela was jarring. Chelsea had somehow forgotten this was all a ruse to matchmake her cousin and get her aunt off her back.

"Yeah, of course. I'll think of something." She shook her head to clear it. "Have a nice time. I bet it will be less of a train wreck."

"And I bet it won't be half as memorable."

He turned and walked down the path, and Chelsea let

herself into her house, struggling with the key as her hands shook. This was all perfect. The date was a disaster; Mikaela would shine in comparison to her. This was what she wanted. She was not suited for Mr. Millionaire. There was no reason for her unease and the vague tang of bitterness in her mouth.

No reason at all.

13

IT WAS A LONG DRIVE FROM WHERE CHELSEA LIVED BACK TO Neil's house at the far end of Auckland, and he found himself trying to think about anything but the date, undertaking every task he could think of to distract his mind, and any potential progress he had made with Chelsea.

Grabbing the laptop he kept in his car, he set about trying to turn his chaotic thoughts into a plan of action. First, he wrote down the things that had happened that evening and a to-do list: the people he had to speak to, reminders to himself to follow up with Holly, and to track down Delta once she was out of hospital. He wrote down the ideas that were swirling around in his head on how to prevent that sort of thing happening again, at least for this city's troupe of independent airborne dancers. A voice at the back of his head pointed out to him that Chelsea would hate it if she found out what he was doing.

So what? It's my money, and I spend it how I like. Besides, it's not like I'm going to run out.

He wondered what he could ever do to earn her trust. Had he really behaved so poorly? It was clear, if he wanted anything to do with her, he'd have to find a way to prove to her that he wasn't whatever she was afraid of. Then again, this emotional contortionism, bending himself into knots to please someone, was exactly what he'd been trying to avoid. Maybe Eddie was right. He couldn't make her trust him. His own wounds were too raw for him to seriously try.

He glanced out the darkened glass as they drove over the bridge to the city's northern shore. Below them, the harbour waters were black, glittering in moonlight.

This country never failed to be breathtakingly picturesque. He began to think of all the places he wanted to visit in New Zealand, writing up a spreadsheet, the numbers and the research helping him keep his emotions at bay. He did some price checks. He added in what it would cost to take an extra person—not that Chelsea would ever let him take her on an expensive holiday.

Not that he was going to take her.

Lastly, he pulled up the Honey website and punched in his login. He saw he had a stack of messages, responses to the ones he had sent out with Eddie's insistences, and others from women he'd met at the soiree Chelsea had organised.

"Rachel... Ashley... Shannon...," he muttered. All of them beautiful, put-together women. Their profiles had looked fun, and they had been eloquent. He checked his replies. At least three of the women said they'd be happy to meet him. Several had rejected him, saying they weren't interested. Neil didn't take it personally.

Shannon seemed nice. Attractive, tall, thick dark hair in waves—she looked like she had a lovely laugh. Her profile said she was looking for fun events, conversation, nothing serious or long term. *That's what I should be going for. Nothing serious. Nothing long term.*

"We're home, boss," his driver said as they pulled into the driveway.

"Thanks, Lance."

"If you don't mind my saying, you seem worried. Did things not go well with the lady tonight?"

"You're not paid enough to hear my whining," Neil replied wryly.

"Just thought you could use a friendly ear."

"I don't know how she feels about me." Neil looked down at the laptop, still open with Shannon's profile. "And I shouldn't be interested in her. But here I am, accidentally planning a trip anyway."

"The heart wants what it wants, boss."

"I sincerely hope my heart isn't involved in this. See you tomorrow."

Inside, Eddie was waiting for him.

Neil took one look at the expression on Eddie's face, an unimpressed glower, folded arms, and an air of petulance that took away from his adult demeanour.

"I don't need mothering, Eddie," Neil snapped as he threw his keys onto the sideboard. Eddie made an exasperated noise. "If you're going to behave like this, you can go get yourself a hotel. Or better yet, go back home to San Francisco."

"Neil, you've got to see it from my perspective." Eddie stood up from the perfect white furniture Neil's house had come pre-packaged with.

"You don't get a perspective."

"Of course I do. I'm your brother."

"You're interfering."

"Because you're making a big mistake. You're just going to get hurt again."

Neil ignored him, stalking across the expanse of the living room to the large stainless steel, designer kitchen. Neil suddenly hated that everything was white or silver. He felt like he was in someone's vision of a futuristic space station.

"Neil, there's a world of uncomplicated relationships out there. Why do you have to pick this unknown quantity?" Eddie continued, following him.

"Honestly? I've got no idea." Neil yanked open the fridge and stared into its depths, as if it would hold the answer. "I've got no idea, and it scares me."

"What are you doing, then? Just drop her before you do something stupid like fall in love."

Neil snagged a beer from the fridge and slammed the door behind him. "Leave it alone. What makes you think you have any right to be interfering in this?"

"Have you forgotten about Florence already?" Eddie demanded. "You don't get to tell me to back off, because the disaster that came out of you and Florence affects my life too. You can't afford to fall in love with this woman. You can't get yourself into a mess like that. Hell, she probably doesn't want to be involved in a mess like that. Then again, who knows what women want. Not you, that's for sure."

"Women aren't from Venus, Edward, but if you don't get off my case, then I'll put you on the first manned mission to Mars, I swear it."

Neil didn't like the look on his brother's face one bit; it was an expression of mingled wonder and horror.

"Are you falling for her?" Eddie demanded. "Is that why you're so defensive?"

Neil didn't answer and all but stomped from the kitchen, heading up the designer wooden stairs that looked as though they floated unsupported in the air. In his room, he threw open the doors of his steel-and-glass balcony and drank his beer, the cold night breeze dishevelling his blond-and-grey hair. Some unknown island loomed in the distance in the middle of the harbour.

Eddie was right, in a way, and Neil didn't want to admit it. He'd told Chelsea he was a problem-solver, that he solved problems one step at a time. How he always found the next most logical thing to do, and he went ahead and did it. Do that enough times, he had always believed, and you'd calmly find your way to the end of the problem. The logic usually worked on people too. People always wanted something, and once Neil was able to figure out what that something was, he was more than able to use it to work with them. Or use it against them, depending on how much of a villain he was required to be. It was useful in business.

It was useless in love.

He didn't believe women were an alien species. He knew they weren't the inexplicable creatures of enigma, of capricious desires, of wilful obfuscation. It was simply that when his own heart was involved, his cool rationale and clarity evaporated. His feelings and desires became a weapon used against him time and time again. He couldn't solve a problem that he couldn't see, and his feelings were like a blindfold over his senses.

Delta, the dancer, tangled up high in the air with a broken leg, that was an easy puzzle to solve.

Chelsea, with her gaudy and blonde hair streaked with colours like a rainbow, that was a much harder problem. Neil had no solution for the problem of Chelsea with her wilful chin and an open face that broadcast her every thought. She was defensive and confusing, and he wanted desperately to understand her. There was a sweetness to her that he found utterly compelling.

Eddie was right. He couldn't afford to fall for her, no matter how compelling she was. Neil had fought too hard to be free of emotional ties that could be used to control. He'd rather take the literal fall that Delta nearly had than to fall for Chelsea.

14

———————

Chelsea arrived at work on Monday morning in an uncommonly good mood. Delta was recovering well. Feedback from the social mixer had been positive. Mikaela had texted to say her date with Neil had gone well. Chelsea was sure she didn't feel jealous at all. Her stomach was queasy only because she'd spotted a man outside Honey's building who looked a lot like the man she'd seen during her date with Neil. She told herself she was being paranoid.

Slinging herself into her chair and positioning her coffee within easy reach, Chelsea's machine had barely booted up before Helen stalked out into the reception area, clad in her usual array of designer garments. Her face was so heavy with make-up, Chelsea wondered if she could recognise Helen without it. She quickly smothered her giggle into a friendly smile at Helen.

"Good morning, Helen. How was your weekend?"

"Chelsea, I need to see you in my office in five minutes," Helen said, ignoring the pleasantry, before turning on her heel and stalking back into the dim light of her office.

Chelsea's mood plummeted. She glanced at her inbox

of emails, then shrugged. No sense worrying about them until she knew if she was fired or not. At least Neil had bought her a whole extra week of employment. Five minutes took forever to tick by. Then, taking a swig of coffee for bravery, she squared her shoulders and marched into Helen's office.

Helen's *cave* would have been a better term for it. There were many reasons Helen made Chelsea roll her eyes so hard she saw her own brain, and one of them was her overwhelming fear of light damage to her skin. Her office was bathed in perpetual twilight, and even the meeting rooms had dim, diffused lights that Chelsea had initially assumed were for "mood," but later learned to be part of Helen's particular requirements.

Blinking in the low light, Chelsea found her way to a chair and sat herself down.

"What's up?" she asked Helen.

"I'd like to discuss your position here at Honey, Chelsea," Helen began. "I have been thinking about our work relationship, and after your behaviour on Friday night at the social mixer, I think a change is in order."

Chelsea thought back to the mixer. What could she have done there that changed Helen's opinion of her?

Neil.

Chelsea felt herself go cold. Dating the clients was probably a bit of a no-no, come to think of it, even if it was to further another client's chances. Was Neil about to get her fired after all?

"I thought the mixer was successful?"

"It was. People had very good things to say about you. They found you personable and memorable." Helen looked pained as she said it. "I have decided I have misjudged you. You have a lot more potential than I have given scope for, and therefore I'd like to discuss a promotion of sorts with you."

"You'd like... What?" Chelsea replied dumbly. Now she was blinking from surprise rather than blindness. This was quite the emotional roller coaster for first thing Monday. "I don't understand."

"There's only the five of us manning this ship, Chelsea, and it's a competitive market out there. We're fighting for market share against regular dating sites, international sites of this nature, those 'hook-up' apps." Helen wrinkled her nose. "What we do here is different to those things. In all manner of relationships, most heartbreak and injury is avoided if everyone understands the nature of the interaction. Therefore, it is important that we keep our line of work separate from those other venues. You understand me, I'm sure?"

Not really, Chelsea wanted to say. Helen sighed audibly, and Chelsea belatedly tried to smooth her frown of concern away. Neil was right about her face.

"I mean, Chelsea"—Helen leaned in conspiratorially —"the users of our services are quite clear that the match-making happens between those who are resource rich and time poor, and the well-presented people who desire a casual relationship in luxuriant surrounds. It's a valuable service, where everyone is clear that these girls are not pros-titutes, nor 'cheap shags.' They are excellent companions for those who are too busy with careers to maintain proper rela-tionships."

Chelsea nodded earnestly. "Sure, Helen. I understand you. I really do."

"I hope so. As part of your promotion, I'd like you to become something of a social media advocate for us. Build and maintain some social media platforms. You know how these things go—news, funny pictures of cats, beauty articles. I'd like you to go on the site and post on our users' profiles enthusiastically, engage, make them feel like our company cares. It's the sort of thing I'd do myself, but it seems overbearing coming from me. I think a young, fresh voice like yours would do wonders for us. I expect you to complete a six-month social media roadmap, including milestones, professional development, and metric tracking and reporting." She smiled at Chelsea, obviously apprehensive about the conversation. "You can do that, can't you?"

Chelsea was beginning to feel like a bobblehead from all the nodding she was doing.

"We both know you are currently being underutilized," Helen said, her charm beginning to wear thin. "I'd like us to be on the same page. If you're not interested, I'm going to have to look for someone who will take the extra responsibility—and your current responsibility with it. I'd prefer to keep you because you have great potential." She pushed a face down piece of paper at Chelsea. "Your new salary."

Chelsea looked at the numbers on the sheet. It would be nice to have more money.

Helen's thinly veiled threat of firing her had not gone over her head. If she was fired, it would be back to Aunt Esme's bed and breakfast, in one of the lower circles of hell.

"It sounds great," Chelsea lied earnestly.

"I look forward to your social media roadmap. I'm afraid if it isn't what I expect, then maybe we'll have to discuss the value of this."

"Sure." She still felt at a loss about the whole conversation. She was expecting to get fired, not promoted. "D'you really mean it, Helen? About the potential?"

"Of course I do. You've got all this... colour and vibrancy, and while I know you do your art stuff, there's room for you to grow here too." Helen stood and made little shooing hand motions. Chelsea gathered the meeting in the batcave was concluded.

She stumbled out of the dimly lit office and blinked in the lights of the reception area. She felt like she'd run a marathon, and it wasn't even 9:00 a.m. on a Monday. She was going to need a lot more coffee.

And then to see what the internet had to say about writing social media strategies.

"The good news is it isn't broken," Delta told them. She was lying on her bed in a colourful silk kimono, her leg bandaged and propped up on a large cushion. "I've done something weird to prang it. Like I twisted my muscles around the bone or something. I wish I'd gotten a picture before they wrapped it up; it's the most disgusting bruise ever."

Chelsea joined the collective shudder.

"How come you're so cheerful, then?" Tony asked, draped on a bamboo chair.

"Painkillers," Delta replied, sipping a mocktail of fruit juices that Kim had whipped up, complete with festive umbrella to celebrate her return home. "Lots and lots of painkillers. And relief. A broken leg would have taken months to come back from; this will only take a few weeks."

"I'm really glad you're all right, Delta," Chelsea said. She was enveloped by a bright pink beanbag in the shape of a cat. Her flamingo dress blended right in.

"Did I tell you guys Chels's date saved me?" Delta pulled a floral blanket over her other leg.

"The suit?" Tony asked, surprised.

Delta launched into the story. Chelsea had to admit that Neil sounded very heroic in Delta's recount, emerging immediately from the audience to take charge of the situation and talk Delta down. Chelsea's heart twisted as the normally imperturbable Delta's voice choked when she talked about her fear hanging in the tattered, tangled remains of her silks, when everything she trusted when up in the air—her equipment, her body—had been damaged.

"I swear, it was just his voice that got me down from there. He just made me feel like I could do it. I didn't even worry he wasn't strong enough, though he looks like a pipsqueak when I think about it."

"Is he a pipsqueak?" Kim asked Chelsea interestedly. Chelsea threw an ornate slipper at her.

"No, I'm serious. You know what he did after? He rang me up and talked to me and Holly about us getting a proper studio and performance space so we're not forever taking our equipment up and down in strange bars. He's working out the details with Holly. He won't take no for an answer." She sipped her drink. "Some asshole monkeyed with my silks after the last check we did and didn't put it back in the right place, so the suit wants to make sure we have our own space."

While Kim and Tony made excited noises, something cold and nasty gripped Chelsea. Neil was setting up her friends with a performance venue? Giving her friend money? When he'd only just met them? Something must've shown in her face, because Kim frowned at her.

"What's eating you, Chels?"

"I didn't know he was going to do that," she said. Her voice was sullen.

"Maybe he didn't want you feeling awkward. You got

pretty upset with him at the art gallery when he bought your art."

"That's because I thought he was trying to buy my interest. How do I know he's not trying to buy my interest by bankrolling my friends?"

"Not telling you about it is a pretty rookie mistake if impressing you was the aim," Tony pointed out.

"I'm happy to take his money, Chels, don't worry. If you don't want to sleep with him out of gratitude, I'll do it just as soon as my leg is working again."

Chelsea shot Delta an unamused look. Unhappiness and something like jealousy prickled at her. She began to try and clamber out of the beanbag, but her struggle ruined any chance of a dignified, angry exit.

"I was kidding, Chels. It was just the painkillers talking, come on," Delta said, seeing Chelsea was upset. "I'm sorry. Look, here, go into my purse. I have two vouchers in there for a trip out to Rangitoto Island on the weekend. I was going to hike up there with a hot guy I met, but I don't think I'll be hiking anywhere. You should take them and take Neil up Rangitoto."

"A Rangitoto walk? I don't know, Delta. That's pretty touristy," Kim said, making a face.

"On the other hand, it's a date where he can't possibly buy anyone or anything," Tony pointed out.

"He'll hate this. It's perfect," Chelsea said gleefully. "And I'm dying to see him out of a suit!" There was a heartbeat of pause before everyone burst into uproarious laughter. "No, not like that. Quit it. What are you all, sixteen?" Her face flamed. "I just mean he can't come hiking in a suit!"

"Oh, honey, we can find you much better ways to get him out of a suit!" Kim grinned wickedly.

Chelsea suffered their giggling for several minutes

before attempting a dignified exit, still accompanied by their hoots and hollers.

Tony was right, it was a pretty perfect idea for a second date. There was no way he'd enjoy it, and it would make Mikaela look even better in comparison. She called Neil as soon as she got home and explained about the Rangitoto trip.

"Would you like to come? Delta's leg's out of action for a few weeks, and it's a fun little trip. You get to see the harbour, climb a volcano—"

"It's not active, is it?"

Chelsea was surprised to hear his voice sounded apprehensive. "Active? Hell no. What, you think I require all my dates to take me to active volcanoes? It's dormant. Hasn't so much as had gas in about six hundred years. Why? You're not afraid of volcanoes, are you?"

There was a long silence. "Not exactly. I simply saw a rather graphic volcano disaster movie in my formative years."

Chelsea laughed. "You are in the wrong city, then, Neil. We're sitting on top of sixty-something volcanoes. You know that very nice lake near where you're staying? Lake Pupuke?"

"I don't think I want to know what you're about to say."

"It's an old crater."

"I was right; I didn't want to know." There was a long-suffering sigh. "Very well. I'll come on this geothermal adventure."

"This isn't even *close* to a geothermal adventure. This is a glorified hike. Don't worry, we'll have you skiing down Ruapehu in no time, and then we'll go see the geysers in Rotorua."

"I'm thrilled that you are planning to spend so much

time with me in the near future, even if I'm dismayed at your choice of recreation."

Chelsea was still grinning when she ended the call. This trip might even be fun. And when they were trapped on a boat, or an island, she could interrogate him about the money he was giving to Delta and her performing friends.

15

———

THE NEXT MORNING BROUGHT WITH IT CLASSIC AUCKLAND summer weather—grey clouds mingled with oppressive humidity. It was the sort of weather where Chelsea hoped for rain to wash all the moisture out of the air. Her garden buzzed with dozens of cicadas, a relentless hum that was the anthem of a good Kiwi summer.

"And I half expected you to wear a suit!" she greeted Neil when she found him awkwardly standing in the shade, wearing what looked like brand-new cargo trousers, the shirt of the national rugby team, a backpack, and a white cricket hat. "I didn't think you owned anything for this sort of activity."

"I didn't," Neil admitted, smiling when he saw her. "There was an emergency shopping trip. My younger brother, ah, insisted on advising."

"If he's anything like my friends, he must have mocked you mercilessly."

Neil laughed and swept his eyes over Chelsea. "You look much more suited to this than me, and no less bright than usual."

Chelsea was dressed in white baggy culottes with a pohutukawa print on them and a bright red top. She had a pink straw hat and a colourful sarong draped around her. Her shoes were sensible sports shoes, even if they were black with neon pink accents.

"I'm surprised you decided to come along."

"I didn't want to waste the good impression I had made on you at the performance. I thought you might find me a coward. I did consider buying the ferry company just so I could redirect the boat, I won't lie to you."

Chelsea's jolt of panic must have shown on her face.

"I'm joking," he said gently.

"That's a relief. It'd be scary to think you could actually do something like that." Chelsea laughed a little.

"Not by this morning I couldn't," Neil said. "A proper corporate takeover would have taken too long."

Chelsea stared at him and attempted a laugh.

"Right. Of course." She glanced behind her and was relieved to see the ferry was bouncing on the waves beside the pier, with the on-board staff throwing ropes to the shore staff as they brought the ferry into dock properly. "We better get in line if we want good seats. You don't get seasick, do you?"

"No," Neil said as they ambled towards the slowly forming queue for boarding. As they stood silently in the line, Chelsea found she couldn't contain her growing awkwardness about Neil's casual quips regarding spending vast quantities of money.

"Why do you talk about buying companies and corporate takeovers like that? Are you trying to be impressive?" she inquired.

"No," Neil replied, his expression hard to read again.

"Then why can't you just be normal?"

Neil looked down at her, his pale blue eyes serious. The unrelenting sea breeze tugged at his new hat, the brim of which cast his face into a shadow.

"Why do you dress like that?" he asked with an easy shrug. "Why do you dress in bright colours? Why do you wear high heels? Why do you put magenta streaks through your hair? You know others will look at you strangely and think you are, at best, desperate to prove your individuality and, at worst, think you're some good-for-nothing layabout without the decency to observe social mores."

Chelsea felt her jaw drop; embarrassment and anger in equal parts flooded her. She wished they were already on board the ferry. Then it would have been easier to shove him into the ocean.

"I don't see any reason to conform to other people's expectations of how I should look!" she replied hotly. "It's my hair. They're my clothes. I think and see and feel in colour; it's part of being an artist. At least, it's a part of the way I express my art. If you don't like it, there's a whole website of bland conformist women who'd love to be blonde and boring for you."

"This is who you are, then, and you refuse to compromise for the comfort of others?" Neil repeated.

Chelsea's reply caught in her throat. This was who she was. She did not compromise. She did not go out of her way to fit in. And it was true, if someone found her too much, she felt it was their loss. She advocated all her friends to take this approach. Life was too short for compromise. If she wasn't herself to protect the sensibilities of others, who would she be? What would she be?

And here she was, expecting Neil to behave differently for her.

"I see your point," Chelsea admitted grudgingly.

"I'm not speaking to make you uncomfortable, just as you do not dress or behave to challenge others. My humour, odd and perhaps obscure though it may be, is my own. Corporate takeovers are something I do. Buying companies is something I do."

"And it'd be more than a bit rubbish of me to ask you to pretend to be Johnny No-Cash, just because I feel weird about you being totally loaded."

"Yes. It wouldn't be honest, either." Neil glanced down and held her gaze. "I didn't take you for someone who valued dishonesty in dating."

With Neil's gaze on her, Chelsea was struck again by how good-looking he was. Even as everything about him seemed the antithesis of what she wanted, she found him compelling.

"Last chance to back out of this date," Neil said, gesturing to the line that was now moving forwards to board the vessel. "I'm going to be pretty unhappy if you throw me overboard because I accidentally let you catch a glimpse of my platinum Visa."

"I'd do no such thing," Chelsea informed him, blushing as she remembered that exact thought crossing her mind only minutes earlier. "I'd still like to subject you to climbing a mountain."

"I'd have preferred something like 'I like your company' rather than an expression of your desire to torture me," Neil complained as they climbed the metal gangplank. He shot her a long-suffering look, but his eyes revealed wry humour.

"There's no one else I'd rather drag myself up a mountain with today," she told him with complete honesty.

They climbed a steep and narrow set of steps to the roof of the ferry. Here, what had felt like a moderate sea breeze on land turned into a cold, buffeting wind, whipping

Chelsea's hair across her face. The brim of Neil's hat bent and twisted under the competing forces of the wind and the tie under his chin. They seated themselves near the front edge and looked out over the expanse of the bay before them. The sea was not its customary cerulean. Instead, it was dark grey and choppy in the wind. The ferry bounced underneath them, and they could feel it straining against the restraints that forced it to remain in place against its mooring.

"Sorry about the weather. With any luck there'll be a good shower to wash the humidity out of the air," Chelsea said. She looked up at the grim sky. She had hoped for tourist guidebook weather—the blue skies and cerulean seas that made the perfect contrast to the primal greens of the native bush that covered the volcanic island. Instead, it was the sort of dismal grey and oppressive humidity that made it feel like they might be in a horror movie.

Chelsea glanced down at the pier below and frowned as she spotted the same dark-haired man with the beard she'd seen twice before. He was in conversation with the dock staff, and as she watched, he wandered over to pick up the timetable for the week's ferry runs while swigging from a can of soda.

She must have frowned, because Neil asked her, "What's wrong?"

"Nothing," Chelsea replied. "There's just a guy I keep seeing around, or maybe it's several guys that look alike. But it doesn't look like he's getting on the boat."

Neil followed her gaze to the dock. "Which one?"

"It's not important," Chelsea said hastily, feeling embarrassed. "It's nothing."

"There's no reason anyone would follow you, is there?" Neil asked, looking bemused.

"Nope. I'm sure it's a coincidence."

The ferry blasted its horn, and within minutes, it began to reverse out of the docking bay and slowly chug its way to the mouth of the marina, where it kicked its engines into high gear and began to plod through the choppy seas with determination. Chelsea began a conversation with Neil about his work, but it quickly ended when the roughness of the seas forced them to simply sit and focus on calming their stomachs. *At least I'm not sweltering*, Chelsea thought. The sweat from waiting on land had long since been chilled by the sea winds.

Neil seemed lost in his own thoughts, alternating between sitting beside her and wandering to the rails to look at the sea below. As they approached the looming island, Chelsea could feel his apprehension rising.

"I can see this from my balcony at home," he told her. Chelsea whistled quietly. A harbour view on the North Shore? It must be a real fancy house. "I never knew what it was. Maybe I should move."

"To get away from the volcano?"

"Yes," Neil said, managing the smallest smile Chelsea had ever seen.

"You're going to have to move quite some way away. About five thousand kilometres to the west." She could see Neil frown. "That's to Australia, by the way. No volcanoes. Just every type of poisonous creepy-crawly Mother Nature could dream up." Neil shuddered visibly. "My theory is that they hate volcanoes too."

"I don't understand how you don't find it distressing that this whole country is so geologically unstable."

"You're from California!" Chelsea was astonished. "California! On the other edge of the same damn tectonic plate. With all the earthquake risks. You have *tornado alley* in your country! You wouldn't catch me living in a place with a name like that."

The ferry chugged closer to the volcano, which looked nothing so much like a slumped giant. To Chelsea, it was utterly familiar and comforting. As a lifelong Aucklander, it was unfathomable to imagine a beachscape without this behemoth watching over it. To see someone react to it with such obvious unease and ill-concealed fear was strange.

"Honestly, Neil, the worst that'll happen is that you'll twist your ankle on a rock," Chelsea said, reaching out and squeezing his hand comfortingly. "It's just a nice hike, and you'll get to see some amazing views. It hasn't done anything for six hundred years, and if it were about to start, we'd have a lot of warning."

She hadn't let go of his hand. It had been cold and slightly wet when she picked it up, and his tight return grip made her feel as though the touch was welcome. He didn't let go either, his eyes fixed ahead.

The volcano was now in front of them, so close that they could no longer see the summit.

A crackling voice came over the loudspeaker to remind them that the island had no facilities beyond some composting toilets, and that this was their last chance to buy water from the ferry's café.

"You've brought water, right?" Chelsea asked.

Neil nodded. "The salesperson at the outdoors shop sold me this backpack with a water bladder."

Chelsea grinned and silently thanked the anonymous salesperson for treating Neil like a complete tourist. Her own backpack had several litres of water in it. She knew her back would complain on the ascent, but rather that than dehydration.

"Trust me, it's a good idea. Dehydration out here isn't fun."

"Surely we could just drink the atmosphere," Neil muttered, and Chelsea laughed. He had a better sense of humour than she had first given him credit for.

They waited while they docked to the island's narrow wooden wharf. A vastly international group of tourists waited to climb aboard, having done the summit climb first thing in the morning before the heat of the day was upon them.

Chelsea snagged a complimentary map of the island and its walks as they disembarked from the ferry, though she knew from memory it was virtually impossible to stuff up. After all, it was a popular tourist destination, even for those who did not speak English. It was probably one of the easiest outdoors adventures the country had to offer.

She dropped Neil's hand as they stepped out onto the solid ground of Rangitoto Island. She glanced around the bare basics of the wharf: some signs, some shade, some seats, some toilets. It couldn't even be called a ferry termi-nal. The concrete ran out pretty quickly, and the ground gave way to raw volcanic rock and the dark sand "beach" where the waves had pounded the dark rock into something smaller and finer, but not quite sand.

Chelsea wondered what it was like seeing something like this for the first time. The dense foliage of primordial rainforest, made up of ferns and palms of different height, was filled with the calls of native birds. Narrow but well-worn paths led into the living labyrinth.

"It smells just like the art gallery's garden," Neil commented finally.

"What?"

"After I left the art gallery, I went through the garden. It smells just the same," he explained. "Like earth, green and damp, and... New Zealand."

"Are you satisfied it's not going to blow up on us?" she asked him gently. She fought the urge to take his hand, to touch him and comfort him. What was wrong with her? Why was she thinking like this?

Neil glanced around, as if judging. The sedate greenery looked the opposite of anything volcanic. "I suppose."

"Good! We'll take you down to Rotorua sometime. You'll get to see what real volcanic action looks like then. Kidding," she said in response to his pained look.

The walk itself was harder than Chelsea remembered. She wasn't in good shape, and being significantly shorter than Neil, she struggled to match his strides even though he was taking obvious care to keep his pace relaxed. The oppressive heat of the day did not improve when the morning's clouds moved on and sunlight began to filter down through the canopy. Whatever coolness the shade might have granted was countered by the humidity that, unlike the clouds, chose to move absolutely nowhere.

Neil found himself enjoying the day more than he expected. The invitation was, just as their first date had been, Chelsea trying to push him out of his comfort zone. It was unfortunate that this particular experiment happened to touch on his lifelong anxiety about volcanoes. He had avoided Hawaii for that reason his entire life. It was true that academically he had been somewhat aware that Auckland had many volcanoes, but nothing he had seen had looked particularly volcanic, and it was easy to pretend that the grass-covered hills that urban Auckland had been built around were indeed just that, not the aging remains of primeval founts of lava.

He was not the type to back down from a challenge though, so he accepted the date. A quick trip to an outdoors sports shop saw him fitted out for the trip. Eddie had accompanied him, and though he honourably obeyed his promise to not cluck at Neil about his concerns for his heart, Eddie chose instead to amuse himself by making fun of Neil's hat. Not for the first time in Eddie's life, Neil contemplated fratricide.

Neil's unease about the volcano was made better when he realised that, like the grass-covered bumps on the Auckland terrain, this volcano bore little resemblance to the landmarks of his nightmare. Aside from its cone shape, it was more like walking through a primeval jungle. As Chelsea had promised, there were no streams of lava or smoke, nor even shakes of the earth, so Neil was able to quash his unease to a mere background noise.

There was plenty for him to think about—the heat and humidity for one. It was hot; the air felt wet on his skin, and each breath felt suffocating. There was no respite from the heat, not even in the shade. Once they left the shores, there wasn't even a breeze.

"It's hotter than hell," Neil commented as they climbed.

"Not true," Chelsea gasped, her face red and perspiration beading on her forehead. "You're thinking of Australia again."

Neil hid a grin. New Zealand's rivalry with Australia was more than the stuff of sitcoms; it was a daily reality. He slowed his pace again, realising he was leaving Chelsea behind, not that she had said a word about it.

"You should tell me if I'm going too fast."

Chelsea looked like she was going to argue, then reconsidered. "Maybe a quick sit-down wouldn't be so bad," she admitted.

They stopped by a likely looking log, and both of them drank water greedily.

"Wait till you see the view," Chelsea said. "It's totally worth all this." She sounded like she was trying to convince herself.

Neil looked down at her. "It's very worth it already," he said. He kept his tone mild. Maybe she would allow herself to understand he meant more than the ferns and the flowers and the native birds. She glanced up at him. His meaning had not escaped her. He smiled.

They reached the top within two hours of setting out, Neil encouraging frequent breaks. He liked it when Chelsea had enough breath in her lungs to chatter to him, and liked it less when she looked like she might drop dead. He didn't find the walk exhausting, but the heat was hard to bear, and his skin felt like it was burning.

As they came out of the path, they found themselves on a small flat section with a concrete pad at the centre and cleared field around it. A cool breeze hit them, and Neil found himself lost for words.

On one side, he saw the city. Small though it was, Auckland's sprawling, glittering mass looked beautiful against the blue sky. In the distance behind the skyline, he caught sight of shadows, looming ranges to the west and to the north. The arms of the bay reached out into the water, creating headlands and peninsulas. The harbour was filled with sailing boats. A cruise ship was heading into the bay. Behind them, facing the ocean, was an expanse of blue water uninterrupted until it reached the shadows of some other island in the distance. The choppiness from the morning had subsided, and the water was faceted and glittering. Occasionally, there was a larger ripple crested by a white foam cap. Everything in sight was in hues of blue or green. Even the city, in the summer light, was a grey that bordered on blue.

"It's breathtaking," Neil said. He was suddenly intensely aware of Chelsea beside him. She smiled at him, her cheeks still red from the climb.

"So's that climb," she said, taking a swig of water. "What a view, eh? I can see my house from here!"

Chelsea's eyes were fixed on the view, but Neil's eyes were fixed on her. In reds and pinks, she stood out against the palette of blues and greens, her magenta-streaked blonde hair whipping in the wind. She made him feel something he couldn't explain. This place here, on top of an ancient volcano in the middle of a harbour, in a country halfway around the world from home, made him feel the same.

Light.

He felt lighter than he had in years. The perpetual tension in his shoulders eased. The fear that lived in the bottom of his stomach went dormant. He stood here, surrounded by his fears, and for the first time in years, he felt light and free and good.

16

GREEDILY SUCKING WATER FROM THE SECOND PLASTIC BOTTLE, Chelsea watched Neil's wonder. She felt her heart swell a little as Neil's expression gave way to joy. It was a look so open that Chelsea felt like an intruder, so she turned away to look at the city and the harbour for herself. She didn't want her own face to betray her.

There was something like wonderment in her chest as well, a joy and a connection that was utterly divorced from the majestic view and breathtaking scenery. The climb up had been hard, but she and Neil had managed it together, communicating in more than just words: in looks and in reading the other's unspoken reactions. The whole journey, it seemed, had been an exercise in trust, teamwork, and supporting the other through challenge and fear.

Chelsea realised, as Neil's joy turned into her joy, that somehow, utterly inconveniently, she was developing feelings for Neil.

It's just the heat. It's just the exhaustion. It's just the overwhelming power of New Zealand's scenery, she told herself as she stared at her home city. *I can't like him. I can't. He's so different from me. He's screamingly rich, and he uses the website. Besides, he has to marry Mikaela.*

"Chelsea?" Neil's voice made her jump. She turned, begging her traitorous face to behave itself just this once.

"How's this, huh?" she asked, smiling widely. Neil smiled back, the most unguarded smile she had ever seen him give.

"It's magnificent. Thank you."

They sat down at the summit with their packed lunch. Eating and watching the reactions of the other tourists as they arrived at the top mercifully mitigated the need for conversation. Chelsea tried to calm herself down.

You have a crush. You don't have to act on it. It's one more date after this. Then you never have to see him again.

Her internal pep talk seemed to work. Chelsea felt rather good about how things were going as they began the descent from the top of the volcano. Checking the time on her phone, she was pleased to see there was ample time to do some of the shorter, more scenic walks.

"Come on, let's go visit the lava caves," Chelsea suggested, instantly regretting her words. "Dried lava! Dried lava! It's just funky rocks!"

"I think I can miss that attraction," Neil said, the edge of his lips slightly white amidst the pink tinge his face had taken up.

"You're burning," Chelsea told him, reaching into her backpack and throwing him a bottle of sunscreen lotion. Neil read the packet and looked up, confused.

"I don't need this," he said. "I have a hat, and we're in the shade."

"You're kidding, aren't you? No, no, no, you have to wear it. No wonder you're so pink; you've burnt."

Chelsea held up a mirror from the front pocket of her backpack. Neil winced.

"It's an attractive look," he muttered, applying the thick white lotion to his skin.

"Tourist," she teased.

He shrugged. "I know how fond you are of the colour pink. Can you blame me?"

Chelsea laughed and, at the same time, wondered at the thrill that those words gave her.

Neil bore the sunburn with good grace, though Chelsea saw that as they walked, the red deepened. She didn't have the heart to push him into coming to the lava caves with her, so she left him sitting a little way up the path while she went ahead to explore.

With her mobile phone out, using the backlight to light her path, she made her way through the lava caves. She wished Neil was with her, but she knew she had pushed him far enough for one day. *I'll let him pick the last date,* she promised herself, even as she panicked internally. *What if he makes me go to a fancy restaurant? What if he makes me go somewhere where there are fancy women and extra forks and they'll look down their perfect noses at me for having pink hair and being chubby and short and an artist?*

She looked around at the other tourists as she came out of one of the larger caves and caught a glimpse of the man with the beard. It was definitely the same man as the one she saw on the wharf this morning, but she couldn't tell if it was the same man who had been outside her building and near Lamplight Club. She ducked off the path, into the dense foliage, and from behind a tree, she watched him meander through the crowd, clearly looking for something.

Chelsea had no way of coming out from her hiding spot and retreating to where she left Neil without being seen by the man, so she opted to wait. He lingered for longer than she could think of a reason for him to do so. As the families left the area, presumably to head back for the sailing, the bearded man waited. Finally, he looked around one last time with clear frustration and headed back through the caves, moving quickly. Chelsea sighed in relief. She'd almost certainly managed to lose him. As she tried to clamber out of the thick foliage, her foot slipped, and she found herself unceremoniously sliding a metre down a bank and lodging in a bush.

Climbing back up the bank was harder in practice than she had anticipated, and after what felt like an eternity of jumping, scrabbling, and falling back down, she realised she needed help. She was almost in tears, and her palms were bleeding slightly.

Swallowing her dignity, she shouted, "Neil! Neil, I'm stuck."

She held her breath.

"Chelsea? Are you okay?" Neil replied, shouting down the lava caves.

"No! I've fallen down a bank, and I can't get back up."

There was a long pause.

"Hold on."

Soon, a pale and slightly shaking Neil emerged from the cave. Chelsea was unbearably glad to see him. "Why is it that I'm always sitting on the ground in some stupid predicament I can't get out of when I see you?" she asked, giving him a watery smile.

"Because the universe loves me enough to want to give me a fighting chance to woo you with my resourcefulness," Neil replied, looking like he was about to be sick. "I was coming after you anyway. My mobile battery died."

"No reception. It drains the battery dry if you don't turn off the network." Chelsea looked up at him from the gully she was in. "I was trying to hide from the man I think is following me, and I fell down the bank."

"You'll have to explain about the man later." Neil sighed and looked down the bank. "I think I can pull you back up," he said, shrugging out of his backpack. Within minutes, Neil had anchored himself against a strong tree and lowered a flexible sapling to Chelsea. She looped it around her wrists, and within a minute, she had successfully hauled herself up the bank again.

"I swear I'm not such a hot mess most of the time," Chelsea told him as she brushed the dirt off herself. "I swear I'm a functional adult."

"I believe you." Neil picked up his backpack. "You'll have to be to get me back through those godforsaken hell caves."

"We need to hurry, or we'll miss the sailing," Chelsea said. "We'll make it. I think." She took Neil's hand, grimy with sweat, sunscreen lotion, and dirt, and began to lead him through the caves with the torch he had the forethought to bring.

The descent took a while, with their growing exhaustion. Neil was hit by sun tiredness, unused to being out in the harsh New Zealand sun for so long.

"Almost there. Almost there," Chelsea kept whispering as she clung to his hand and they walked down the path. She was unnerved by the lack of others around them. The crowds of the day had vanished, and it felt like it was only them on the island.

When they reached the bottom of the volcano and hobbled over to the wharf where the ferry was to meet them, they were greeted by silence. There were no other people there. Neil pointed out to sea. "Is that the boat?"

"It must be on its way in...," Chelsea muttered. They watched it for a few minutes, and there was no denying it was growing smaller. "I don't understand. We had plenty of time." She pulled out her mobile, and with growing dismay she checked the time.

"What's wrong?"

"We missed the ferry," Chelsea said, her voice disbelieving. "We're stuck here."

17

––––––––

Hysterical peals of laughter bubbled out of her.

"When's the next ferry?" Neil asked, looking at her strangely.

"Tomorrow morning. That was the last sailing for the day." She was laughing harder now.

"Right. Fine." Neil glanced around the spartan wharf. "We'll just stay the night somewhere. Is there a motel?"

Chelsea shook her head, her shoulders shaking with soundless hysterics.

"A campground?" Neil asked, eyes widening a fraction too wide.

"Nothing. This is just a big old lump of rock for the tourists to climb!" Chelsea finally stopped laughing and wiped her eyes.

"I'm stuck, overnight, on a volcano with nowhere to stay because we missed the last ferry off this island." Neil shook his head. "I don't believe it. There has to be a way off this rock."

Neil stalked past her to the edge of the wharf, shielding

his eyes as he stared at the city in the distance, as if trying to eyeball what it would take to swim there.

"You can't swim. It's a pretty strong current, and the water is freezing this time of year."

Ignoring her, he took off his backpack and pulled out everything he had, looking at each item one by one.

"What on earth are you doing? Trying to MacGyver us out of here?" When he didn't reply, Chelsea tried again. "Neil, are you okay?"

"No, I am not okay. This is not okay. I am stuck on a volcano with no way to get home until the ferry turns up sometime tomorrow!" Neil wasn't shouting. His voice had not risen in volume, yet there was a force, a heat in it that made Chelsea take a step back. "I don't want to be here overnight. I don't like being this close to it. And I don't like being trapped!"

Neil was breathing heavier than he should have been, and Chelsea could detect the edge of hysteria in his voice. He really didn't like volcanoes, she began to realise. Then why did he come along?

"Please, just let me think." His face was an alarming shade of red, and with his stubbornly set jaw, it gave him a look of, ironically enough, a volcano preparing to blow. Chelsea watched him stare at all the items, then slowly replace everything in his pack, leaving only his mobile in his hand. He stared at its dark screen, pressing the power button a few times before he threw it into the pack too. He covered his face with his hands.

Chelsea reached into her back pocket and pulled out the scrunched-up map she had grabbed before she left the ferry. Examining it for a few minutes, she approached Neil.

"Okay. I have a plan," she started.

"Is it for us travel back in time and not come here?" Neil asked, not opening his eyes.

Chelsea bristled. "Look, I feel terrible. You didn't have to come on this stupid trip. You could've just told me how much you hate volcanoes, and we could've just gone to Melbourne instead!"

"And the entire flight, you'd have been in my ear about the fact that I could buy tickets? No thank you." He spread his hands. "Here we are. I'm on equal footing. No Amex to save me now. I'm sunburned and thirsty, and the only thing that could make this worse is if you tell me this is the island where the New Zealand government keeps their cloned dinosaurs." He finally opened a single eye to look at her.

"Look, I have a plan." She shoved the map at him. "There's a causeway that connects to the next island over. It's got everything we need. We'll be able to cross. There are campsites there, and best of all, it's not a volcano."

At this, Neil definitely perked up.

"It does mean a two-hour walk," Chelsea continued, wincing as she thought of her blisters, "and we'll have to ration the water, but it's our best chance of getting off the island before 9:00 a.m. tomorrow."

"You had me at 'not a volcano.'" With a grimace, Neil got to his feet, donning his backpack and hat.

"It's right next to a volcano. How can it be so different?" Neil gave her a look that reminded her of an offended cat. "Forget I asked," Chelsea huffed, hurrying to keep up with him. "Wait up, Moneybags McLongshanks."

It took them three hours to make the two-hour journey, neither of them being physically fit and both already tired from the summit hike.

Neil walked slightly ahead of Chelsea, trying to burn off his anger and frustration. He knew it wasn't her fault they were stuck here. He should have just hired a boat and a skipper and brought them out here with their mode of transportation entirely within their power. Neil did not enjoy being powerless, nor did he enjoy feeling emotions he knew better than to have. He didn't want to hear Chelsea's apologies. It made him feel churlish for his anger. His anxiety about the volcano—stupid, childish, useless fear as it was—was a constant noise in the back of his head. He didn't like being affected by Chelsea's moods. She wasn't doing it deliberately. None of this was deliberate. But even more than the volcano, the niggling fear that his emotions were being plucked at and tweaked like an instrument made him feel half inhuman.

It was past six o'clock in the evening when they finally reached the eastern wharf of the island. Chelsea sprawled on a bit of shaded grass and pulled off her shoes, looking mournfully at the bottom of her feet. If her feet looked anything like his felt, she had his sincere sympathy. He took himself off to a different patch of shade and looked out at the sea while slowly and sparingly drinking water.

This is why I didn't want to have feelings for someone again. I end up trapped, physically and emotionally. She's doing this to make me feel weak and powerless.

You forget yourself, a quiet, rational voice at the back of his mind said. *This was an accident, a careless mistake at worst. She doesn't deserve your temper. Anger is a waste of energy. It's a long night ahead if you can't get off this island, and probably another walk in the morning to the other wharf. Just let it go.*

She apologised, the rational voice reminded him. *She apologised and meant it.*

Putting the water away, Neil took a deep breath. The air tasted of salt, the bitter tang from the sunscreen lotion, and the sweet scent of greenery in the shade. If he had to be stranded somewhere, this was as close to paradise as he was ever likely to get. He let out the breath and walked back to Chelsea.

"I'm really sorry, Neil. I should have been better prepared and more organised. I really thought..." She trailed off and shook her head. "I'm sorry."

"It's fine," Neil said, surprised at how gentle his voice came out. "I shouldn't have lost my temper. I don't like to be out of my comfort zone. And I don't like to depend on others. This situation is everything that scares me."

Chelsea's blue eyes looked a little watery, but she didn't cry. "I'll do what I can to make it as bearable as I can," she promised him.

Neil shook his head. "Come on. When your feet feel better, we'll go and look for that crossing to the other island."

In obvious pain, Chelsea put her feet back into her shoes and hobbled towards the large sign bearing a map for the tourists. Not far, there was a sandy beach and a channel separating them from the next island.

"I know it's around here somewhere," Chelsea muttered, scanning the tourist sign and squinting at the landscape. "Hmm."

Neil looked over her shoulder. "It should be right—" He looked at the channel of water where the crossing was meant to be. "—right there."

"Oh. It's only there during low tide. This looks like high tide."

"When does it stop being high tide?" Neil asked.

"Within six hours, definitely."

"So, a bit of a wait, then." Neil walked up to where the path stopped abruptly on the edge of the water.

"It says not to cross in high tide. I can't swim so well, so if you go in, I can't pull you out," Chelsea called.

So close, Neil thought before turning back.

"Come on. Let's get some rest."

They trudged towards the patch of grass that grew well back from the high tide mark, ringed by trees that clung in equal parts to the ground and the bottom of the cliff face that rose behind them. Chelsea found a spot where the gnarled roots formed a gentle grassy hollow, shaded by the trees, that had obviously been used by people as a respite from the open conditions before. They lay down in the cool, soft space.

"We should stay awake, so we can sleep through the night," Neil murmured, feeling acutely aware of how close Chelsea was to him. He rigidly shuffled as far to the side as the hollow would let him. Chelsea sprawled freely, wiggling this way and that until she had some semblance of comfort on the grass.

"It'll be fine." Chelsea yawned. "We'll get up when the tide is low, cross over, and find one of the camps there."

Neil wanted to argue, but the exhaustion of the day was swallowing him whole. His legs ached, he was tired, and his face felt burnt. He didn't manage to say whatever he intended in reply. After a yawn that stretched his burned face, he became insensible to the world.

18

———

WHEN NEIL AWOKE, THE SUN WAS HALFWAY DOWN AND twilight was creeping across the island. The temperature had dropped. In the shade, it was now cool with the evening breeze. He sat up and saw Chelsea sitting in one of the last patches of light on the beach, facing their destination.

"Everything all right?" Neil asked, approaching her. She half turned, smiling, her face and hair bathed in the brilliant hues of the setting sun.

"I woke up just as the sun was setting," she explained, scooting over and making room on the dark rock for him. The rock was still warm with the day's heat. He settled himself down gingerly, trying to avoid the worst of the spiky bits. "I thought I'd let you sleep. Just been doing some thinking."

"I'm sorry to have interrupted."

She shook her head. "I was thinking about you, actually." She didn't look at him, keeping her eyes fixed on some remote point at sea.

"Yes?"

Chelsea shrugged and half turned away. "I was just

wondering why you're bothering. With me, I mean. I'm not even trying to sabotage the dates and look at this. Two for two, complete disasters."

"You can't say that," Neil said, looking at Chelsea intently. Something cold and unpleasant emanated through him, starting from his sinking stomach. Was he getting dumped, stranded on the shore of a volcano? That'd be the most fitting end to this terrible day. "We don't know how today ends yet."

"This would never have happened with Mikaela, or any of the other girls from Honey." Chelsea shook her head. "I know they wouldn't constantly be at you over money. To them, that'd be the best thing ever. They love men with money, power, and prestige. They would love that when you wave money around, things happen."

"No, they wouldn't be like you." Neil paused for a moment, then continued tentatively. "When I met you, you were a blur. You were colour, movement, energy, noise. You were crying, and it was so natural." Neil wasn't looking at Chelsea anymore. He too was looking towards the setting sun, now only a fraction above the horizon, the glow deepening to pink. *Everything is very beautiful, even to a dirty old cynic like me.* "You don't pretend. You don't pose. You can't even hide what you're feeling; it's all over your face, even if you somehow manage to keep the words inside. I like it that you are honest with me. I like that you don't want anything from me."

He had so many doubts about this fledgling courtship. The constant battle over his intentions, his money, Chelsea's defensiveness, it had all made him repeatedly wonder what drew him to continue trying. Here in the sunset, he knew what he had told her was true. She was so different from everyone he knew. She was so different from what he was allowed to be.

Maybe it's better I said all this. Now she can end it.

"So, you like me for me," Chelsea said. "*Because* I'm a hot mess of tears and anger and nonsense."

"Yes."

They both fell silent.

The cicadas had stopped some time ago. Now, the night choir had taken over, the same rhythmic hooting he always heard outside and a quiet chirp of insects. The sun was gone, and the dark blue sky was devouring what was left of the golden splash above the horizon.

"Thanks," she eventually replied.

"Can I ask you something?" Neil shifted his weight on the rock.

"It's only fair, I suppose."

"Why are you so afraid of me?"

"I am not afraid of you," Chelsea said hotly, looking at him with such deep offence in her eyes that Neil almost laughed.

"Yes, you are," he said quietly. "You wouldn't yell at me so much if you weren't. You're obsessed with my money."

"It's just... I'll never be able to be on equal footing with you." Chelsea rubbed her legs. Goose pimples ran up and down her bare limbs. Neil just waited. With a sigh, she continued. "I'm afraid I will never have any power in any relationship we have. Because of money. Because you can do so many things I can't. Because if you buy me something, I'll never be able to repay you."

"But I don't need you to repay me. I don't *want* you to." Neil turned Chelsea's words over inside his head and tried to find some scrap of experience he could relate them to. Was there any terrain on which he had felt the same? He had never felt that way about money, had he? Well, he would never want to be in a rival's debt, but the sums they were discussing here were not of that magnitude. What's a boat ride, a few art pieces, dinner, gifts? He could, academically, see the gulf between them, but he couldn't figure out a way to express that, for him, these acts were the equivalent of her buying a coffee for a friend.

"I don't want to be owned," she replied, hunching her shoulders. "You say it's free, but how can I be sure there's no strings? More than enough men in the history of the world have felt 'repayments' necessary for gifts."

"I am not those men," Neil said, white-hot fire in his voice.

"Yeah," Chelsea said non-committally. "All right." Standing, she brushed the grass off her feet and strolled off towards where the land sloped downwards and a stretch of water—shrinking as the tide ebbed out—separated them from their destination.

Neil remained on the rock. Maybe he did understand. "I don't want to be owned," she'd said. She might as well have said, "I don't want to be controlled."

Neil knew something about *that* fear.

Maybe it is better if we don't pursue this. Had he said that before? He must have.

Trying to resist her was like trying to eat a bowl of bran cereal instead of the *pain au chocolat*, like drinking the cheap soft drink instead of the champagne.

Neil shook himself. Retrieving his backpack, he walked down to the edge of the water with her. To him, in the darkness, the stretch of water seemed ominous, a glittering black ribbon moving slowly but intractably. He scrutinised it closely for several minutes.

"Water looks all right to cross," Neil said. "It most likely won't go past our waist, and the current doesn't seem strong."

"Definitely won't go past *your* waist, Legolas." Chelsea frowned at the water. "I don't know, Neil. We might want to give it another hour, just to be sure."

"If we wait too long, then there'll be no way to get off the damn island. Nothing operates at night in this country."

"Yeah, but at least we'll have a bed, or a campsite or something, and we can go home tomorrow. It's camping. It's an adventure." When Neil sighed, Chelsea relented. "Fine. If we put our shoes in your backpack, we'll even have dry shoes at the other end," she said. "As long as we don't get swept away, we shouldn't drown."

With shoes stowed safely, Neil began to wade into the channel slowly. Beside him, Chelsea yelped at the cold water. Neil grimaced. It was a mixed blessing. It felt cool on his burned skin, but the salt was less than kind.

A swell came from the ocean, catching Neil by surprise as it pushed the cold water from his thigh to his waist, chilling his delicate regions rather suddenly. Yelping and leaping into the air, he felt his elbow connect with something soft, and Chelsea squeaked in pain.

"For God's sake, watch out for my boobs!" she cried, wrapping her arms across her chest.

"I'm so sorry," Neil replied, embarrassed. He realised he had misjudged the depth of the water terribly. "Perhaps we ought to turn back."

"In for a penny, in for a pound," the normally sunny Chelsea snarled from beside him. He stumbled, giving opportunity for a larger swell to knock him down.

Saltwater filled his mouth, nose, and ears. The world was replaced by a roar as Neil tried to get his footing, but he had never been dumped into the ocean before, not like this, in the dark out at sea. He had swum only in pools and had never set foot into the wild ocean. He didn't know which way was up, and when he tried to breathe in, his body began to burn, and a vice-like force began to tug at his torso.

"This way, come on!" Chelsea's words reached him as his head broke free of the water. Her arms were wrapped around him, and she was attempting to bodily haul him towards the opposite shore. "Come on. On your feet, long legs. At least try to stop breathing underwater, you stupid millionaire."

Neil wanted to laugh and cry at the same time. Finding his legs, he managed to gracelessly propel himself along, though standing was out of the question as his stomach and lungs still heaved to evacuate the seawater from his body.

"My date is vomiting in my arms. This is just like being back at university," she said, but her voice was gentle. "Get it all out. We're almost there; we're in the shallows."

She was right. When she lowered him, he was able to support himself on his hands and knees, still retching painfully as the saltwater came back up out of him.

"It's all right, moneybags," she teased him softly, her hand rubbing his back. "You're all right now."

"Never been in the ocean" were the first words Neil managed to gasp out as his retches subsided and his lungs tenderly refilled with air. Another coughing fit overtook him.

"You could've mentioned that! I guess I won't be taking you to any of the surf beaches, then. We'll stick to some nice placid bays; you'll learn to swim with all the Kiwi kiddies." He managed to crawl onto the grass, where he collapsed. "We should've waited an hour," Chelsea repeated.

"I concur."

"So much for dry shoes," she sighed sadly. "We'll rest

here until you can walk. But we better hurry. We're both drenched, and the night's not going to get any warmer."

Neil almost wished the volcano would erupt and end this humiliating evening. Almost. Face down on the grass, focussing on breathing in and out without spasms of coughs, he felt Chelsea stretch out beside him. One of her hands continued to rub his back comfortingly.

This is nothing that bran cereal will do for you. His breathing stilled, and chills began to come over him.

19

———

CHELSEA'S ANGER AT HIS SULKY MOOD THAT AFTERNOON disappeared rapidly with Neil's unplanned swim. When he fell and slipped under the waves, she was sure he'd regain his footing quickly. After all, who hadn't taken a tumble into the sea unexpectedly? Hadn't everyone been caught unawares in the surf and been sucked under only to be dumped, coughing, spluttering, nose and eyes streaming, onto the sand by a wild wave? There wasn't even any surf to speak of, just the odd swell and the steady ebb and flow of the water as it made its way back out to sea with the tide.

Only Neil hadn't come back up, and his thrashing limbs against her shins made her realise he might be in trouble. She had no idea where she got the strength to haul him out of the water. *It must have been like when grandmothers lift cars.*

It was cold now as they lay on the grass, both of them sodden. Her arm had been over his back, soothingly rubbing to calm him as he regained his breath, but now she found herself drawing slightly closer. They were both so cold...

"We're taught body heat is excellent against hypothermia," Chelsea heard her voice say, as if from somewhere else.

"Do you think we're getting hypothermia?" Neil asked, his voice hoarse.

"I think we're well on our way."

There was a long pause. Groaning, Neil shifted his weight first onto his back, then, as though it took Herculean effort, onto his other side so he faced her.

"I'm happy to see if the advice works preventatively," he said softly. Chelsea scooted into the embrace of his arms, shivering even more violently when they touched. "You don't need to worry about my... my conduct," he reassured her.

"You've already grabbed my boobs," she said through chattering teeth.

"That was my elbow!" he replied, indignant as tremors ran through his body.

They lay there for some time. The touch was nice, and though they were wet and the breeze was cool, they were beginning to dry off.

"We can't sleep. We might not wake up," Chelsea murmured, fighting off her body's desire to hibernate. Neil was here and he was so warm, and neither of them had the energy to argue. *We might never get another chance to cuddle like this without arguing,* her hazy mind thought. *You definitely won't if you die of hypothermia, you silly woman.*

Suddenly, Chelsea sat bolt upright. Her body flooded with adrenaline.

"Chelsea?"

"Shhh! I heard a voice! Man's voice!" She scrambled to her feet, Neil not far behind her. "There's someone here."

"Well, this island is populated, isn't it?" Neil said. He

rubbed his burnt face gently, obviously trying to come to his senses.

"What if it's him?" Chelsea asked, scanning the darkness. The line of the bush was not far from where they had been resting. Slightly balefully, she noted that the water between the two islands was down to a shallow stream. There was no time to think about that. Motioning Neil to follow, she moved towards the line of the bush, keeping a careful eye on the path.

"Who are you afraid of?" Neil demanded.

"The man with the beard."

"Who?"

"He's been following me! I told you! I've seen him around, and he was up at the lava caves. That's why I slipped. He's here. He's looking for me!"

"Chelsea," Neil began in what sounded like a tone of rationality.

"Woman with pink hair? Yeah, they might've come this way. How hard can they be to miss?" a deep male voice with a thick New Zealand accent said. The man had a light trained out in front of him.

"They're looking for me!" Chelsea hissed. Neil motioned for her to shut up. Her heart raced. Who was looking for her? Why? Her mind raced through the plot of every thriller novel and film she had ever seen. She quietly unzipped Neil's pack and pulled out their shoes.

The silhouette stopped and swung the light towards them. Neil and Chelsea shrank into the bushes.

"Anyone there?" he called.

20

———

"Let me go out and I'll do the talking," Neil whispered. The man came closer.

"I won't be taken!" Chelsea said. Part of her realised that her paranoia was unreasonable. "Avenge me!"

"Chelsea!"

"Is there someone there?" the man called out.

"Get away from me!" Chelsea screamed, hurling one of her pink sneakers at the figure. "Who are you? What do you want? Who do you work for?"

The first shoe missed, but the second two found their mark, and the man approaching them dropped his torch and cursed a blue streak.

"I'm looking for some lost tourists. What the hell is your problem?"

Chelsea wavered. Neil clamped down on her arms. "Are you mad?" he hissed. Louder, to the victim of Chelsea's shoe missiles, he said, "It's all right, officer. I've got her; she won't be throwing any more shoes at you."

"You don't speak for me," Chelsea informed him, shrugging out of his grip. He looked down at her, his face clearly querying her sanity, but let her go.

"I'm not a cop. My name's Bruce. I'm one of the rangers on this island, and I'm looking for a Neil O'Connell and a Chelsea Lambert. That you two?"

Up close, Chelsea could clearly see that the tall, clean-shaven Maori man in the ranger uniform was not the man who had been following her.

"Why are you looking for us?" she asked.

"A bloke called Edward O'Connell noticed you two didn't make it back on the last ferry from Rangitoto. He's got a boat out looking for you guys. They radioed me to check out this way. Moira back at the camp thought you might try to come across here. Most folks who get stranded on the island do. Didn't expect shoes thrown at me though, missy."

"Sorry," Chelsea said, genuinely remorseful and feeling quite stupid. "I thought you were someone else."

"This is Chelsea, I'm Neil, and Edward is my brother," Neil told the man, stepping in front of Chelsea. "I'm sorry for my date's missiles."

"I think the hypothermia confused me," Chelsea offered. Both Bruce and Neil gave her a look. Chelsea decided quiet was a good course of action. Now that she was moving and no longer flooded with adrenaline, reality was beginning to set in. She could see how her behaviour might appear a tad unreasonable.

"Right," Bruce said, giving them a look that suggested he might have wished he had not found them. "Come on, then. I've got the Range Rover parked just over that hill. There's a blanket and some water in there. You look half frozen and well cooked. I'll drive you back to Home Bay where there's a boat waiting for you."

Chelsea walked silently, so tired she could hardly see

straight. Neil conversed with the ranger, explaining some of the less embarrassing parts of their adventure. She couldn't help but smile as she heard Bruce's polite responses, nevertheless holding a tone that New Zealanders reserved for tourists who fell afoul of nature, unaware of the rules of interacting with the environment they had learned as children.

Of course, I can't be too smug, she thought, trudging along in her retrieved shoes. *I'm a local, and it's not exactly like I've been a prize-winning Girl Scout today.*

The drive to Home Bay was quiet. Neil ran out of conversation, and Chelsea decided against speaking and embarrassing herself further. Huddled under a blanket, she acutely felt every bump in the unsealed track that passed for a road. Bruce sang along with his radio. At long last, they arrived in Home Bay.

They gave profuse thanks, refused Milo, and before long they were huddled under different blankets below deck of a small boat, watching the dark shape of the islands grow smaller and smaller behind them as the lights of Auckland grew closer.

Their boat took them to Devonport on the North Shore.

"Come back to my house. Have a hot shower, a drink, and then take a taxi home from there," Neil said as they waited beside the road for the taxi that the skipper had called for them. He looked at Chelsea almost imploringly. "You can even sleep there. I have so many bedrooms, you won't even have to be on the same floor as me."

"So romantic," Chelsea said with a tired smile. She wanted to demur, but the thought of a hot shower, a cup of tea, and falling asleep for a really long time was overwhelmingly tempting. She glanced at Neil. The man was almost asleep on his feet. "Thank you. I'd like that. Just so long as we're clear—nothing sexual."

"That is the spirit in which I offered it," Neil replied. "When I say come to my house, use my shower, sleep in a spare bed, I mean exactly what I say. Besides, should our relationship ever progress to a point where I would feel comfortable making sexual overtures, I would be much more romantic, much less smelly, and much, much less tired."

Despite her exhaustion, Chelsea had to admit she was more than a little curious about seeing Neil's house. Was it as prim and proper as he was? Would it be like something out of a magazine, or would there be something of him in it? She tried to picture what sort of house she would put Neil in.

She couldn't picture it. All she could think of were cars and suits. Did she really know him so poorly as to not be able to fathom his environment?

They arrived outside a multiple-storey house, new and fashionable with tidy, well-maintained gardens. As Chelsea clambered out of the car, she didn't even bother arguing with Neil over the fare. She looked at the house.

"Looks like something from a magazine," she said as Neil dug around inside the damp backpack for his keys. He glanced up briefly at the house with its white exterior, land-scaped gardens, and lawn lighting.

"I suppose," he agreed, thrusting the house key into the lock and opening the heavy polished wooden door. As she looked inside, Chelsea felt her jaw drop.

21

"Jeez, Neil, do you get snow blindness living here?" she asked, unable to keep the disbelief out of her voice. She shook off the feeling that she was talking like a hick. The house was pristine—white walls, white carpet, white tiles. Silver- and black-edged fittings broke up the blinding whiteness. She stood frozen on one spot on the white tiles just inside the front door, clutching her shoes in her hand. She and Neil were both filthy, and everything in the house was white. She couldn't bear the thought of traipsing her dirty, muddy footprints across the pristine carpet.

"Come on, I'll show you where you can stay," Neil said. Chelsea winced as he stepped onto the carpet, leaving behind a trail of mud and sand. She tore her attention from the decor and noticed that the house was lit up. Every light was on. From deeper inside the house, she could hear muffled voices and music.

"Sounds like there's a party on," Chelsea said, frowning. Neil too turned his face upwards in confusion. One of the doors on an upper landing opened, and the noise of the party spilled out unmuffled. A man with floppy blond hair, black shirt, and black slacks ambled out, a crystal wine glass in his hand. His face lit up when he saw them.

"Neil! They found you. Good, I thought you were going to miss the whole thing," the man said, grinning widely. "You're late, but the night's still young. And who's this?" His eyes fell on Chelsea. They were the same shade of blue as Neil's eyes, and now that she looked a bit closer, there was more than a shadow of resemblance between them.

"Eddie, are you having a party?" Neil asked, his voice tight.

"Yeah, like I said yesterday. You're going out on this... volcano climbing thing, then we were going to have a party." Eddie leaned over the bannister, still smiling widely. He beckoned to them. "Come have something to drink. We'll sort it out." He vanished back into the room he had come from. Neil headed up the stairs after him, and Chelsea, not wanting to be left standing in the entranceway, followed, still wincing internally at the thought of the perfect carpet beneath her sandy feet.

The room they stepped into looked like it was built for entertaining. It was about the size of the entire Lamplight Club. At the far end, a glass and stainless steel bar was well stocked with beverages. A woman with the air of a professional bartender was shaking a cocktail shaker while smiling disarmingly at the three women who lounged next to the bar. Two other women were draped on a long, white couch, watching two women play pool. Music played from a fancy stereo system built into the wall, and a flat-screen TV mounted on the wall played music videos with the sound off. Chelsea watched it for a few moments before realising that the music video and the music didn't match up. It was disconcerting.

The room had the air of a private club, and Chelsea did

not feel invited. The occupants of the room looked over at them, the women peering out from below long lashes, everyone posing as artfully and elegantly as if they were photographers who had walked onto a set. Chelsea felt even more acutely aware of her dishevelled, sunburnt state, and wondered if she smelled as terrible as she felt.

"Ladies, my brother finally made it home from his outdoor adventures," Neil's younger brother announced, smiling winsomely, gesturing in the same easy manner that Neil had. "I can't wait to hear what wonders he discovered in that harbour out there, and I hear that Kiwi girls like a rugged man with a fondness for the outdoors."

The women laughed delicate tinkling sounds, with just a little bit of artful eye rolling between them. *"Oh yes,"* they seemed to say. *"Oh these men, saying what they think we want to hear."*

"Eddie, I need to have a word with you," Neil said.

"Let's get a drink, Neil. You need one; it's been a long day. And..." Eddie trailed off, looking at Chelsea.

"This is Chelsea," Neil informed him. "You and I will speak outside." Neil's voice was made of steel. It was clear even to Eddie that Neil would brook no argument. The brothers stared at each other, Neil towering over Eddie in more than mere height.

"All right, all right," Eddie relented with another boyish smile. "You all keep on having fun. We'll be back in a minute. Bailey, get Chelsea a drink, would you? Something nice."

"We're still heading out tonight, aren't we, Eddie?" a woman with a sleek dark bob and long, tanned legs asked.

"Sure, Susie, of course we are. Don't worry, babe," Eddie said as Neil, with one hand on his arm, hustled him from the room. As soon as they were gone, everyone in the room looked at her. Chelsea shifted awkwardly from foot to foot.

"Oh, honey," one of the women said, her voice full of pity. "What *happened* to you?"

"We went to Rangitoto. We misjudged the time and missed the ferry back. Eddie sent a boat to grab us. It's been a bit of a long day." Silence followed her threadbare summary of the day. Chelsea's stomach knotted. This was a nightmare, these glamorous women were the sort that Neil should be with. They were all looking down on her, and now they had started sniggering and laughing. She was scruffy and she didn't belong. Tears pricked at her eyes. Should she retort? Should she run?

"Thank god you're here, this is the most boring party ever, Eddie just talks and talks and *talks,*" said a woman with gold-blonde hair that flowed in thick waves. "Mostly about himself, and how great he is. Occasionally he remembers to mention how great his brother is." The room erupted in laughter, and Chelsea realised the sniggers hadn't been directed at her. The women were laughing at *Eddie.*

"You have to sit down," a small woman with wispy blonde hair said, abandoning the pool table and the women cleared a place for Chelsea to sit. "You look ready to fall down."

"Here, I found some moisturiser, you should put this on." The woman who had first spoken handed Chelsea a small tub of cream from her handbag. "We've been waiting for hours for this brother to get here, it's been too awkward to leave. From the way Eddie was talking up his brother, I was expecting him to be eight feet tall and made of solid gold."

"We should just run for it, while Eddie's out of the

room," the wispy blonde said. Chelsea found herself smiling.

"Here you go, babe," Bailey, the bartender, said, thrusting a tall glass with a wedge of lime on the rim towards her. "And when you've finished that, you can drink this." She had an identical drink in her other hand.

"What are you *giving* her?" the golden-blonde woman asked, looking aghast.

"The only thing she should be drinking right now, which is water," Bailey replied. "Drink up, babe, you're dehydrated."

Chelsea obeyed, gratefully draining both glasses of water, as the women chattered around her. They were nothing like she expected them to be. They were nice. Two remained snootily stand-offish in the corner, but rest, were clustered around, making sure she was okay. *I can't believe I assumed they would make fun of me. When did I get so judgy?* Now she felt like she was going to cry again.

"Thanks for the water, and everything," Chelsea said, finding her voice. She handed the small moisturiser tub back. "You're all really kind, but I'm wiped out, I think I'll just go home."

"Great," the wispy blonde said, snagging her handbag from by the foot of the couch. "I'll call us taxis, we can all get out of here."

"Speak for yourself, I'm staying," It was the dark-haired woman called Susie that had spoken, for the first time since Eddie had left the room. The other women paused for a moment, then shrugged.

"He's all yours, hope you enjoy yourself," said the woman with the moisturiser. "There's plenty more fish in the sea for the rest of us."

"Yeah," replied the golden-blonde. "Less irritating fish."

"I'll just tell Neil I'm going," Chelsea said, getting to her feet, and padding out of the marble-tiled room while the women rounded up their shoes and coats.

As she shut the door of the lounge, the voices of the women were muted, and from the next floor up, she could hear male voices coming from a partially closed door. Heading up the stairs, she froze as she heard words coming out.

"...trying to help you, Neil. You're making a mistake."

Chelsea reminded herself that eavesdropping was not a cool thing to do, but her curiosity won the confrontation with her morals. She strained to catch more of their conversation. She guessed they must be pacing around and sometimes speaking in the wrong direction for her to be able to hear.

"...not your business... shouldn't be here..." That was Neil.

"You're forgetting about Florence." Eddie was talking louder. *Florence?* Chelsea wondered. *Who was Florence?*

"...why I'm in New Zealand... never going to look here... couldn't find out..." Neil, again.

"...in big trouble... you need to end it..." Eddie's words were vehement.

"...won't let it... go badly... what am I going to do about all these women..."

"...waiting for you for hours. You said you'd be back in time for the party..."

"...you said friends. You knew I was going to be with Chelsea."

"She can come too. You'll see how much better... won't let her into any club dressed like that..."

"Where exactly do you think we should go?"

Chelsea let out a breath and began to quietly ease her

way down the stairs. She didn't want to walk in on that discussion. There would be no way to pretend she hadn't heard any of it, since her face was as expressive as everyone said it was.

Who the hell was Florence? Were they talking about the city in Italy? Had Neil done something in Florence that Eddie was reminding him of? Or was Florence a woman? Eddie seemed insistent that Florence was important. Was she family? An ex? Had she died? Or worse... was she current?

Neil doesn't seem the sort to cheat, she told herself as she reached the bottom of the stairs and, in that stark white entranceway, started to wrestle her damp feet into damper, muddier shoes. *You don't know that,* another voice in her head pointed out. *You couldn't picture any version of what his house would look like. Why do you think you have any kind of insight into what kind of man he is? You know as well as anyone that it's not uncommon for the men on Honey to not be entirely single. You're being naive to think that it's not possible that he's got a girlfriend or a wife.*

I don't want to be a mistress, Chelsea thought. *And to hell with them for talking about me like I'm some kind of hag that won't be let into clubs.*

"Chelsea? Where are you going?"

She looked up at the sound of Neil's voice. He and Eddie had emerged from their conference and were looking down on her from their vantage point at the top of the third landing. Neil's face looked stony; Eddie's was a look of poorly feigned innocence.

"Please stay," Neil said. "We've had a rough day. I promised you hospitality."

"Your brother promised a lot about you to the party in

there, I'm sure he doesn't want you to let them down."
Chelsea glared at Eddie.

"I'm sure it's just a misunderstanding," Eddie started, a
glib smile on his lips.

"Oh, go jump off something high into a giant pile of
money," Chelsea told him waspishly.

She wrenched open the door and ran out, slamming it in
her wake. She made it as far as the footpath before she had
to pause; the adrenaline of confrontation could only carry
her so far given how exhausted she was. Her legs shook
beneath her, and she fought the urge to sit down there on
the sidewalk in front of his house and just sleep.

Behind her, she heard the door open. She turned
around, gripping the letterbox. Neil walked out onto the
footpath.

"Please wait," he said softly.

"Well? Not going to your party?" she asked, trying to
sound as though she were strong and giving him a chance,
instead of staying in place because she wasn't sure she
wouldn't fall over if she tried to walk away.

"My brother and I are very different people," he said,
walking closer to her. She could not miss the exhaustion
and pain in his gait. "He asked me yesterday if it would be all
right if he had a bit of a social gathering here. I said it would
be fine, but to not expect me. I had plans with you, and if
our plans went beyond climbing a volcanic island in the
harbour, I would prefer it to socialising with strangers."
There was a ghost of a smile on his face. "My brother said I'd
be welcome to join them when I returned. Regrettably, what
I said and what he thought were not the same thing. I think
he intended to organise entertainment for me after my
'ordeal.' He expected me to have a bad time. He did not
expect me to have brought you with me."

"That much is obvious."

"You look very tired. Please come back inside," Neil said. "My offer to let you clean up and rest stands.

"Not with your brother there giving me snooty looks."

"He's leaving." Neil stepped closer to her, putting his hands on her arms. It was hard to see his face, as he was lit from behind by the square of light from the door, but he looked so very serious. "He won't be back until tomorrow afternoon, on pain of being thrown out to fend for himself for the rest of his visit. I'd rather you were comfortable than soothe my presumptuous brother's ruffled feathers."

"I just want to sleep," Chelsea whispered. "I'm so tired of fighting. This whole day has been a battle."

Neil leaned down and gently kissed her forehead. Chelsea's insides fluttered, and she leaned against his chest, releasing the letterbox and wrapping her arms around him for support. They stayed there for a few moments. Chelsea's wildly beating heart picked up pace when she realised that she could hear his heart beating just as hard. She wanted to stay.

But she couldn't now.

"No," she told him. "Thank you, but I want to go home."

She felt him slump slightly. "Of course."

Chelsea shivered, from both tiredness and cold. Neil pulled her even closer, his hand running up and down her bare arms, gently comforting and warming. *I could almost fall asleep here,* she thought. He smelled like a hot day at the beach, all sweat, sea, sand, and sunscreen, with an echo of his cologne applied many hours ago. He smelled like summer and man... like Neil.

Chelsea jerked awake at the happy buzz of cheerful people getting closer. The party from the white salon was descending the inner stairs and spilling out onto the front patio in front of the house, with ladies shrugging into coats and rummaging around inside handbags. As they streamed past them, they gave perfunctory goodbyes to Neil, while Chelsea received chirpy farewells and wishes for her swift recovery from the ordeal, and one request to know where she had gotten her hair dyed with pink streaks.

At last, the parade ended with them all tucked into cars, and the host of the ill-advised party brought up the rear, with the sullen Susie clinging to his arm and with a tall, red-haired woman on his other side.

"Neil, my treasure," she said, stepping forward to kiss Neil on the cheek. She was tall enough to be eye level with him. "You didn't think I'd leave without saying something, even after you snubbed me upstairs?"

"I didn't see you, Rachel," Neil said. Chelsea felt his body relax. Hers tightened in response. Who was this woman? "I didn't know you enjoyed attending Eddie's getting-laid parties."

The woman, Rachel, laughed, full throated and delighted. Eddie looked murderously at his brother.

"I was misled. I was told you'd be here. Still, even a fleeting glimpse of you is more than I've had in months." The tall woman turned to Chelsea, smiling and extending a hand.

"And you must be Chelsea," she said warmly. "It's nice to finally meet you."

Chelsea tried to take in everything about this woman. Her clothes were fashionable and expensive. Her nails were manicured. Her diamonds were real. Her red hair probably had its own Facebook page. She was smiling with genuine joy.

"I didn't mean to be rude, before," was all Chelsea could

think of to say. "There were so many people talking upstairs."

"Rudeness seems to be in vogue tonight." Eddie sniffed, giving his brother a dark look.

"Hush, you reprobate. You know you were making trouble," Rachel told him before turning back to Chelsea. "You both look dead on your feet. We'll have to do this again when you two are less exhausted. I, for one, am about to turn into a pumpkin myself. Goodbye, Chelsea. I think we're going to get on just great." With an air kiss and a grin, she all but glided down the sidewalk.

Eddie gave her back a baleful look before turning back to Neil.

"I wasn't *actually* trying to get you laid," he said to Neil with an air of being much put upon. "I was just trying—"

"Whatever you were trying, I'll pass on my share of the favour. I already have a date."

"Your loss." Eddie shrugged.

"Charmed to meet you too, Eddie. Thanks for getting us off that island, but next time, if you're just going to be rude, you might as well leave us there."

"Ouch, the rose has thorns," Eddie replied sarcastically.

"She says what's on her mind. She's a lot like you that way." Neil ignored both of their indignant squawks. "Go partying, Eddie."

Throwing his hands in the air, Eddie left. Susie followed him, glaring daggers at Chelsea. She ignored her. Neil looked down at Chelsea.

"You're mean when you're tired."

"I'm mean all the time. I was mean to you most of today," she said softly. "Sorry about that."

Neil chuckled. "Come on. I'll call my driver for you."

"Who was that woman?" Chelsea asked, part curious, part worried, as she and Neil staggered back into his house.

"Rachel? A very old friend and my business partner," Neil said. Chelsea sighed with relief. "I'm flattered you're interested enough to be jealous."

Chelsea wanted to argue, but instead she sank onto the steps to sit for a minute. Then Neil was showing her into his car, his driver ready to take her home. "Sleep well, Chelsea," he said, stroking her arm gently and leaning down to kiss her forehead.

Then the door was shut and the car pulled away. Chelsea turned to watch Neil standing in a pool of light until they turned and he was out of sight. As the car drove through late-night Auckland, Chelsea wavered on the edge of sleep, enveloped by the sensory memory of Neil's gentle touch on her arm and the soft brush of his lips against her forehead.

Strange, she thought as she drifted, *that of all the sensations today, that's the one that stayed.*

22

"So, are you going to pretend that last night didn't happen?"

Neil looked up from tying his necktie. His younger brother was framed by the doorway, looking petulant.

"Did you learn that from the women you have one-night stands with?" Neil asked. Eddie couldn't hide his smile. "You can't be that mad if you're laughing at my stupid jokes."

Eddie shrugged. Neil wasn't too surprised; his brother was quick to anger but even quicker to forget.

"Yeah, okay, I was an asshole," Eddie said. "I mean, I didn't mean to be, let's get that straight. I was trying to do a nice thing for you. But when I saw how awful you looked, I should've just packed up the party and cleared out. And, even as much as I think you're making a mistake with her, I should've respected the fact that you brought Chelsea home, and it wasn't cool to try and get you another hook-up. So, I'm sorry."

"Either you're maturing," Neil said, feeling himself smiling as a shrewd thought occurred to him, "or Rachel's been in your ear."

"I plead the fifth."

"God bless that woman." Neil checked his cuffs as he spoke.

"I suppose this is you getting ready for going out with Chelsea again?"

"No. This is me getting ready to go out with another woman from Honey."

Eddie's face lit up. "*Finally.* Who's the lovely lady?"

"Chelsea's cousin, Mikaela."

Eddie's face was remarkable, and Neil barely kept from chuckling. And to think people accused him of having no sense of humour.

"Her cousin." His brother followed him out onto the landing as Neil headed for the door. "Brother of mine, I don't understand this strange and dangerous game you are playing, but having more than one woman always ends badly. Trust me on this."

"Listen, this really hasn't worked out between us, has it?" Chelsea's cousin sat across the table. She had finished her second glass of wine and looked down at their newly arrived mains.

"I wouldn't say we have an extraordinary spark, if I am honest," Neil said gently. Mikaela had looked glum all evening and had been difficult to engage in conversation. Certainly, she was, as promised, beautiful, well put-together, and intelligent, but there was a distance from her that Neil did not feel invited to try and bridge. "I'm not certain why Ms Lambert felt we would be well suited to each other."

"Probably because I told her you were the only one I wanted to date. But only because I didn't think you'd ever agree. No offence." Mikaela looked embarrassed. "I don't know how she talked you into it. I guess she's much better at her job than Mum gives her credit for."

"No offence taken," Neil replied. "I'm perfectly happy to have made your acquaintance regardless. I'm glad we can end this amicably."

Mikaela nodded and started eating. Neil felt that distance again, as if offering that brief connection had exhausted her.

"Ms Lambert is very insistent to find you a date. May I ask why you were there?" Neil focussed on his own food while Mikaela fumbled for a reply. "If it helps, I wasn't there for a date either. My brother insisted I sign up for the website. It was easier to say yes than to argue in perpetuity."

"I know that feeling," Mikaela replied. Some of the unease and tension had drained away from her face and shoulders, and she was looking at him as though he were someone else. "My mum made me sign up. She wants me to get a man. A rich man, preferably. She's got some entitlement complex. Like after all she's invested in me, I can be cashed in like some kind of fund." Mikaela shook her head and poured herself another glass of wine.

"And your mother is Chelsea Lambert's... aunt, correct?"

"Yeah. And Mum is leaning on her to use her job to sort me out with a rich husband. Mum's got some screwy ideas about how the world works."

"You don't want to get married?"

"I don't want a husband, no." Mikaela looked away. "Sorry I wasted your time."

"I'm not looking to get married either, so I don't consider this time wasted."

"Just so we're clear, you and I aren't going anywhere after dinner."

Neil choked slightly on his food, and once he'd coughed his airway clear, he looked at Mikaela in genuine confusion. "I assume from your intonation you're indicating there will be no intimacy between us, but given that we had already agreed neither of us is interested, I can't imagine why you thought I would assume that. After dinner we will shake hands, bid polite farewells, and see what's on late-night TV in separate houses."

"Just making it clear." There was a defensiveness in Mikaela's eyes that looked familiar; Neil had seen it in Chelsea's. He was aware the modern dating scene placed certain expectations on women, but this went beyond that. There was caution of social debt that tied Mikaela and Chelsea together.

"You are not in my debt, Mikaela," Neil said gently. "I've noticed Chelsea express similar fears in conversations."

"It's one thing you learn quick around Mum—you don't get something for nothing. Everything comes with strings. She's nice enough and means well, sort of, but it's like she can't help herself. When she wants something, suddenly she'll remind you of every glass of water you've ever had from her tap, you know? I don't think she knows how to ask for things without making it impossible to say no." Mikaela paused her eating to look at Neil. Her cheeks coloured slightly. "You don't need to know this. It's just family stuff."

"We have agreed to end a potential relationship, not sit in silence while we eat. I welcome conversation." Neil considered his next question carefully. "Is she quite hard on you and Chelsea?"

"More her, I think. We were about thirteen when Aunt Vicky got sick. Really sick. She and Chelsea moved in with us. Mum said that, because Aunt Vicky was a layabout, they didn't have anywhere to go. But the sicker Aunt Vicky got, I think she just wanted to be around family. Makes sense, right? Even if family is as tricky as my mum."

Neil nodded.

"Aunt Vicky died when we were about seventeen, and things got worse. Chelsea left as soon she was eighteen. Mum feels like she left us after we gave her so much, but the thing is, you never really get out of owing Mum. But then, Chelsea just pretends like we never did anything good for her." Mikaela pushed away her empty plate. "I don't think it's fair of Mum to use that to make her find me a date, but I think Mum would calm down a lot if Chelsea was just around more, you know?"

"Emotional extortion is not the same as love," Neil replied, keeping his voice steady.

Mikaela shrugged. "Chelsea's desperate to give us both the flick. It's why she's hustling so hard to get me married off, to settle scores with Mum so she never has to see us again. Family, huh?" She shrugged. "What about you? Why is your brother forcing you to meet women? Does he think you might be gay?"

"No. It was his solution to my dilemma that I'm lonely, but I don't want to fall in love." Neil felt strange admitting that. Mikaela was unaware of how profound this moment was. She had lost interest again and looked down at her phone, becoming visibly distressed.

"Dammit. I have to go. I'm sorry." Mikaela leapt to her feet and ran from the table. It happened in barely the blink of an eye, and suddenly, Neil was alone, clueless as to what caused Mikaela to depart in such a hurry.

Regardless, the dinner had had a profound effect on him. The unexpected insight into Chelsea's fears was a gift. He too knew what it was like to have a loved one keep a ledger of debt where things that should be given freely were weighed, accounted for, and always found wanting.

Perhaps I should be less surprised it is so hard to convince Chelsea that she owes me nothing. It was a long time before I believed myself to be debt free.

And if Neil was honest, he knew nothing would erase the debt he owed.

23

"Thank God you two are here," Chelsea said, hugging Kim and gently half hugging Delta, who was precariously balanced on crutches. "I spent this morning reading a book called *Reaching Out to Maximise Engagement* for work. I really don't think the authors had the dating industry in mind. I've been working on my 'voice,' which really just means coming up with how many corporately mandated kisses I leave on the profiles of men old enough to be my father."

"Was that what you were doing? You were so slow replying to messages, I thought you'd died," Delta said.

"Doll, I wish my job was entertaining your poor bedridden butt. But until you pay my bills, I'm still Helen's minion."

"And as much as I love you, if I had to choose someone to entertain my bedridden butt, I'd want someone more like the suit. Anyway, we're here. Someone hold the door for me."

Chelsea and Kim held the doors of the charity shop open so Delta could lope in on her crutches.

"Remind me why we're here at lunchtime," Kim said, trailing along behind Chelsea.

"I have a date tonight," Chelsea said, stopping to flick through a rack of dresses. Her friends gave her an impatient look as she continued to push hangers aside. "With Neil. At Queen's Grill."

"With Neil 'Moneybags' the Millionaire," Delta clarified. "At the poshest, most highly rated restaurant in all of Auckland. I think there might be a restaurant in Wellington with a better reputation, and that's only because Wellington starts with bonus hipster points."

"Yes, that's the one," Chelsea said serenely. She looked up from a crimson mass of silk, edges embroidered in gold. "What's the problem with that?"

"And you're buying your dress in a charity shop." This seemed to be the crux of the argument. "We're trusting the gods of opportunity shopping that not only will we find something that fits, but that it will be posh enough to wear to dinner."

"Yes," Chelsea chirped in reply. She held up the garment. "Do you think it would be inappropriate for me to wear a sari?"

"Yes, it would. This isn't a Bollywood movie," Delta said.

"Or maybe it is, I don't know. I lost track of what this all was quite some time ago." Kim put her hand on Chelsea's arm. "Chels, I've missed something. I thought you hated this guy."

Chelsea looked up at Kim's concerned face and sighed.

"We've had a nice time together. We've gone on two dates that have been my pick—mostly ones where he can't wave his credit cards around and use money to make things happen."

"Like the Rangitoto disaster," Delta interrupted.

"That's more of a funny story than a disaster," Chelsea told her. Kim arched her eyebrows. "Okay, it's a funny story *now*. And it was pretty funny when Neil's face peeled."

"Okay, so, Neil's face falling off aside, why are we here? Why aren't you mortgaging a kidney or robbing a bank so you can get a dress you can wear to that place?"

"I'm trying to be cavalier. If I think too hard, I freak out, so I'm just pretending it's no big deal. I thought about this for ages and looked at what I had in my bank account, and also what designer dresses cost even second-hand, and the short answer is that I'm not getting one without doing either of the charming things you suggested."

"Honey should invest in a wardrobe," Kim suggested.

"Helen's thought about it, believe me." Kim and Delta both made a face. "I realised I was going to be panicky about how I looked anyway. My hair's *pink*. I'm not the sort of person that fits in at a posh place like that. I don't want to look like the Cinderella whose fairy godmother forgot to show up."

"So that's why we're here? You're just going to look shabby?"

Chelsea shot Kim a disapproving look and shook her head. "No. I'm going to dress like *myself*. I always like dressing for a fun date in fun clothes, and this is where I find fun clothes. So there."

"I almost feel sorry for Moneybags," Delta said, trailing her hands along a rack of blouses, absently glancing over them.

"He says he likes me for me," Chelsea told them. "I still don't understand it. Why me and not one of the well-coiffed, expensively perfumed women that his brother keeps chucking at him? I can see his Honey profile analytics. They're all gagging for him."

"Who knows, maybe he likes you because you're the kinda class act that will rescue him from drowning and then pick a fight with his brother," Delta said. "You're pretty special, Chels. Don't get all wibbly wobbly on us."

"Hey, how about this one?" A dress had caught Chelsea's eye, wedged between an 80s polyester wedding dress with leg-of-mutton sleeves and a bright orange sundress. She gave it a solid yank, pulling it out, and held it up for her friends to see.

"Looks good," Delta said, eyeing the elegantly cut satin dress patterned with birds of paradise. "I mean, if you were going to drink cocktails on the beach."

"Perfect," Chelsea told her. She glanced at the pile on her arm. "Time to hit the dressing room."

Opportunity shopping, Chelsea reflected as she tried on one dress after another, wedging herself into dresses that were too small or finding herself lost in dresses that were too big, really was aptly named. You never found what you were looking for, but always found something that would do just as well, if not better. And this time was no exception.

She was down to the final dress. She slipped easily into it, the lines of the garment hugging her figure as she zipped it up. She smiled at her reflection.

"Well?" Chelsea asked her friends, throwing the curtain open. "Fourteen dollars." Kim and Delta stared, then grinned and whooped.

"You'd make the worst trophy wife ever," Kim told her friend.

"And I won't let him forget it," Chelsea replied cheerfully.

Despite her cavalier words, Chelsea was a mass of nerves as she waited for Neil to arrive. She was dressed, her hair curled, her make-up applied, her shoes on, and her walking practiced. With no tasks left to do, her anxieties crowded her, surging over the barriers she put up to protect herself.

You're going to look stupid. Everyone will laugh. They will know you don't belong.

She was paralysed by horror visions of stuffy butlers giving her disapproving looks as she reached for the wrong fork, of sniggering diners pointing and giggling. Neil's brother and the women from the party were sitting at a nearby table live-tweeting the whole debacle...

"Oh, get a grip," she whispered to herself. "We don't have butlers in New Zealand."

Her doorbell rang, and with shaking knees, she rose to answer it. Neil stood at the door with a bouquet of outrageously colourful flowers in his arms, a cerulean shirt that brought out his eyes, and another one of his dashing tailored black suits.

"Chelsea," he said, a small smile managing to light up his face. "You look beautiful."

And just like that, at Neil's obvious happiness, Chelsea imagined herself grinding her anxiety under her heel. She accepted the flowers, pausing briefly to run her fingers over the soft petals before putting them in some water.

"Sorry about the bucket," she said as she eyed the plastic bucket that currently made a home for the bouquet. "I don't have a vase big enough."

"Would you like to make one, or should I risk your wrath by offering to buy you one? You can have one from my house. I'd feel better with less bouquets of dead flowers around my house, truth be told." There was a ghost of a smile on Neil's lips.

"Dead flowers. So romantic."

"So I am told," Neil spread his hands before offering her his arm. "Your dress is lovely. Puts the flowers to shame."

"Shush," Chelsea said, taking his arm and sweeping him from her little home. "Aren't you going to ask who I'm wearing?" She grinned as she pulled the door shut behind her and checked it had locked.

"I don't think it matters. You've made it very much your own."

The dress she found at the charity shop was a 1940s shape, with a pencil skirt and a trapezoid upper. Chelsea had fallen in love with the print, an impressionistic floral that started black and white at the bottom of the dress and slowly transitioned to full colour by the time it reached her neck. It summed up her relationship with "high society" well: in a world of dour blacks and whites, she was a splash of colour.

Her chest felt fluttery, and her manner was giddy. What was she doing, acting like she was back in high school with her first crush? She'd plenty of dates, of boyfriends, of experience...

It must be the nerves. The anxiety. Wasn't there a science article somewhere about people confusing fear for love?

Oh, don't even think that word.

"What happened? You've gone silent." Neil opened the car door for her. Chelsea slid in, trying to keep her legs closed to avoid giving Neil, the driver, and her neighbours a view up her skirt

"Have I?"

"Yes. It's quite noticeable when you stop talking, because you do it almost non-stop." Neil slid into his own seat.

Moments later, the car started moving towards the central city.

"I'm just nervous about tonight."

"Why?" he asked, looking at her. Chelsea was glad that there was no recrimination in his voice, no demand in his face. He looked as though he simply wanted to hear what she had to say.

"You're taking me to a really nice place. I don't go to really nice places. I might..." Chelsea trailed off, feeling a faint blush rise and hating herself for it. "I might embarrass you."

"To embarrass me, I'd have to care what people think."

"Don't you?"

Neil paused and considered for a second. "It depends on the people. For example," he said, taking her hand and letting the corners of his mouth twitch upwards, "you."

Chelsea was not entirely comforted. When they arrived outside the restaurant, the valet opened Neil's door first, then hers, and Neil helped her from the car. Chelsea straightened up, fussing with her dress for a minute before Neil touched her gently on the arm.

"Are you all right?" he asked softly, looking at her intently.

Chelsea forced a smile. "Grand."

"You're a terrible liar." Neil pressed her hand briefly against his lips before squeezing it reassuringly. "I promise you that you have nothing to worry about. Do you trust me?"

"Yes." Chelsea's response was uttered before it truly registered. It had come from some instinct that was more certain than her quavering rational mind. Yes, she trusted Neil. He was on her side. He'd help her with the forks. Hell, he'd probably pay for a worldwide change in how forks were used if he thought it would make her feel better.

"If I use the wrong fork, you'll buy me a fork etiquette company that says I did it right, won't you?" Chelsea whispered as they walked towards the restaurant's doors.

"At last you begin to see the potential that my wealth holds for you." Neil's taciturn reply still somehow held the tone of laughter.

As they stepped through the double doors, Chelsea could only bring herself to look at the floor, watching her black shoes strike the marble, unable to look up and meet the eyes of the other patrons who would surely recognise her for the imposter she truly was.

"Mr O'Connell, Ms Lambert, welcome to Queen's Grill. If you will follow me to your table."

The hostess's voice echoed slightly. Curious at the lack of other sounds, Chelsea finally looked up, wondering how the popular restaurant could be so quiet on a Friday night.

The restaurant was empty.

"Where the hell is everyone?" Chelsea asked as she clutched Neil's hand, following the server to a table for two in the middle of the room. "It's summer and Friday; this place should be packed with a queue outside the door."

"I knew how nervous you were," Neil said as they sat down. "It was good of you to agree to come to an outing of my choice, so I wanted to make it as easy as possible for you. So I booked it for the night."

"Every table? For a Friday night?" Chelsea looked around. A waitress stood next to them, not quite able to hide her smile.

"Yes. It was cheaper than buying the restaurant, and I know how you admire fiscal responsibility," Neil explained, scanning the wine list. His selection made, he looked at Chelsea with the half-hidden smile he favoured. "I hope you'll be able to relax now that we are unobserved. Feel free to use any spoon or fork you like. Katie here is being paid extra to nod and say, 'Very good, ma'am.'"

Chelsea shot a look at their waitress, who gave her a small wink. "I don't like the forks either. If you ever get stuck though, you can't go wrong with from the outside in."

"*You* can't go wrong maybe, but I'll bet you I can," Chelsea muttered darkly, surveying the cutlery situation.

"Very good, ma'am," Katie said with a straight face. Chelsea couldn't help but smile. Once Katie had taken their orders and left, Chelsea looked at Neil opposite her in the empty restaurant.

"Delta confirmed your anxieties," Neil said.

"That traitorous wench!"

"Don't blame her. She's been going mad cooped up at home."

"Tell me about it. I hear from her all day long." Chelsea shook her head. "She'll start bothering me for date updates soon. Anyway, how is your brother?"

"Eddie?" Neil shrugged. "He's well enough. Recovered from the ordeal of being unceremoniously thrown out of my house. I hope he doesn't get too attached. I'd really prefer it if he went back home to California soon."

"Are you not close?" Chelsea toyed with her water glass. They had not discussed the disastrous return from Rangitoto since watching Eddie and his guests file out into the night.

"We get on well enough. I understand that he, in his own way, has my best interests at heart." Neil shrugged. "Whether he has an inkling of what those best interests might actually be, well, that's a different question. I care about him, I really do, but I came to New Zealand to get space, and I can't get space with him in my house. However roomy that house might be," he added with a ghost of a smile.

"Isn't he as loaded as you? Is he mooching? Seems like a party boy like him would want his own space."

Neil shook his head. "Not at all. Eddie is very wealthy in his own right, and he's got a bigger hand in our parents' interests than I do. He's staying with me because he likes company. Familiar company. He doesn't particularly like new or unfamiliar things. It was a big enough move for him to come to a country he doesn't know. Staying by himself would have pushed him too far out of his comfort zone."

"He's an adult though," she pointed out, watching him. Neil, as always, was hard to read. Chelsea had begun to recognise his facial expressions, the small changes that heralded his moods. In many ways, his means of expression was the opposite of her own. While she favoured bold open-ness, Neil's expression was subdued. It wasn't fair to label him as unfeeling or stony, though. He felt things; he just didn't shout it. The tiniest movements of his face had big meanings.

"He is. He is *able* to stay by himself. He just prefers not to if he has an option. I don't mind. He's my little brother. It's part of the package to have to deal with him annoying me and wanting to look out for him at the same time." He shook his head a little ruefully.

"I don't mean to pry, but Eddie seems very invested in your personal life. He doesn't like me, does he?"

"He doesn't know you. He's judged you on what he thinks you are." Neil rubbed his face. "He likes predictability. He thinks you're unpredictable. He's right, of course; you are unpredictable. However, I like that, as we've established."

"But he seemed really worried. I haven't done anything for him to think I'd put you in harm's way. Is there some-thing he's afraid of?" She ached to ask him about the conversation she had overheard, and it was nigh on painful to keep the questions inside. How to ask about Florence?

"Well, I think getting me stranded on a volcano might be considered *harm's way*," Neil said with a small laugh. "You have no siblings, is that right? Just your aunt and your cousin?"

Chelsea stared at him for a beat, wondering, before she realised why he might know. "Mikaela's been talking?"

"Talking is something that's been known to happen on dates." He smiled briefly. "She told me about you and your mother. I'm sorry."

Chelsea looked down at her array of cutlery and shrugged, her good mood deflating slightly.

"It wasn't like she said." She wished he hadn't heard the story from Mikaela; she was certain to have painted Chelsea and her mother in an unkind light.

"From what she said, she'd been raised by someone whose only understanding of interaction was transaction." Neil's voice was soft and kind.

Chelsea inexplicably blinked back tears. "There was this movie we watched one night when we were teenagers, me and Mikaela. It was some horror about these people that end up in fairyland. Not like pixies and things, but these old-school evil fairies. Every time you took a gift from them, even if you didn't realise, they got more power over you. That's my aunt."

"I know," Neil said, reaching across the table and taking both her hands. "Chelsea, believe me, I know. There are people like that. People to whom you are in perpetual, inescapable debt. Obligation as affection. There's only one thing to do with those people."

"Yeah?" Chelsea's voice was barely a breath.

"You leave. Because as long as they keep taking, you will

never be able to give." He winced. "That sounded trite. Did it make sense?"

"I guess." Her chest was tight.

"Chelsea, please look at me." He squeezed her hands. She dared to look up and hoped desperately the movement wouldn't dislodge the tears balancing precariously. "You have no debts as far as I am concerned. Everything I give you, I give you freely. Always. All right?"

Chelsea nodded and tried to surreptitiously wipe her eyes. Something about Neil's words dislodged something heavy and painful in her chest. There were just two more things.

"Are you and Mikaela...?"

"We ended it amicably. Neither of us was interested. She was only seeing me for her mother."

Chelsea made a face.

"And what about... Florence?"

24

———

NEIL LOOKED WINDED. IT REMINDED CHELSEA OF HOW HE HAD looked when he realised they were trapped on a volcano.

"I overheard her name when you and Eddie were arguing last week, when I was trying to leave. I wasn't trying to eavesdrop," Chelsea said in a gabbled rush.

"She is someone I owe a debt to," Neil said finally, with obvious difficulty, "that she will never let me repay." He took a deep breath, refilling his lungs.

"Is 'us' a problem for her?" Chelsea asked, no clearer on their relationship, but worried by the obvious pain the name caused for Neil.

"She doesn't get a say. I'd rather forget her." He gave her a small smile and lifted his wine glass. "To unpredictability and all the excitement it brings."

"If you insist," Chelsea said, lifting her own glass. "And then let's toast to... trust. To trust and the stability it brings."

Neil's blue eyes met hers. "Hear, hear," he said softly.

Dinner passed with no etiquette disasters. Chelsea's relief was almost indescribable, and their affable waitress made the evening even more relaxed. They returned to the car just as the late-summer sun was beginning to set.

"I hope you're not ready to go home," Neil said, holding her hand as they strolled along the urban waterfront.

"Hardly," Chelsea said. Relief and wine made her feel giddy. "I'm still in the mood for fun."

"Good. Let's go back to mine. I had something special arranged, in case dinner wasn't to your liking." He smiled at her worried expression. "I promise it does not involve extraneous forks or my brother. Trust me?"

Chelsea barely heard the question. Her eye had been caught by a man talking on his phone across the road. She stopped in her tracks and stared. It couldn't be the man again.

"Chelsea?"

"It's him. The man who's following me!" Chelsea grabbed Neil's arm. "Over there. On the phone, outside the Indian restaurant." The man continued to talk into his phone. He seemed agitated and oblivious to them. "Have you ever seen him before?"

"No," said Neil, sounding mildly concerned. They were both staring at the man, who ended his conversation, checked the time on the phone, shrugged, and went into the restaurant.

"I'm not paranoid. It's the same guy," Chelsea insisted.

"I believe you. Do you want us to approach him?"

Chelsea's heart skipped a beat. *Us.* He didn't offer to do it for her. He didn't leave her unsupported. *Us.*

She shook her head.

"No. We're not far from the car. I'd rather just leave," Chelsea said. Neil kissed their joined hands, and they quickly turned down a side street towards the waiting vehicle. "I'm happy to go to your house."

"Excellent. I had hoped you were feeling adventurous." Neil smiled again, this time wider, more than the tiny quirk of the corners of his mouth. "With such faith in me, we shall go far indeed."

"As a woman, I always have to worry what your intentions are when you invite me back to your house."

"I hope you would know by now that my intentions are of no consequences without your own intentions to join them," Neil said, looking out at the harbour.

"Well, good," Chelsea told him, trying to recover her glib manner after his thoughtful response. "I spent a whole fourteen dollars on this dress, so I'll be damned if you're going to peel me out of it in such a hurry."

Neil, to her surprise, laughed loudly.

What *would* she do if he had intentions? Chelsea found herself pondering this question as the driver took them over the harbour bridge to his North Shore mansion. She rolled her eyes internally. "Having intentions" was, in her humble opinion, an incredibly euphemistic and dated phrase. He probably did have intention; at the least, he probably had attraction, didn't he? Did *she*?

Chelsea considered it. Well, yes, she concluded. Yes, she did find him attractive. She thought fondly of their moments of intimacy, stolen between arguments and other dramas. She enjoyed his warmth on Rangitoto, a thousand little touches and small chaste kisses on the forehead or the hands, and standing exhaustedly outside his house, his hands gently tracing her arms.

She promptly made up her mind to kiss him that night. She definitely liked him more than enough for that, and who knew, she might find she had intentions to make known to him after all.

She smiled the rest of the way.

As they walked up to the house, Chelsea again appreciated its beauty, in a magazine sort of way.

"How do you stand living in a show home? Don't you worry about spilling something or messing something up? It's too perfect," she said, pausing to admire the picturesque view in front of her.

"I have two cleaners that come in every day. I don't know why. I think they came with the property. They're very nice. They're responsible for a lot of the flowers. Don't forget to steal a vase before you go home tonight."

"But it's so impersonal. How do you stand all the white and steel?" Chelsea pressed.

Neil smiled and unlocked the front door.

The two doors swung inwards dramatically, and in the middle of the entrance hall, on a small plinth, stood one of Chelsea's vibrant sculptures, only just shorter than Chelsea herself. It was a fantastical tree made of fabrics and magazine pages, with the leaves woven in bright colours. It was as if the earth itself cracked under the pressure of the whiteness and this explosion of colour thrust forth from beneath it.

"I've found a few ways to make it my own," Neil said.

"I forgot how lovely that piece is," Chelsea said.

"I enjoy how dynamic it is. It looks like it's in motion, like it's a living part of the house." He looked down at her. "Do you want to see where I've placed the other one?"

"Do you really think it belongs here?" she asked him, stepping closer to the piece, gently running her hand over one of the fuchsia woven leaves occupied by a bird made of blue buttons.

"Yes," he said, gesturing easily. "It brings the room to life."

"But it doesn't fit," she whispered, unable to raise her voice for fear of him hearing it quaver.

"I think it looks grand," he replied.

Chelsea stepped away from the sculpture and put her hands on his shoulders. He looked down at her, his face hard to read as some emotion that she had not seen before crossed his features. It looked something like anticipation. Or was it fear?

"Yeah," she whispered. "I think so too." Stepping up on her tiptoes, she tilted her face up towards him.

Warmth spread through her as his lips touched hers, a softness she knew from his gentle kisses on her face and hands. For a single second, Chelsea thought she forgot how to kiss, startled by the sheer joy of contact. She found herself stepping even closer, her arms going around his body and his like so over hers, pulling the embrace tight. Chelsea savoured the softness, the kindness, and the comfort she found there, the sparking touches of passion that had begun to build.

He broke away after a minute, breathing harder than usual. Chelsea herself was breathless, and she smiled brilliantly up at him.

The silence stretched between them, and suddenly she could hear soft noise from above them, of people talking behind closed doors and music. Neil's gaze followed her eyes.

"I have some guests," he explained. "Though I sincerely wish I didn't right now."

"Guests?" Chelsea's heart dropped. Her disappointment must have been palpable to Neil, who leaned down to give her another quick kiss.

"Not like last week. Regrettably, we should go and say hello." Taking her hand, he led her upstairs to the door of the same room that had hosted the party last week.

"I see we've returned to the Salon of Disappointing

Social Graces," Chelsea remarked wryly. Neil gave her an equally wry glance as he opened the door. Music spilled out, music she liked, and from inside someone shouted, "They're here!" and there was a small cheer. Chelsea gasped.

"What the hell are you guys doing here?" she shouted at her gathered friends. Delta was behind the bar with a crutch under her arm as she mixed up drinks. Kim and Tony were there, as well as Neil's friend Rachel, and they were playing a game of pool. Holly, Delta's organiser friend from the Lamplight Club, was sitting on the white couch with Marian from the art gallery. This was a strange assortment of her sort of people.

"You couldn't keep the high life all to yourself, sweets," Tony drawled as he lined up a shot and missed, much to Kim's delight.

"Yeah," Delta chimed in. "You've told us so much about the suit here and his giant house, we just had to come see." She didn't even wobble on her crutch as she shook a cocktail mixer vigorously.

"Seriously!" Chelsea felt overwhelmed between the dinner, her art, the kiss, and all this.

"I thought it would be nice to socialise with your friends," Neil said in her ear, and she could hear his smile. "I expect you will all be at home in the, what did you call it, Salon of Disappointing Social Graces?" Chelsea drove her elbow into Neil's ribs, and those who'd overheard laughed.

"An apt name," Rachel said, having excused herself from her conversation with the art gallery curator. She smiled warmly at Neil and Chelsea. "Fitting after your last experience here. I hope we can get to know each other better tonight; our last encounter was fleeting, and you already had a poor taste in your mouth."

"You seemed nicer than the other women," Chelsea

offered. "Less... waspish and vapid."

Rachel laughed. "Neil, make sure they put that on my tombstone. Let's get you both a drink."

Hours later, well into the night, the moon hanging high in the dark, dark sky, Neil sat back from the party that continued around him. He had had a thoroughly enjoyable evening, first the dinner with Chelsea, who, despite her glib comments and her attempt to downplay care for her appearance, looked radiant and had not yelled at him at all for making an effort to make her feel more comfortable. It had been a gamble, buying out the restaurant, but when he questioned himself over his intentions, he was certain his goal was only to make Chelsea feel comfortable. The mention of Florence had startled him, almost broke him, but Chelsea had seemed willing to take him at his word and leave the matter. He wondered how long Florence's icy fingers would continue to clutch his heart.

The stroll along the waterfront had been equally nice, barring the encounter with the man who Chelsea believed to be following her. He had certainly given little credence to it before, especially with her hypothermic hysteria on Rangitoto, and he still didn't know what to make of it. He had trouble believing there would be some stranger following her. More likely, they were following him. He wondered for a moment if Florence's hand was in it.

No. He shook his head and dragged himself back from the dark precipice. He forced himself to look at the party. The atmosphere in the salon was, for the first time, warm. The company was relaxed; even Rachel had slid seamlessly into the group. Hopefully Chelsea's memories of the previous visit to this room would be replaced by good drinks, good company, and good music.

"Want to show me the balcony?" a quiet, familiar voice asked. Neil looked up to see Rachel draping herself over the back of the couch he occupied.

"Yes, I think you would like it." He glanced at Chelsea, who was absorbed in a story being told by Marian, and rose from his seat. Outside on the glass balcony, the sea breeze gently tousled their hair, but the night was balmy.

"Actually not bad for an Auckland night," Rachel said, leaning on the chrome railing of the balcony. "I'm far more used to California summers, though."

"It's too humid here," Neil said. "There's so much water here, around us, in the air..."

Rachel laughed. "I hear it gets even worse in January. So," she said, looking at him, "you looked a million miles away in there. Is everything all right?"

Neil considered the question. "Yes, I believe so. I was just reflecting on the evening. Giving thanks for your ability to seamlessly integrate into any social situation."

"You flatter me. How did the dinner go?"

Neil told her all about it, as well as his thoughts. He paused when he finished, unsure whether to mention the kiss and the uncertainty that it fired up in him.

"Hey, Neil, you haven't been listening to Eddie, have you?" Rachel said, her voice so understanding that Neil's resolve wavered. "It's not about Florence, is it?"

"This wasn't supposed to happen, Rachel. It wasn't supposed to happen at all." Neil shut his eyes to try and defend himself against the onslaught of fears and memories that had suddenly overcome his barriers. "I'm still afraid," he told her quietly, "that I'll never be free."

Rachel sighed. "Neil, Neil, don't. Just take it one step at a time. Don't go spooking yourself."

"It wasn't meant to be serious. That's why..."

"The site?"

"Yes. Only I'm not Eddie. I don't think like him. I can't relate to people like him."

"I know. You are the one with an actual heart, despite your stone face."

"Eddie has a heart, you know that," Neil said, feeling pained. He looked sideways at Rachel.

"I know, I know. He just keeps his heart in a box. You're a good person. You stick up for your pig brother, and for all that you don't go shouting your feelings from the rooftops, you've got a lot of them inside you."

Neil shook his head. "I'm not a good person."

"Don't start with that. I've known you for a really long time. We've worked together. We've been friends. I'm qualified to say you're a good person." Rachel grabbed his arm.

"Rach—" Neil felt lost. All he could do was shake his head.

"There is a woman in there who is interesting, intelligent, kind, strong, independent, and beautiful. She's got soul. She's obviously very interested in you; she can't keep her hands off you. She's giving you all the right signals. Whatever reservations she had about you, she's obviously decided to give you a chance. She's trusting you, Neil." Rachel's eyes were imploring. "She's taking a risk. Don't let her fall."

"No," Neil replied, harsher than he intended. "Don't talk like that to me. I don't want to be—"

"Trapped, yeah, I know. I'm sorry." Rachel lifted her hands in surrender. "I chose my words poorly. All I meant was, if you decide you don't want this thing, whatever this thing is, you need to tell her so she can walk away."

"But I do want it." The admission was like a weight falling off his chest. The strangling power of a secret kept hidden and denied was cut, and Neil was able to breathe freely. "I do want it."

"Then you need to trust her too," Rachel said. "You have to trust she's not going to take advantage of you, the way she's trusting you to do the same."

"I think I picked someone difficult because I wanted it to not work," Neil said, looking out at the dark harbour. If he concentrated, he could just pick out the shape of the island, their island, the volcano, as a darker black against the sky. "Every time she shouted at me, I thought, 'This is great, it didn't work, I can leave.' And then we'd sort it out, and she'd make me laugh, and I knew I couldn't just walk away."

"You didn't *pick* someone difficult," his oldest friend told him soberly, looking out at the harbour too, contemplating her own thoughts in meditation of the view. "You were attracted to someone who is just as passionate as you, just a lot more expressive about it." She glanced sideways. "Yep. There you go with that stony face of yours. There's spies out there with less of a poker face than you."

Emotions churned inside Neil. He could hardly believe they weren't written on his face. He cared for Chelsea. It was more than just interest and curiosity, or some fit of pique. It was something deep and powerful, and the admission whipped away the comforting veil that he had thrown over his feelings.

"Rachel, you'll help me, won't you?"

A serene, warm smile split her wide mouth, a patronising smile that was only shared between the best of friends, friends who had seen each other at their stupidest and still wished to keep company.

"Darling, I love it when you ask me to do things like that.

Try to remember this later when you yell at me for interfering."

"I have never yelled at you," Neil protested.

"You're right, actually, you haven't. You've talked to me in tones that were worse than yelling." She patted his arm. "Neil? A word of advice for you? Forget Florence." Her voice was like steel. "Forget. Florence."

Neil was about to reply when he heard the noise of the sliding door. He turned to see Chelsea coming out onto the balcony with her friends in tow and a drink in hand.

"Oh! I'm sorry, I didn't mean—"

"By all means, join us," Rachel said, turning to face Chelsea. "Neil and I were just catching up. Come." Rachel took Chelsea by the arm and steered her over to stand beside Neil. "A perfect night for young love."

It was the sort of night where time seemed to become completely irrelevant. Cold eventually drove them all back inside, where more music, more drinks, and more chatter created a celebratory atmosphere. Neil felt Rachel's eyes on him as she deftly engineered situations to leave him and Chelsea together, but he could see that it was superfluous. Chelsea seemed to end up in his arms no matter where in the room the party rotated to. Neil knew it was in equal measure him seeking her out.

It was in the small hours that he was sending the guests home in taxis, before the only two left in his house were Rachel and Chelsea.

Rachel hugged Neil warmly in the entrance hall and gave him a meaningful look that recalled their earlier conversation. Soon she was swallowed by the night, and Neil was standing in the doorway of his entertainment room, looking at Chelsea half asleep on the chaise lounge.

"Would you like me to call you a taxi?" Neil asked, tentatively brushing her hair out of her face.

"No," Chelsea said, smiling sleepily. "I'd like to see you in the morning."

"Come on, then. I have a guest room for you."

They wandered upstairs to a guest room, Chelsea relaxed and half asleep. As Neil helped her into the room and prepared to bid her good night, Chelsea turned suddenly.

"Neil, I have a question about Florence."

"Florence is not in our lives, and that's all I wish to say. Please forget you ever heard the name."

"You're... single though, right?" Chelsea asked.

"Am I?" Neil asked. Chelsea blinked. Emotion filled her face. "It's up to you, Chelsea. Am I?"

"No," Chelsea replied, reaching up to kiss him, her fingers winding their way up his neck and into his hair before sweeping down his back. Chills spilled over Neil, and he pulled her closer, mouth moving gently, eagerly over hers. He wanted to wash Florence from her lips, from his, from their union.

He wasn't sure how long they stood there, desperately kissing, and it wasn't until Chelsea started tugging at his clothes that he recovered some sense of himself.

"No, Chelsea," he said, taking her hands in his. "Not like this. You've been drinking. I've been drinking."

She made a disappointed noise and buried her face in his chest.

"You're right, dammit, dammit, dammit," she said, then looked up at him. "What a pity for both of our intentions."

Neil leaned down and kissed her again before he tore himself away. "Well, let's say instead that, now we know what our intentions are, we have a very, very fun morning to look forward to."

25

WHEN CHELSEA WOKE IN A SEA OF WHITE, ALONE IN A luxurious bed, it took her only a second to remember the previous night and her parting from Neil. She carefully re-examined her feelings, prodding at them gingerly, waiting for embarrassment or regret to leap out and ambush her.

They did not.

Instead, there was only warmth and a yearning. Her chest ached slightly to finish their conversation, and her only fear was that he did not feel the same way in the light of the morning, in the absence of alcohol.

After a quick shower, Chelsea went to find Neil, wandering barefoot through the palatial corridors and landings before finding him in a sun-drenched kitchen, drinking a coffee and looking out at Rangitoto.

"Hi," Chelsea said awkwardly. "Any of that coffee going?"

"Of course." Neil went over to a stainless steel coffee maker that looked like it had been made for a spaceship. While it whirred and churned, he didn't take his eyes off her, looking at her in something like wonder.

"What?" she finally asked. "Am I wearing my dress inside out or something?"

"You're here," Neil said simply.

It startled Chelsea to realise she hadn't thought about leaving in the middle of the night, slipping out after she thought he'd gone to bed, or running from the house in the early hours. And Neil had not even checked she was still here; he had simply given her space and hoped she would trust him.

Chelsea did run then, but her feet carried her towards Neil, and a second later she pressed her lips against his as his arms enfolded her, holding her fiercely. His lips moved over hers with gentle eagerness, and she shivered, a delicious shiver of delight and anticipation.

"Chelsea," Neil whispered against her mouth. She pushed herself closer to him. His hands were on her shoulders. And then he gently pulled himself away. "I need to tell you something."

She felt her heart sink.

"I know about your aunt, Chelsea. And your mother." Neil looked solemn. Chelsea did a small double take; these weren't the words she had expected to hear. "No, don't panic. Please listen. Mikaela told me a little of your family history. I understand that your aunt's relationship with your mother might have had an impact on your fears."

"Look, you can't just take Mikaela's word for it. Mum was sick; I promise she wasn't freeloading—"

"Shhhh." Neil leaned in and kissed her.

Chelsea felt herself bristle and pushed him away. "Don't you shush me!"

"Please let me tell you what I heard before you start arguing with me." Neil looked so serious and so tender, Chelsea felt her annoyance begin to ebb. She nodded.

"Thank you. Mikaela never implied you or your mother were freeloading. And many people would not use those terms to describe an ill adult seeking to spend the end of their life with their family. Most importantly, whatever the relationship between your aunt and mother, you are not the heir to it."

Chelsea's heart hammered, and she felt like she was about to cry again. There were so many feelings and memories being stirred up. Her mother's death would always be a hole in her life, it was true, but it was the memories of her aunt that caused her the most pain.

"No matter what your mother has taught you, Chelsea Lambert, you don't just get to keep taking from family and giving nothing back." Aunt Esme's words rang in Chelsea's ears. Her mum had been so sick, and Esme had been at her about some bill. Chelsea had been sixteen.

"I try to make sure I'm not a burden on people, you know," she suddenly heard herself saying. "I don't leave people in the lurch. Not family. Not friends. I don't take anything I can't balance, and I don't have that much to give, so..." Chelsea ran out of air; her chest felt tight.

"You have so much to give." Neil kissed her forehead. "You are selling yourself short. Chelsea, you are one of the most generous souls I've met. Your instinct is to give. Your aunt is not the authority on you; you don't have to listen to her petty evaluation of your character and nature. I know it's a lot to ask. People like Esme are so capable of getting in and setting down roots. Let me ask one thing, then, one thing. Let others be generous with you. Let me be generous with you," Neil whispered. His eyes were fixed on hers, and his fingers ran through her hair softly, caressing, stroking. "Everything I give you, I give you as a gift. Free and without obligation, now and always."

For a moment, Chelsea allowed herself to fantasize about a life without worry of obligation. Her mother's sweet and open nature was alien to her. Vicky Lambert had been generous to a fault. She shared what little she had generously, with Chelsea, with Esme, with friends. In turn, she accepted generosity without hesitation. She had no sense for when it wasn't genuine. But then, why should she? Chelsea wondered. Why should Vicky have assumed her sister's care for her in her final years was laden with strings and guilt, to be inherited by her only child? For the first time, Chelsea was struck by the thought, Neil's words breaking through years of doubt and reinforced beliefs, that maybe it was Esme who was wrong.

Now here she stood in front of Neil, who looked so vulnerable Chelsea couldn't fathom it, clinging to each other in a kitchen, the coffee maker long since silent and the coffee cooling rapidly, forgotten. All he asked for was that she trust he wouldn't call in his gifts as debt later.

All he asked for was her trust.

"What do you want to give me?" Chelsea asked.

"Love," he whispered. "I want to love you. I want to give you happiness. Security. Laughter. I've wanted to take away your pain and unhappiness since I saw you crying on the pavement that morning you brought my phone back. I want to do it because I love you, not because I want anything back."

"Too bad," Chelsea whispered, rising on her tiptoes to kiss him. "Because I want to love you back."

In Neil's arms, she suddenly found she felt the safest she had in a long, long time. Her body ached to be close to him, to express her emotions by pressing them into his skin, and the fervour of his touch and kisses told Chelsea that he felt the same.

Neil's room was more colourful than the rest of the house, and it wasn't just due to the presence of Chelsea and one of her sculptures. There was gentle clutter that made the room feel lived in, unlike the showroom feel of the rest of the house. There were several framed photographs on the wall of friends and family. It felt homey. Neil liked it here.

He liked it even more now with Chelsea beside him. He knew how hard it was for her to confront her demons and her fear, to trust him and let him be generous with her. And though he couldn't explain why what he was about to ask was such a big deal, he wanted to open his heart the same way.

"It's my birthday soon," Neil told her, still holding her against him.

"You'll have to tell me when. We can go and do something fun," she said against his chest.

"That's what I wish to talk about. I always spend my birthday with my family in San Francisco. I'd like to take you with me."

He felt her tense but didn't say anything. Either she'd say yes or she'd say no. Either way, it would be fine.

"When would we go?" Chelsea asked.

"In about two weeks. It won't be any trouble to add another ticket, and I'm staying in a hotel anyway. I would like to introduce you to my life in San Francisco."

Looking down at her face, he could see conflict warring there.

"Isn't it a bit soon for me to meet your family?" she said finally.

"If you feel that way. But I've already met your cousin, and you've met my brother."

She laughed. Neil liked that she knew when he was teasing her. So many people didn't understand his jokes.

"All right," she said. She smiled widely. "I'd love to go with you."

He kissed her mouth and hugged her tighter.

"Neil, will you move back to California soon? How long are you planning to be in New Zealand?"

"I don't know," he said, looking at her again. "It was meant to be a visit, but I think I've fallen in love with the country."

"That's what all the tourists say," Chelsea said smugly, and Neil laughed.

As he held her close, Neil wondered at his decision. He had come to New Zealand to get away from his San Francisco life, to hide from all the ghosts that haunted him there. Eddie would tell him this was a bad idea. That alone seemed like a good enough reason to do it.

She trusted him, Neil reminded himself. She was risking her heart for him. It was his duty to do the same, even if she didn't know how risky this was.

26

———

CHELSEA KISSED NEIL GOODBYE ON THE PAVEMENT OUTSIDE her house late on Sunday evening. She watched until his car was out of sight, aware she had a slightly dopey grin on her face, and then almost skipped down the half-overgrown path to her flat.

"Goddammit, you bitch!" The angry accusation came from behind her as she turned the key to open the front door. She ducked as something flat and soft-ish hit her over the head, and she turned to see her assailant.

Mikaela stood behind her, clutching the large paperback she had walloped Chelsea with. Her make-up was streaked, and she looked furious.

"Mikaela? What?" Chelsea put her arm up to fend off Mikaela's renewed bibliographic battery. "Ow, quit it. What's the matter with you?"

"What's the *matter* with me? *With me*? You have no idea what a huge mess you've made of my life, do you? You never think about anyone but yourself. I've been trying to get in touch with you all day, and you ignored all of my calls."

"I haven't been ignoring *your* calls. I've been ignoring *everyone's* calls. I've been busy."

"I can certainly see that now. Aren't you going to ask me in?"

"Not if you're going to keep hitting me and being horrid, I'm not."

"You ruined everything! You were supposed to help me get Neil, not take him for yourself! You're always taking things from me. Since you were a kid. I didn't have all the regular things growing up because my mum was spending all of her money on you. And you've never done anything for me. This would have been so easy for you, but you had to take him too." Mikaela started crying.

Chelsea stared at her cousin in a mix of confusion and guilt.

"Neil told me he had ended it with you. He told me you were fine with it. He said it was amicable."

"I thought he broke up with me because of me. Not because of you. If you hadn't been in the picture, I would have been able to keep him."

"Look, Mikaela, I honestly don't know why anyone would pick me over you. I hardly think I'm much of a threat to your dating prospects, but look, I'll find some other nice men and we'll organise something with them, okay?"

"You better," Mikaela said, her face distorted by anger. "Or I'll tell Mum you took my man."

"Oh, for God's sake, Mikaela, you don't have to blackmail someone when they're offering to help you," Chelsea snapped, more annoyed than upset. "Just quit it, all right."

Mikaela looked taken aback at the rebuff. "I just got broken up with," she told Chelsea, though her tone was milder. "You should have more sympathy."

"Ending things after a few dates doesn't really merit this sort of tantrum," Chelsea told her.

"It does if you live with my mum."

"Ain't that the truth." Chelsea sighed. "Look, stop hitting me and you can come inside for a cup of tea, and we'll figure out how to handle Esme, okay?"

After a pause, Mikaela nodded. More quietly than Chelsea had expected, she followed her into the cramped lounge and perched herself on one of the stools at the counter.

"What are you looking for in a boyfriend, Mikaela? Is it just because of your mum? Because she's not right, you know. You don't owe her a rich husband or whatever else she's telling you."

Mikaela shook her head. "You wouldn't understand. You've always done whatever you wanted. You don't know what it's like to not be able to be the person that you are."

"What do you mean?"

Michael just shook her head again. Chelsea sighed. It had been such a nice weekend. Delta would have told her to just send Mikaela away. But Chelsea couldn't. For the first time in a very long time, she felt a sense of kinship with her cousin. *Maybe I should try to see her as her own person and not as a tool of her mum's more often.*

As she put the cup of tea down in front of Mikaela, there was a knock. Chelsea answered the door.

"Hi, can I help with something?" she asked.

"Are you the one that's stealing my girlfriend?" the woman on the front step demanded.

Chelsea stared. "I think you have the wrong house."

"Don't deny it! Her car is parked right out front, and I know you've been seeing her and she's been calling you."

The angry woman pushed forward, forcing Chelsea to open the door wider.

"For God's sake, I don't know your girlfriend!" Chelsea turned and looked for Mikaela. "Mikaela, do you know this woman?"

"Well? Do you, Mikaela? Or are you going to deny my existence again?" the woman demanded, successfully pushing past Chelsea.

Mikaela was on her feet. "Stacey, don't do this."

"I just want you to be honest with me!" Stacey shouted.

Chelsea looked from the angry woman to her cousin and back again.

Oh.

"I told you I wasn't happy with you seeing a guy, even if it was just to put your mother off, and now I find there's a woman involved too?"

"I'm her cousin," Chelsea interjected. "I'm definitely, definitely not sleeping with Mikaela. She's my cousin. I can go get photos of family Christmases when we were kids if you want."

Both women stared at her for a moment, then looked back at each other.

"Why do you care so much? You broke up with me, even though I told you I ended it with the guy."

"I don't know. Because I'm stupid or something. I thought we had something special, and you want to throw it away on pleasing everybody else instead of me. Instead of *us.*"

Chelsea tiptoed past Stacey to her bedroom. She made a half-hearted attempt to look for some family photos while they argued in the living room, but soon she gave up and flopped on her bed.

So, Mikaela liked girls. Assuming she didn't also like

guys, that would definitely interfere with her mother's plans of getting a rich husband. Chelsea tried to remember what Esme had been like about homosexuality. Esme's circle of friends was so judgy, and whatever they said, went. Mikaela being into women would, to Esme's eyes, make her "look bad." Chelsea winced. Mikaela's situation was not a fun one.

After twenty minutes, Chelsea heard the front door slam. Waiting another a minute, she cautiously opened her bedroom door and saw Mikaela sitting on the couch crying.

"Do you still want to find a rich husband, or should we switch it up to finding a rich wife?" Chelsea tried, wanting to lighten the mood.

Mikaela glared daggers at her. So much for that idea.

"I suppose you're really happy now, aren't you? You think you've got all the aces now, haven't you?"

"What the actual hell are you talking about? You can date whoever you want. If you like women, we'll find you women. If you like men and women, we'll look at both. If you need time to get over Stacey, then that's—"

Mikaela leapt to her feet. "If you tell Mum about this, I'll tell her about how you sabotaged my relationship, and I'll tell your work. You sabotage my life, I sabotage yours. Not a word. Do you hear me?"

"You don't need to threaten me. I'm not going to do anything!" Chelsea's sense of kinship evaporated as Mikaela wrenched open the door and departed.

Great. That's what I get for trying to be nice to Mikaela. Chelsea was shaking from the adrenaline of the encounter and the fear that Mikaela knew exactly how to ruin someone in the eyes of her mother.

Chelsea's mood did not improve with the arrival of Monday morning. Today was the day she'd have to ask for time off to go to San Francisco with Neil. She self-consciously glanced around the office. It felt wrong, somehow, to be thinking of her weekend with Neil here. It felt private, personal, and not a little as though she had poached from Honey. After all, Neil would no longer pay the outrageous fees for 'personalised access' to the Honey dating register.

Chelsea quickly tapped out an email to Helen and sent it. Before she had so much as a chance to start mentally composing prayers, the door to Helen's office swung open and she stalked out, perfectly balanced on her towering heels, her golden curls bouncing with the movement. It seemed every light in the reception area was trained on her, and she looked perfect, golden, sweet... *Dare I say it,* Chelsea thought, *just like honey.* Her perfectly contoured face was set in displeased lines. *Honey,* Chelsea amended mentally, *but poisoned honey.*

"You want to take time off?" Helen demanded, tapping her long nails on the glass reception top.

Chelsea folded her hands together nervously.

"That's right."

"To San Francisco, you said?" she demanded again.

Chelsea winced. This was not going well.

"It's fine if you can't spare me, Helen. It doesn't hurt to ask. I am legally entitled to time off, you know."

Helen's mouth pressed into a thin line as she regarded her.

"I am aware of my legal obligations" was all she said before she turned and stalked back into her office. The door slammed. Chelsea sighed and pulled up her to-do list for the day. Three hundred lapsed users to send flirty personal messages to, inviting them back.

"Hobbies: golf, busty blondes, financial analysis. Great...," she murmured as she worked.

She was a quarter of the way through her list when an imperious email landed in her inbox. Helen requested her presence in her office.

27

"You wanted to see me?" Chelsea said, opening the office door a crack.

"Come in. You'll be the death of my vision."

Chelsea slipped into the batcave, shutting the door quickly behind her to block out the light.

"Yes, well, sit."

Chelsea sat in the chair indicated by the manicured hand. Helen smiled at her. It looked forced.

"I have decided to grant your request," she said with an air of benevolence. "You may take the week off to visit San Francisco."

Chelsea stared, lost for words for one of the few times in her life. "Are you kidding?" she finally blurted out.

"You're confusing me with one of your friends. My time is too valuable for 'kidding.'" Helen sniffed and resettled herself into her chair. "You understand, of course, our business is competitive. We must stay ahead of the competition at all costs. The dating website market is a tricky enterprise." Pausing, she swallowed and looked around the room as if for assistance before glancing back at Chelsea. "You don't like this job, do you? You don't like me or the site or what we do."

Chelsea had not been expecting that question. She stared at Helen, who seemed to have something like fear in her eyes. Leaning forwards across her desk, Helen continued.

"It doesn't matter what you say. I'm going to be terminating your contract anyway. It would just make us both feel better if we could just say out loud that you're not in the best place here." Helen got to her feet and stalked across the dim office to unlock a cabinet. "Drink?" she said, holding up a bottle of amber liquor.

"No thanks," Chelsea said, frowning.

"I'll have one for both of us." Helen returned to the desk with the liquor and some shot glasses. Chelsea, meanwhile, was trying to understand the words that Helen had just uttered.

"Am I fired?" Chelsea finally said.

Helen knocked back a shot. "I suppose. It's more of a redundancy. I don't think the company will be here for much longer. I'm letting you get out of it while the going is still good. You'll get your notice paid, you can take your holiday, and you don't have to deal with all this." Helen waved her hand and poured a shot. "You sure you don't want one?"

"Helen, what are you talking about?" Chelsea's blood was running cold in her veins. She ignored the offer of alcohol. "I thought we were okay now. I've done some good work."

"You hate it here. You hate me. We're just a pay cheque. You turn your nose up at my business. You turn your nose up at the ladies who use the site to go into these relationships. You turn your nose up at the men. Well, let me tell you, you're not that different from them, are you?"

Had Mikaela told Helen about her and Neil? "Is this about my personal life?"

"No, it's about mine." She put the cap back on the bottle and put in her desk drawer. "You have bills to pay. So you're here not because your heart is, but because you know I need someone just pretty enough to sit on that desk, answer phones, post messages, and generally do all the little things I don't have time for because I'm trying to manage us from collapsing." She leaned forwards over her desk, with Chelsea pulling away as much as she could. "So, you're here because I don't have time, just like our wealthy clients. You're here because you have no money. And together, our relationship sort of works, or at least it worked enough that we didn't feel overly compelled to end it."

"You were going to fire me a whole bunch of times," Chelsea felt obligated to point out.

"And yet here we are." Helen shook her head. "You'll get paid out. I'll even tell people what a great employee you were. But we're done here."

"This has to be illegal," Chelsea said, not moving from her chair.

"You'll have more than your fair payout in your account tomorrow. Sometimes, Chelsea Lambert, you have to know when to let a bad relationship go. We tried something. It didn't work. Let's move on to somewhere we can both be happy, hmmm?"

"You have some pretty warped ideas about relationships, Helen. Really warped." Chelsea stood from the chair and looked at the beautiful woman hunched over the table nursing a shot glass with a look of abject defeat on her face. "Whatever. Fine. I'll figure it out. Thanks for everything, I guess."

Still bewildered, Chelsea stomped out of the office and

back to her desk. *Good riddance too*. She threw her belong-ings into a bag and cleared her history and her emails off the computer. Checking her work area to make sure she left nothing behind, she slung her bag over her shoulder and knocked on Helen's office door.

"Here's a list of passwords for the next girl, assuming you're still in business. You're right though," Chelsea said, eyes fixed on Helen. "This wasn't great for either of us. Thanks for sticking with me, I guess."

Helen sniffed. In the dimness, Chelsea couldn't tell if she had been crying or if it was a sniff of disdain. "I'm sure our lives would have been better without us crossing paths. Goodbye, Miss Lambert," Helen said, pointedly turning away.

"I'll try not to let the door hit me on the way out." Chelsea could, after all, no longer see the point in keeping her mouth shut.

As she left the building for the final time, she realised there was one good thing that had come out of her time at Honey.

Neil.

Warmth flared inside Chelsea, and she grinned widely, alarming a passer-by as she thought that, yes, through a happy accident, it was Honey that had brought her and Neil together, even if it wasn't in the manner that Honey had intended.

Her smile faded as another thought followed hot on the heels of the first. Now she was out of a job, with only a few weeks to get another one. Neil would undoubtedly try to help her. He might try to pay her rent and her bills, or to give her a job, or simply just gesture with magnificent care-lessness and sweep her into one of his spare rooms, and smile as she shed glitter and colour all over his pristine mansion. It would probably work at first, but then how long before it stopped working and she realised she was trapped in a cage of stainless steel and magazine whites?

He would just want to help, and she'd be in no position to say no.

Maybe she could just not tell him. Not lie, just not mention it until she had a plan. An alternative other than his kindness.

You said you'd let him be generous with you. You could also trust him to not give you anything you don't want, a little part of her whispered.

It wasn't him she didn't trust, she argued back. It was herself. She didn't know how she'd react to being offered solutions. Would she have the strength to resist? Would she break down and accept and slowly resent it all?

Thinking of Neil made her so fiercely happy, it hurt. Their relationship couldn't possibly survive the threat of her destitution, the threat of his generosity.

All right, then, Chelsea decided. *I'll just tell him later.*

28

CHELSEA'S FIRST SLEEP IN WAS RUDELY SPOILED BY THE WAIL of her ringtone.

"Is it true you've been fired, you lazy, irresponsible girl?" Aunt Esme all but shrieked down the phone. Chelsea winced. This was one hell of a way to wake up. "Is it? Don't even contemplate lying to me."

"It was more of a redundancy, Aunt Esme," Chelsea mumbled, rubbing her face, trying to get her bearings on the day. She squinted at the clock. It was just past eight thirty.

"That's you all over, isn't it, Chelsea? Redundant. Get used to that word." Aunt Esme took a moment to refill her lungs. "There I was, calling you at the office to give you a second chance at finding Mikaela a decent man, and your boss tells me you've been let go. Imagine my surprise. Imagine my humiliation."

"I really don't see how it should humiliate you. Loads of people ring up asking for people that have moved on."

"Sarcasm and lip. Is that what I deserve after the years of care and devotion I've shown you and your mother?" Aunt

Esme sighed. "I don't know why I'm surprised. I really don't. Maybe if you'd had a proper father, things would be different."

"That's not fair, Aunt Esme."

"Life's not fair. What am I to do now? Mikaela told me that the first man you got her didn't stick around. What are you going to do to find her a suitable boyfriend now?"

Chelsea noted that Mikaela hadn't told Esme why her man hadn't stuck around—neither the part about Chelsea being together with Neil, nor the part about her romantic preferences.

"It's not my job to find her a boyfriend, and it's not yours either. Just let her find herself a partner at her own pace, Aunt Esme. She doesn't need you or anyone meddling in it."

"I can't believe you're going to be so irresponsible. This might have been her only chance."

"That's selling Mikaela short. She's nice and intelligent and fun to be around. She'll find someone who makes her happy and that she makes happy. And she doesn't owe it to you or anyone for them to be rich."

"You have a very poor understanding of how the world works, but that is not a surprise." Aunt Esme took another breath and let it out slowly as though keeping herself calm. "Very well. I will make other arrangements for my daughter. You are obviously going to be no help. So, the next matter. When will you be coming here to work?"

Chelsea's eyes popped open and horror blossomed in her. Working for Aunt Esme? Surely she didn't expect...?

"I wasn't planning to, Aunt Esme. I was hoping to get other work."

"That's very irresponsible of you." That seemed to be her favourite word. "You are extremely unlikely to find anyone to take you on with your history and appearance.

The most sensible thing you can do is to come and work for the family business. It would take care of your bills, and it would contribute something to the family. You know how hard things have been since we took care of you and Vicky."

Maybe if Esme had called later in the day, Chelsea would have been better prepared. But as it was, first thing in the morning, her emotional guards were lowered, and her aunt's words were adept at homing in on her sore spots. To remind her of being a helpless teenager with a dying mother and no autonomy. To be utterly reliant on Esme, and to have to pay the huge emotional toll that incurred. That, at least, was what she thought later when she tried to dissect why she did what she did.

"No, Aunt Esme, I won't let you. You've been making me feel like rubbish since I was a kid. You don't get to use my dead mum to guilt-trip me. You don't get to call me names and expect me to show up."

"How dare you," Esme said. "I am simply trying to keep my family together. It is not wrong of me to expect everyone to contribute. You and your mother were freeloaders. And you still are. You never visit. You never do anything for us. You never even call."

"Maybe you should be kinder."

"Kinder!" She gasped. "After everything I have done!"

"I don't know what to tell you, Esme. I'm not coming to work for you. I'm not finding Mikaela a husband. If you want to see me, maybe you should ask me, like a regular person."

"I am not a regular person. I am your aunt. I took you in and clothed you and fed you and looked after your ailing mother. I am owed something."

Chelsea said nothing. Her hand gripped her phone so

tightly her knuckles had turned white, and her stomach twisted. She fought the urge to apologise to Aunt Esme.

"Very well, Chelsea, you leave me little recourse. I had hoped it would not come to this, but if you so absolutely refuse to help, to contribute, to work, then there's nothing for it. I will have to sell Vicky's art."

Chelsea sat bolt upright in bed. "No. You can't. Some of that is mine."

"It's all about what you want, isn't it? Well, I don't quite see the charm in Vicky's hodgepodge, but art dealers have assured me these works of hers are valuable enough."

"Aunt Esme, they're all I have of her. You can't do this."

"If you want them, then you are welcome to submit a tender for them. I'll make sure my art dealer calls you. Goodbye."

The line went dead. Chelsea felt cold even in the humid heat of the summer morning. Could she ask Neil to buy her mother's art? Transfer that power from Esme to Neil?

Could she trust him that much?

29

______

Even though Eddie had left for San Francisco only hours ago, the house already felt much emptier without him. Neil found himself at a loose end. All the arrangements were ready for his and Chelsea's departure the next evening. Packing had been easy; Neil had a whole life over the Pacific Ocean.

Neil was looking forward to showing Chelsea his home and introducing her to his family. He hoped they would do silly tourist things together. He hoped he could show how much he cared for her.

His phone rang.

"Don't bring her here," Florence said when Neil answered the call from an unknown number. "*Hello, how are you?*" was for lesser mortals. "You don't want me to see her. You don't want me to even be in the same city as her, Neil."

Dread seized Neil's gut. He had been with Chelsea barely a week and had told his parents of his bringing her to San Francisco only days ago. And somehow Florence already knew.

"You don't control my life, Florence." Neil fought to keep his voice even.

"I don't want to. I just want you to come home. I miss you so much."

"Stay away from me. Stay away from her."

"You can't hide from me, Neil. And you can't hide her from me either. I will tell her everything."

Neil hung up.

How could she have known? Neil wondered briefly before his thoughts turned to damage control. It was a mistake to think about taking Chelsea to San Francisco. He'd been in New Zealand for months because he knew he could not be happy in his home city, not while Florence waited for him. He knew just how poisonous she could be. It was irresponsible to take Chelsea there, at least without a warning...

But if he warned Chelsea, he would have to explain who Florence was and why she was so mad. He'd have to admit everything that had passed between them and all the terrible things he'd said and done. He thought he had put it all behind him, but hearing Florence's voice brought back all the fear, all the guilt, and all the misery.

No. She shouldn't come. He was going to have to disappoint Chelsea.

He didn't know how long he'd been sitting on his bed, trying to control his breathing, trying to stop himself from sinking into that hole of inertia and depression that hearing Florence's voice forced him towards. He only became aware of his surroundings when his doorbell rang.

Chelsea was on his doorstep, smiling, bright, and happy. She gave him a hug and a long kiss.

"I'm so excited about this trip! I packed a million things; I hope you don't mind. Don't panic when you see my luggage." She must have spied something on his face. Either he was getting more expressive, or Chelsea was learning to read him nearly as well as Eddie and Rachel. "Is something wrong?"

"No," Neil replied instantly. "Nothing is wrong. It will be a good trip." He smiled.

"You haven't changed your mind?" Insecurity was beginning to creep onto her face. "D'you want to check the clothes I've packed? I mean, if you're worried."

"No, nothing like that. I received some frustrating work news. It's nothing to worry about. Come inside."

As they walked towards the lounge, Chelsea suddenly stopped him, both arms on his.

"Neil, I've got to ask you something. You can say no, absolutely. It's just, I need help with something, and I can't ask anyone else."

"Of course. Name it."

"My aunt is... punishing me, I guess, by selling my mum's art off. I was wondering if..." She took a deep breath. "If you might be able to buy it and keep it safe."

Neil reached out and touched Chelsea's uncertain face. Florence was driven from his mind, his worries about the trip gone, and all he could focus on was the gentle, tremulous trust Chelsea was offering him.

He had asked her to let him be generous, and here she was. He did not miss the significance of the request. She was asking him to safeguard something precious and trusting him to not use it against her.

She was trusting him. He'd be a fool to not trust in them too.

"Of course. I'll have someone on it right away." He leaned in and kissed her forehead.

"Thank you," she whispered.

30

THE EVENING FLIGHT TO SAN FRANCISCO WAS COMFORTABLE, and as she sprawled in a large seat and sipped wine, Chelsea was glad she hadn't tried to talk Neil into downgrading from business class. He slept on the flight, but she was far too keyed up and instead stayed awake, making the most of her in-seat entertainment. When they left the airport and climbed into a waiting car, Chelsea fought her drowsiness. She tried to take everything in: the cloudless sky, the massive highways, the sheer size of most of the cars on the roads.

"I thought big cars were one of those stereotypes that isn't true," Chelsea said to Neil, whom she found watching her with a sort of wonder.

"I'm afraid to say, even the most environmentally conscious of us likes our big cars," he said with a rueful smile.

Chelsea dropped off briefly and awoke as they were arriving in the city proper, driving through streets with terraced villas on steep hills, which eventually gave way to traffic jams and towering high-rises. As she clambered out of the car in front of their hotel, she couldn't help but look up. On all sides, beautiful buildings soared into the blue sky. She breathed in a great lungful of foreign air and smelled coffee, food, fumes, and a hint of marijuana.

From the balcony of their five-star hotel room, she saw American flags fluttering from the top of every building. It was skyscrapers as far as the eye could see, and in the distance, San Francisco Bay. To the west, glowing gold in the setting sun, the famous Golden Gate Bridge itself.

"This place is incredible," Chelsea said. "No wonder Americans always say Auckland is small."

"It means a lot to me that you like it."

"This hotel seems a bit much for the two of us. You sure we couldn't have just stayed at your parents' place?" she asked, looking over her shoulder. Neil was carefully hanging up his suits in the armoire.

"Very sure. Apart from the fact that it's distressing to return to my parents' keeping, they will feel they have a right to pry into all manner of my business. You would have been a nervous wreck. You don't like going to fancy restaurants for fear of looking out of place; you would not have survived a week with my mother and father. I would have woken up to find you stealing all of the forks, spoons, and knives simply to avoid having to choose between them. Then I'd have to deal with my mother lecturing me on coming home with a starving artist who resorts to stealing the silverware." He grinned, or at least gave the slightly wider smile that passed as a grin for Neil.

"Is it really going to be that bad?" Chelsea asked, ambling back inside, clutching her vintage wool cardigan tightly. California might be a state with amazing weather, but it was still the middle of their winter.

Neil shrugged and came over to kiss her. "They're very

comfortable with wealth. It will never occur to them that you may not be. You can wear, say, do whatever you feel necessary to express your individuality. I would never ask you to change. They're perhaps going to deal with it less... elegantly than I have."

"What have you told them about me?" Chelsea asked as she wrapped her arms around him and put her face on his chest.

"I've told them that you're an artist. That you've really made me enjoy New Zealand. That you are someone very special to me."

"I'll try to live up to being the interesting artist attaché," she said, forcing a smile. "Is Eddie there?"

"Yes."

"Is he likely to try and embarrass me in front of your family?"

"No." Neil seemed so certain of this that Chelsea didn't question it. "Some time I would like to try and introduce the two of you properly. He labours under some misconceptions I won't be able to clear up without you there to prove him wrong. And while your dislike of him is entirely under-standable given your poor introduction, there is more to him than he demonstrated that evening."

"All right," Chelsea said. "He's your brother. I'd much rather get on with him than not. Besides, I'm sure he'll find me just as charming as you do!" she said with an impish grin.

Neil laughed.

"Well, I hope not *as* charming," he said, leaning down to kiss her softly. "I wouldn't want to risk you preferring him to me."

"Never."

The next day, Neil took her on a tour of his home city, showing it off with every bit the same pride Chelsea had taken in showing him Auckland. They eschewed a driver for the day and travelled about in the old trams that ran along the middle of busy roads. None of the trams looked younger than fifty years, and Chelsea was delighted by the eccentricity each different one had. They drank the most hipster coffee that Neil could find, visited several art museums, and he even took her to the tourist trap at Pier 39, where Chelsea squealed over the sea lions. She found more offbeat diners and shops than she could have ever dreamed of.

They did a night tour of Alcatraz. From the prison island, San Francisco was a visual feast, the whole glittering city laid out in front of them, the steep roads visible as a string of lights curving up into darkness.

Despite Neil's jokes, they didn't miss the ferry back to the mainland, and as they made their way back to the hotel, she thoroughly bewildered Neil when she posed for a photo with a steaming grate.

"We always see these in the movies, but we don't have them in New Zealand!" she explained as she sent the photo to all her friends. Neil just shook his head in good-natured bemusement. All in all, Chelsea was having a wonderful time. She had banished all thoughts from her head of her lack of employment, Aunt Esme, her future, and how she was going to tell Neil about it all. They were having a nice trip in a foreign country, and he cared about her. He wanted her. He made that much clear.

That night, in the luxury of their hotel room, Chelsea enjoyed Neil's company to the fullest extent. In the privacy of the opulent room, they wrapped themselves in each other, their barriers lowered, and embraced the intimacy of their relationship.

Chelsea lay in silence afterwards, listening to Neil breathe beside her. She wanted to fix this moment in her mind forever, this moment of peace and love, where the only sound was the quiet murmur of the city beyond the soundproof glass. She wanted to remember the feel of the sheets against her legs as she breathed in the scent of Neil's soap, aftershave, and sweat. Wrapping herself in a lush robe, she padded out to the main room, where she quietly unlatched the double doors that led to the balcony, and stepped out into the winter night. Wrapped up warm, she looked out over the twinkling city and felt incredibly alive.

How wrong I was to fear this, to fear him, she thought exultantly.

She stood on the balcony until her feet were too cold, and then she went back inside and slid back into bed.

"Where've you been?" Neil murmured, turning over and wrapping himself around her. "Your feet are freezing!"

"I was outside on the balcony," Chelsea murmured against his neck. "Thinking about freedom. About how together we could fly so far."

"Oh, good" was all he said before sinking back into his dreams. Chelsea followed soon after.

With Neil called away the next day to check in on his businesses and how they fared in his absence, Chelsea was left on her own. She spent the morning walking through the streets of San Francisco before being joined for lunch by Rachel, who had also come to California to celebrate Neil's birthday. The more time Chelsea spent with Rachel, the more she liked her. Lunch buoyed Chelsea's spirits even more, as had Rachel's reassurances that she would be at the "soiree" that night hosted by Neil's mother.

"You'll like them," Rachel said as she saw Chelsea back to her hotel. "Henrietta and Colin—that's Eddie and Neil's parents—are interesting people. I think you'll challenge them. You're pretty different from most of the people they meet, but I think you can win them around. Colin works with all kinds of people. I think Henrietta is a little more... hoity-toity." Rachel flashed a rueful smile at her choice of words. "Just be yourself. They value kindness."

"How close is Neil to his family?"

"Very. You may not have seen it while he was hiding out in New Zealand, but the family is very close. Eddie barely moved out; he's only a street or two over from his parents."

"They both seem very self-sufficient."

"They are," Rachel replied with a laugh. "The whole family is incredibly self-sufficient. But they're still close. Henrietta loves her two boys."

"Rachel, what did you mean, just before, when you said he was hiding out in New Zealand?"

"Did I say that?" Rachel's smile wavered for a moment. "I misspoke. It's more of a working vacation. It's nice for him to go and spend some time away from here."

Chelsea stared at her. "Okay. That's fine. You don't need to tell me."

"Look, I have to dash." Rachel came in to give Chelsea a quick half hug. "I'll see you tonight at Henrietta's, all right?"

Chelsea spent the afternoon preparing for the birthday party in the evening. Even though she had no interest in appearing as something she wasn't for the sake of Neil's rich family and friends, she did want to look her best. The afternoon vanished in making use of the hotel's massage, facial, and manicure facilities, with a cocktail or two to assuage the guilty niggle that perhaps she was taking advantage of Neil's wealth.

This is probably the longest I've ever spent on my hair, Chelsea thought with the curling iron in her hand, winding her salon-washed, tasteful fuchsia-and-teal ombre around the hot metal. The king-size bed was littered in the accoutrements of preparation: nice stockings, underwear, new shoes, and a dress.

Tonight, she was wearing a black silk evening gown with green and pink parrots woven in and a sequined design of tail feathers spilling down the sweetheart neckline and down the sleeves. Her necklace was colourful crystals, and her chandelier earrings dazzlingly reflected light in the same colours. Her heels were covered in emerald green satin with small stones set into it, giving it the impression of a coiled dragon.

She pinned her curls up, letting the coloured ringlets fall to her neck, spilling around the large clip with colourful butterfly wings that spread out to adorn the back of her head and frame her face from the front. When she looked at herself in the full-length mirrors inside the walk-in wardrobe, she felt as though she had a grace she did not normally possess.

I still look like me, and I've managed to dress like a million bucks, she thought, turning this way and that in the mirror. Snapping a picture to send to her friends, she also checked the time and was relieved to see she was running early.

Just as she was wondering what to do with herself for the next half hour, the room phone trilled.

"I'm sorry, Ms Lambert?" an unfamiliar woman's voice said on the phone. "This is reception. Your driver and car are downstairs now, ma'am."

"I'm sorry, are they able to wait? My date hasn't arrived yet," Chelsea said, apologetic, unsure how to dictate instructions to drivers and receptionists.

"The driver says that Mr O'Connell has asked you to go ahead. Mrs O'Connell wants to meet you before the evening's engagement. This car has been sent for you."

Nerves flooded Chelsea. Of course Neil's mother would want to meet her before the party. Rachel had made her sound protective. Or perhaps she wanted to put her at ease? Either way, she wished Neil had given her a heads-up about this.

Scooping up her fake jewelled handbag and a white woollen coat, she hurried downstairs to the lobby where a tall chauffeur in an impeccable uniform waited, holding a small sign with her name on it.

"Sorry! Sorry! Didn't mean to keep you waiting. I didn't realise there was a change of plan," Chelsea puffed and smiled brilliantly at the driver.

"This way please, ma'am," he said with a professionally distant smile and wave that made Chelsea awkward. She didn't like it when people had to treat her like she was above them. This guy probably had more money than she did. She trailed along behind him, wiggling into her coat before they hit the cold December air and climbed into the car.

"Will Neil—Mr O'Connell be joining us too?" she asked, hoping desperately that the answer would be yes.

"He has regretfully been delayed by business," the driver said.

Chelsea made a few attempts at conversation, but the driver's professionalism or her awkwardness stymied any chance of it. They rode in silence. Chelsea felt her earlier confidence melting away. She couldn't even make conversation with a driver. How was she going to make conversation with the O'Connells? Especially if Neil was late?

The driver pulled onto a wide gravel path leading up to a lovely trim cottage. It was single storey and beautifully kept. Chelsea was halfway out the car door before she remembered the driver was meant to open it for her. She followed a member of the staff into the house and was startled firstly by how modern and minimalist the decor inside was, then by the fact that it appeared empty.

She looked around. There had to be some mistake. There was no sign of a party or a soiree or anything. She could hear a clock ticking, for goodness' sake. She pulled out her phone to message Neil.

"Excuse me, Ms Lambert?" An older man had appeared at her elbow so suddenly, Chelsea jumped. "Mrs O'Connell would like to see you now, ma'am."

"Oh! Thanks." Chelsea jammed her phone into her bag and self-consciously touched her hair. She tried to not let her legs shake as she followed the servant down a narrow corridor. The room she was shown into was as minimalist as the front room. It was also pink and decidedly feminine and not at all what Chelsea had expected from the "hoity-toity" Mrs O'Connell. Through a double door to a patio, beyond billowing curtains, she could see a figure.

"Mrs O'Connell is just through there, ma'am," the man said, indicating the patio before taking her coat and letting himself quietly out of the room. Taking a deep breath, smoothing her dress, and finding a smile to put on her face, Chelsea walked across the pink carpet and stepped out. She shivered violently in the winter chill. The woman on the balcony had her back to her and was looking out over the grounds.

"Mrs O'Connell?" Chelsea asked, trying to sound chirpy. The woman turned. Chelsea extended a hand.

"Yes, I am. You must be Chelsea." The winter wind had nothing on the chill in the woman's voice. Chelsea's extended hand hovered between them, left hanging and unaccepted as the woman cast her eyes down at the hand and did nothing. She was the same height as Chelsea and wore an obviously expensive, fashionable black dress. She was adorned with gold jewellery, an expensive watch, and her short blonde hair was immaculately dyed and styled. She leaned heavily on a crutch. Chelsea blinked. Her face was smooth, fashionably made up, and she was, all in all, far too young to be Neil's mother.

"I'm sorry, I don't understand," Chelsea blurted out.

Another wintry smile passed over the other woman's lips. "I'm sure you don't. That's why I diverted you here before you went to the party. I thought it was time you and I had a chat."

"I'm sorry, I'm not sure who... I thought you were Mrs O'Connell?"

"I am," the woman said harshly, losing her veneer of politeness for a moment. "But I'm not Neil's mother, if that's what you were thinking. My name is Florence. Florence O'Connell."

Florence. The world made a roaring sound in Chelsea's ears. Finally, she had found the mystery Florence.

"If you're not his mother..." Chelsea whispered, trying to think of some way this could end that wasn't the horrible conclusion she had come to. Did he have another brother who could have married? A cousin? Stepmother?

"I'm Neil's wife."

Chelsea felt sick, and the world tilted for a second. The cold that now spread through her had nothing to do with the brisk weather. It spread through her chest into her limbs, permeating her stomach with disappointment and horror. She was aware her mouth was hanging open and could feel tears pricking at the bottom of her eyelids. Florence looked at Chelsea with mostly disdain and dislike, but there was some touch of patronising pity in the turn of her mouth.

"I'm... I'm so sorry. I had no idea," Chelsea whispered finally. "He said... he was single." *Did he though?* a part of her wondered. *Did he ever actually say as much, or did you assume?* "At least, I thought, because of the website—"

"Yes, the website." Florence sighed. "That is where it gets complicated." She pinched the bridge of her nose. "Neil and I have been together for a long time. As you can imagine, no relationship is perfect. There are... ups and downs." She paused again and looked out over the balcony. "Forgive me, this is difficult."

"No, no, it's... it's me that needs..." Chelsea trailed off. Florence looked so frail and so sad when she wasn't gazing at her with that frosted look of hatred.

"We are quite strong, in a way. We have overcome things that most other couples would crack under. And I know that Neil likes company when he's abroad on business. I don't follow him. I am not... I am not healthy, you see." Florence's eyes fell pointedly to the crutch. "The website you mentioned—Honey, am I right?" Florence raised a perfect eyebrow. Chelsea could only nod. "I knew he was intending to use it. That's fine. We agreed that when he is abroad, he should be able to have companionship without the complication of an emotional involvement."

Chelsea found herself nodding again.

"Yes, you understand, you worked there. That's the complication. You were outside the arrangement. And you coming here is definitely outside the arrangement." Florence shuddered, on the verge of a sob. Chelsea was shaking, from cold and from horror and humiliation. She hung her head, looking away while Florence regained control of her emotions.

"I'm sorry," Chelsea said. "I didn't realise."

"I think there is rather a lot you don't realise," Florence said, her voice frosty still. "Of course, I can see what you're thinking. Perhaps you're thinking if he prefers you, maybe the old has-been wife, the crippled wife, should step aside—"

"No, not at all!" Chelsea's interruption was a half-breathless gasp.

"—but I wanted you to have all the facts so you could decide whether this is something you want to keep being a part of. He's not an honest man. He can't help it. Money makes everyone believe they are completely in control at all times." She held out a slim folder. Chelsea took it with shaking hands. She flipped it open.

The first few pages were banking records. They showed thousands of dollars being transferred to Honey. Behind it was an email exchange between Helen and Neil.

"He organised your promotion. He was paying Helen to keep you on. You know that Honey was in dire financial straits, don't you? Neil was paying for it to stay open while he won your trust. You lost your job a few days ago, didn't you?"

"Last week," Chelsea whispered, looking at the emails. She looked up at Florence. "But how did you find all this out? You snooped through his email and bank accounts?"

Florence fired her a frosty glare. "They are also my accounts, and it is also my money. The rest, well, Edward is a soft touch, in his own way. He always felt badly to watch me be betrayed."

And Eddie doesn't like me one bit. He would have happily done the snooping.

"Unless I'm much mistaken, he's also ingratiated himself with your friends. He's played the fool a bit to let you think he's not all that perfect after all, and he's told you how much he values your independence. Let me tell you something, Chelsea Lambert. You're not unique. He has one of you every six months."

Numbly Chelsea tried to hand the files back. Florence waved her hand.

"Keep it. You'll want to look over them later, when you're feeling disbelieving. There's a USB in there too."

"He brought me here... Why would he...?"

"He can't resist showing off," Florence replied almost wearily. "Listen, Chelsea." The other woman took a step closer. She was pale, made paler by the dark gown, and everything about her was taut and frail looking. "I honour the arrangement I have with my husband, though sometimes it sickens me. I love him, and sometimes we have to do things that aren't easy for the ones we love. I'm not asking you to leave his life. You can have him when he's in New Zealand, enjoy the gifts he gives you for as long as he feels inclined to shower you with them. It's only money. But here, don't make a fool of me. Let me at least have him when he's here. That is what he agreed to."

"I don't want him," Chelsea said. All she could think about was how stupid she had been. "I don't want him at all. Not if he's married. I thought... I thought..."

"That he was different. That you were different. That he loved you," Florence said pityingly.

"I have to go. I have to get out of here. How am I...?" Chelsea staggered back, almost slipping, catching herself on the balustrade. How was she going to get away? All her things were at the hotel she shared with Neil. Her plane ticket was with Neil. She had so little money of her own. This was everything she had been so afraid of with him. She was trapped with him, because he had all the power.

"I'm going to be sick," she whispered.

"Here," Florence said from beside her, her hand on Chelsea's elbow. "This way. Let's get you a drink." They stepped inside.

Chelsea was grateful to be led out of the cold. Her whole body was shaking violently, so much so that the folder visibly rattled in her hands. A tumbler of brandy was pressed into her hands by Florence. Chelsea swallowed it at once, feeling numbness and warmth spread through her. Tears were coming out of her eyes, from anger, humiliation, and heartbreak, but she didn't feel like she was crying yet. It was as if her tears were making a head start on the sorrow while her brain was still catching up.

"I'm sorry we had to have this talk," Florence said. She sounded sad.

"I'm the one that's sorry. I've been such an idiot." Chelsea buried her face in her lower arms, wiping it across her nose, feeling like a snivelling child. Her hair had come down in the wind. She didn't know where her butterfly hairclip was; it had fallen and flown away. Her silk dress was damp. Probably ruined.

"I'll get out of here," Chelsea babbled to Florence. "I should have known. I should have known it was too good. I should have known, but I wanted it to be true. I'd heard Eddie say something about a Florence... He wanted me to stay away because of Florence, you know, but I didn't ask enough, and I should have..."

"Here," Florence said, her hand on Chelsea's shoulder.

She held out an envelope. Chelsea took it and peered inside. It was filled with cash. "Enough to get you home. Enough for taxis, a few hotel nights, and an airfare. Let me just never, ever see you again." She turned away from Chelsea, her barriers going up visibly around her. She took a limping, halting step away. "The driver is waiting for you downstairs."

Too shamed for words, Chelsea put the glass down on a little side table, shaking so badly it didn't stay and slipped off the edge, bouncing on the carpet. Florence didn't turn around. Chelsea fled the room, raced downstairs, hiding her face in her curls, feeling ridiculous suddenly with her colourful hair and her sparkling shoes. She didn't even stop to collect her coat.

She fell into the waiting car and started crying. Great, soul-rending sobs came out of her, shaking her entire body. The driver was professionally neutral and did not say a word, even as Chelsea's sobs did not stop the entire journey.

31

———

NEIL FELT UNEASY AS HE ARRIVED AT THE PARTY. HE HAD GONE through the hotel to pick up Chelsea, but she was nowhere to be found. She had, by all appearances, gone ahead without him. His messages were left unanswered. Rachel, most likely, had taken her ahead, but why, he couldn't guess. Changing his clothes lightning fast, he made his hurried way to his family home in an area called Atherton, an hour out of San Francisco. When he arrived, he found his mother's soiree in full swing.

He tried to slide anonymously through the crowd, looking for Chelsea. There was no sign of her, and Neil felt worry begin to grow in him. How hard could she be to miss, with her coloured hair and her coloured clothes and her youth and exuberance, in a room full of people who were mostly his parents' generation, or his own, and none with Chelsea's verve and panache? On all sides, he was peppered with questions, handshakes, and good wishes. Then his mother herself glided forth from the crowd.

"Neil, darling, you've been so absent," Henrietta complained, though her tone was affectionate. She was a tall woman, only an inch shorter than him, and had no trouble leaning in to kiss him on the cheek. "Where is this date of yours? You have told us so little; we are so curious to meet her."

"She came ahead. Isn't she here?" Neil asked.

His mother shook her head. "Well, I haven't seen her, darling, but then I don't know her from a bar of soap. You've been very mysterious about her."

"She's short, has blonde hair with pink and blue streaks?"

His mother laughed. "Very funny. Neil, my darling, you have always had such a dry sense of humour. Do introduce us when you find her." With a pat on his arm, she vanished into the crowd.

"Hello, Neil" came a familiar voice from behind him. Every muscle in his body seized at its sound, his stomach felt sick, and fear crashed through him. He made himself turn around.

Florence stood in front of him: petite, fragile Florence, pale in all black, her hair tousled and windswept. She wore flat shoes. She had loved her high heels before the accident and never failed to remind him how much she missed them. She leaned lightly on a crutch. She looked forlorn but resolute. She looked like she expected him to be angry.

Well, in that case, Neil thought, *she was right.*

"What are you doing here, Florence?" he asked, his voice tight.

"Your mother was kind enough to invite me."

Dammit, Henrietta.

"What did you say to her to make her feel that was necessary?" he demanded. "I told you to leave my family alone."

"Our conflict is between us. Besides, for a time, they

were my family too." She sighed, and his stomach clenched. "Can we sit down?" She gestured lightly at the crutch. Guilt twisted in him, followed by anger.

"No," he said.

"Fine," Florence replied, looking hurt. "Of course. We'll stand. I only wish I could pretend as much as you that I am whole and well."

"What do you want from me, Florence? I told you and I told you, it's over between us. I'm not in love with you. Our break-up was final. I don't want to be with you."

Florence looked down at the floor. Her legs shook a little. Neil suppressed the urge to pick her up, carry her somewhere safe, and promise to look after her. *That's what she wants. That's all she wants. She's just playing games.*

"I understand that," she said softly. "Neil, I know you don't want to be with me anymore, and I know you know I never stopped loving you. This isn't about that. This is about her. Chelsea. The pretty butterfly."

"Don't you dare talk about her!" Neil all but shouted. People turned to look at them, frowning, muttering. He took a deep breath and smoothed his face. "Let's find you somewhere to sit, in private."

Neil led her into a side room and helped seat her. He wished he hadn't. He wished he didn't fall into old habits the second he caught sight of Florence. When she was seated, with her pale hands clasped in her lap, she looked at him, her blue eyes serene and serious.

"I know how you feel about me, and that's fine, but I thought I would watch your back anyway. I did some research. I watched her on the site. I found a few ex-boyfriends of her own." She took a deep breath. "She's flighty, they said. She flits to and fro, but never really being faithful."

"You're lying," Neil said through gritted teeth.

"Of course you would say that. Here's the thing, Neil. I thought I could save the two of you from each other. I thought Chelsea and I ought to have a chat too. I told her all about you."

"About what?"

"I told her about you and me. About our relationship." She looked at him from below her lashes. "I told her about the accident. I told her about what you did to me. I told her how you treated me after, and I gave her a choice."

"You did what?" Neil whispered hoarsely. His throat constricted painfully. He couldn't even bear to look at Florence.

"I solved all her financial problems for her, in exchange for leaving you alone. She was glad to take the money after she learned what a poisoned chalice you were. Do you know she's been fired? She's been out of a job for a week or more. I think it was unexpected. I think she was desperate. Was there financial trouble in her life, I wonder? Well, either way, when it came to choosing your help or a stranger's, she chose a stranger. Because she was afraid of you. Like any sensible person ought to be." Florence's lip shook slightly as she looked at him. "But I'm not. I love you, Neil. You're never going to be happy without me."

"Because you won't let me."

"No, I won't. I deserve you more than anyone else."

"Get out of this house." He locked eyes with her finally, and Neil prayed that his face was a taciturn as everyone told him it was. He didn't want to betray any of the feelings and thoughts that were pouring through him.

Florence was first to look away.

"Happy birthday, Neil," she said quietly, without looking at him, as she hobbled out of the room.

Neil stayed seated. Any mood he might've had for socialising had vanished. Any encounter with Florence usually left him shaken all on its own, but the things she had said about Chelsea affected him even worse than usual.

She was lying. She had to be. Chelsea was bright and open and honest. She was fiercely independent. Had she cut and run?

He buried his face in his hands and shook slightly. Maybe Florence was right. Maybe he was an awful person. Maybe he deserved to be with Florence.

Where was Chelsea, dammit? Had she truly left? He needed to talk to her. To be reassured she didn't believe the things Florence had said. Their relationship had been going so well recently... Could it be because of what Florence said, that she was out of a job and forced to change her plans? Was her sudden warming to him a ploy for financial security?

At least one part of Florence's story would be easy to check out. Neil pulled out his phone and surfed to the Honey website. Logging in, he began to look through the profiles of the men on the site. On the third one he checked, he saw a public post from Chelsea. Cold gripped him. The post was friendly, chirpy, asking how he was finding the site, inviting a message.

Be reasonable. It was just part of her role at Honey.

He checked through more profiles. He found more messages. The more recent ones were flirtier. He began to wonder if it was true. Had Chelsea lost her job?

Uneasily, he checked the time. It wasn't late in New Zealand. He quickly composed a message to Delta and sent it.

Neil felt sick. His nerves hummed, and he felt as though a swarm of bees had taken up residence just under his skin.

He felt like the world had turned slightly around him, and now he wasn't quite in his place. He wanted to talk to her, to hold her, to hear her say that this was all madness. That she wanted him genuinely. That she cared. That her big smile and her joyful laughs, they hadn't been faked.

"There you are!" Eddie strode into the room, drink in hand, smile on his face. "Mom's favourite birthday boy. What are you doing hiding in here?"

"Shut the door," Neil said quietly. Eddie paused, raising an eyebrow, then did as he was asked. Sitting himself down in the chair that was recently vacated by Florence, he eyed his brother.

"What's happened to you? You look like you got some hellish news. Where's Chelsea?" Eddie asked, looking around. "I haven't seen her all night.

"I don't know," Neil said tartly. "Look, Eddie, you might have been right."

"Me? Right?" Eddie blinked. "Should I check outside for flying horsemen?"

"Be serious," Neil snapped. "You might've been right about Chelsea being bad news."

Eddie's eyebrows vanished into his hairline. "Whoa."

"Lost her job. Posting flirty messages all over Honey. She hasn't been here tonight. She's been... very close to me recently. She could have been reeling me in. Her aunt's been wanting to sell her mother's art. Maybe that's why she's been letting me close."

"You're rambling, Neil. I don't understand what you're saying. Where's all this come from?"

"Florence told me."

Eddie's eyebrows made their second rapid sojourn to the roots of his hair. "Okay, let's back this up just a bit. If this information comes from Florence, it's more than a bit suspect. You remember what she's like, don't you? She's basically a witch in pretty girl skin. If she told me the sky was blue, I'd go outside and check. I've never seen Chelsea posting on Honey."

"That's because you don't look at the men's profiles, do you," Neil said bitterly.

"Oh," Eddie said. He chewed on his lip and screwed up his face in thought. He slowly shook his head. "I can't believe I'm taking her side, but let's not leap to conclusions."

"You just like her better than Florence," Neil said with a small snarl.

"I would like Medusa better than Florence. Have you talked to Chelsea?"

"No. She's gone. That's the worst part. Florence told her all about me. Our relationship. What happened. Everything I did. Chelsea decided that I wasn't worth bothering with. Took cash from Florence and left."

"Neil, listen to yourself. Don't make me slap sense into you. We've been over this. It was a car accident. You and Florence were arguing. It was a wet night. You had an accident. You didn't hurt Florence on purpose. You can't keep letting her sell that story. Neil! *Neil.* You did everything for her. You arranged care. You gave her everything she asked for. You stayed with her for years even as she drained your soul."

"I did not give her everything she asked for."

"You did *not* break up with her because she couldn't walk properly. You broke up with her because she's a manipulative witch, and she was a manipulative witch before the accident, and all she did was make you feel abjectly miserable. That's why you were breaking up with her that night in the car. Why do you *still* believe a single word she says?"

"Chelsea agrees with her."

"Florence *says* Chelsea agrees with her. Please, Neil. Talk to her." Eddie looked at him with frightened eyes. "I've had to pull you out of this hole before. Don't go back into it. Stay away from Florence, all right? I think you should—" Eddie started, but Neil was half out the door already.

He passed like a ghost through the crowd in the main room, phasing out everything around him, looking desperately for a glimpse of telltale bright colours with no luck.

His phone buzzed in his pocket. Checking it, he saw it was a text message.

Delta: Umm... maybe you should talk to Chels about this? I know she was waiting for the right time to talk to you about it, but yeah, she did, about a week ago. She's real cut up about it so, yeah, maybe talk to her?

The doubts he had kept at bay, locked up behind bulkheads and storm walls of Florence's previous lies and treacheries, suddenly flooded through him. Why wouldn't she tell him she had lost her job? And if she was able to keep this from him, what else was she hiding behind a face he had thought so honest that it couldn't deceive him?

He walked insensibly through the crowded room, through the front foyer, and out into the night.

Where was his driver? He needed a driver.

He screamed in frustration at the night, startling several guests and the valets.

"Excuse him. He didn't like the socks he got for his birthday. Don't worry, we've got him. Here's a tip. Let's forget about this." It was Eddie's voice, and then Eddie's hand on his shoulder.

"You can't *drive*. You've been drinking," Neil said.

"Yes, but Rachel hasn't. Let's get you back to your hotel. Who knows, maybe Chelsea will be there and we'll get to the bottom of this mess."

Neil didn't bother hoping. His lack of faith was rewarded, in a way, when he walked into their suite, where they had shared meals and made love only the day before. All her belongings were gone. There was no note.

"Just call her," Rachel told him, handing him a phone already ringing.

"Hello?" Chelsea's voice came over the line, wary and defensive. Behind her, Neil could hear the sounds of an airport. She was running fast.

"Chelsea," Neil said, but faltered.

"Neil, she told me everything. How could you even bring me here? I am so humiliated. She was so humiliated. I can't be with someone like you. I can't trust you."

"So you just took her word for it all? You won't give me a chance to explain? You just took the money and ran?"

"Money?" Chelsea repeated in disbelief. "It was never about money, Neil. Never."

"Then why didn't you tell me you lost your job?" Neil interrupted her.

She was silent for a moment. "I was going to tell you after the trip. I didn't want to spoil things." Her voice was embarrassed.

"You still didn't trust me, did you?"

"Should I have, with what you did? With who you are? With her? I can't be what you're looking for. Go back to Florence. She loves you and needs you." Chelsea hung up.

Neil threw the phone on the bed and sank into a chair. He saw Rachel and Eddie trade glances, but he was too drained, too hurt to read it. "Aren't you going to crow about being right? Where are the lectures for your stupid friend with more dollars than sense? Just leave me alone. I want to be alone."

The door closed quietly behind them, and Neil fell deep

into himself, trying to wall his heart off from the tidal waves of pain assaulting it, an endless and fruitless task. This was the pain he had tried to spare himself all along, the pain of a broken heart, the pain of offering himself up to someone with openness and trust and love, and being betrayed.

I should have known better, he repeated to himself until he fell asleep. *I should have known better.*

32

———

"Chelsea, wake up!"

There was a hammering on her door. Chelsea groaned as she shifted in her bed, peeking through mostly shut eyes at the gloriously sunny day outside. The sun was momentarily blocked by someone standing outside her window.

"Oi! Lazybones! Up!" shouted Tony, hammering on the window.

They're never going to go away. Chelsea lurched out of bed. It was too hot and humid to throw on a dressing gown. She opened the door. Kim, Delta, and Tony filed in. Kim had a bowl of strawberries, while the others had bacon and eggs.

"It's too hot for a dressing gown," Chelsea informed them. "You'll have to cope with my nightie."

"If you're going to be showing those legs off, we need to get you out for a tan," Kim told her.

"Lay off it." Delta swatted at Kim. "Patriarchal rubbish, that is. You can show off your legs however you like, Chelsea. Don't listen to her. You don't need skin cancer to prove your looks!"

Kim stuck her tongue out. "I'm just trying to get her out of the house. She's been in here for weeks. Missed Christmas. Missed New Year's. And now she's missing prime beach season."

Kim wasn't wrong. Chelsea had arrived home on the first flight she could get out of San Francisco after the horrific revelations on that rain-swept patio. Her friends collected her from the airport and sat with her as she cried for hours, dragging the story out of her piece by piece. Since then, she'd stayed in her house, stayed offline, and didn't pick up her phone. She knew her friends were worried, and she knew her behaviour wasn't healthy. It didn't matter to her. She was consumed by abject shame and embarrassment.

"And I'm staying in here," Chelsea told them, sitting down on her couch. "I don't want to go out."

"That's why we're here. You can get reacquainted with society through us. Tony is making us breakfast. It's like a feminist utopia. And you'd starve if we didn't bring you food. Honestly, girl, you're worrying us."

Chelsea managed a weak smile as Tony shouted something back from the kitchen, and her friends' banter continued. When they were around, the noise of their friendship managed to mask the awful feelings and thoughts that crowded her head constantly.

"Come on, Chels," Kim said, noticing Chelsea withdraw from the conversation. "You couldn't have known. No one thinks anything bad about you. He's the rat."

"Have you heard from him at all since that night?" Tony shouted from the kitchen over the sound of bacon frying.

"No, and I'm happy with that," Chelsea said. "I don't want to talk to him."

"Not even to give him a piece of your mind? Tell him what a scumbag he is?" Delta sat on the floor with her legs stretched out in front of her. It looked like she was doing gentle stretching exercises on the damaged leg.

"No. I just want to forget this ever happened. I can't believe what a fool I was."

"Sweets, what were you supposed to think? He was pursuing you. You can't be expected to do a background check on everyone you meet."

"Yeah, but all the warning signs were there. He was a Honey client, for God's sake. Look at his brother! And even his brother warned him to remember... remember his wife." She pushed the words out of her mouth with difficulty.

"It's also not expected to eavesdrop on conversations," Kim pointed out. She shoved the bowl of strawberries at Chelsea. "Come on. We've let you cry yourself to sleep for two weeks. We need to get you dressed and out into the world. You're unemployed, remember? You're going to run out of money eventually, and you don't have a sugar daddy anymore."

Chelsea glared at Kim. "Why don't you give me a papercut and pour lemon juice on it while you're here."

"I'm just trying to normalise what happened," Kim said, taking a strawberry for herself.

"You're an idiot," Delta informed her. "Hey, Chels, I heard from Neil the same night you left San Francisco. He was asking me if you'd lost your job."

"What was he asking you about that for?" Chelsea shifted uncomfortably in her seat, looking at Delta.

"Seemed like he'd heard about it. It was a text message, so it was hard to read the tone, but he seemed a bit miffed you hadn't told him." Delta shrugged. "I didn't mention it before, but I've been thinking, and it seems like a weird message. Where would he have heard from?"

"What did you tell him?"

"I told him yeah, but to talk to you." Delta was not intimidated by Chelsea's glower. "Don't look at me like that. I told you you should have told him."

"It ended up being pretty moot, in fairness," Kim said.

Chelsea just shrugged and flopped down onto the couch, burying her face in a cushion.

"I just don't want to exist right now. I wish the ground would just swallow me up. I really, really cared about him. I thought... I thought maybe he was different."

"Look, Chels, I realise this might be not what you want to hear—ow, quit hitting me, Kim. I'm not going to drop it. Stop it. But, Chels, I've done a bit of research. I can't find any evidence that Neil was married. Are you sure that the woman you talked to was on the level?"

"What are you taking his side for?" Chelsea sat up, furious. She got up and stomped to her room, returning with the files and the USB drive that Florence had given her. She threw them at Delta. "Here you go. Research this, if you're so fired up to get all Sherlock Holmes on me. There are the emails and the bank records, go crazy. As much as I'd like to think that maybe there's some misunderstanding, you weren't there. You didn't see the look she gave me. She looked like a woman whose partner had been cheating. There was hurt and anger and sort of embarrassment. She really hated me."

"You don't have to be married to someone to hate a guy for sleeping with someone else," Kim said.

"I thought you were on my side," Chelsea said.

"We're all on your side, doll. We're just, well, just as surprised as you, that's all. Have a strawberry." Chelsea obeyed. "And Tony's almost done with the bacon and eggs. Then we're going for a walk. You'll see that you're not branded as some sort of scarlet woman, and the general population won't bother you."

"Then what?" Chelsea said.

"Well, you're going to do something useful, like make angry art or apply for jobs. You can't wallow in this forever, sweets. The world goes on. It's not like you to get knocked down for so long. We're worried."

"I don't need to apply for jobs," Chelsea informed them. "I'm going to work for my aunt."

Everyone squawked in surprise, Kim briefly choking on a strawberry she had inhaled.

"Chelsea, is this some kind of masochistic self-flagellation? It's dumb, that's what it is."

"I'm pretty stuck for options, guys. It's a guaranteed job, and she's still threatening to sell my mother's art. Maybe if I'm around more and do some work, she'll relent."

"Chels, you don't need her approval, and you're never going to get it."

Chelsea silently ate more strawberries. She felt her friends exchange looks above her head. She knew it didn't make sense to them, but she had tried doing the opposite of everything, going her own way, trying her own thing. She took risks. It was just time to give the devil her due.

At the end of breakfast, Chelsea did feel slightly better, better enough to allow her friends to bully her into wearing clothes and take her for a drive to the beach. At the end of the day, as Chelsea wandered back to bed, she noticed Delta had taken the files with her.

I guess she really does mean to do some research. She couldn't fathom why; her best guess was that she felt some lingering loyalty to Neil after he helped her down when she was stuck. They just didn't understand how foolish she felt.

And that deep down, underneath the anger and embarrassment, there was something worse: longing. She missed Neil. And she didn't want to.

Leave it alone, woman. It's over. Let him go. He's got his wife, and who knows how many other bed warmers around the globe. I was just a bit of fun, a challenge, and I didn't see it.

It was a blustery, grey day in San Francisco. Cold, but as dry as ever. Neil navigated his way through his umpteenth meeting for the day. With great energy, he handed out piles of papers, set up follow-up meetings, deadlines, and timelines, then sent everyone on their way with their heads reeling. Heading back to his well-appointed office, he updated his planner, both paper and electronic, before he took a look at the day's schedule. He had another appointment in fifteen minutes to discuss a new venture. Excellent. New ventures took up a lot of time and energy. Rachel was involved with this one. He always liked working with her.

Fifteen minutes was just enough time to eat a sandwich. As he reached for the desk phone to call his PA, it rang before his hand touched the receiver.

"Mr O'Connell, your brother, Edward, is on the line. Will you take his call?" Marlene inquired with cool professionalism.

"My brother?" Neil glanced at the computer clock. "Yes, fine, all right."

"Kia ora, bro!" Eddie enthused down the line in the most atrocious imitation of the Kiwi accent that Neil had ever heard.

Neil sighed. "What can I do for you, Eddie? I have fifteen

minutes until my next appointment, and I have to find time to eat."

"Marlene told me this was your only free spot. You're harder to get hold of than the president. Anyway, I'm going to need you to come back to New Zealand."

"I don't think I will be doing that," Neil said, his voice expressionless, even as his heart began to hammer in his chest. Even the thought of returning to New Zealand filled him with anger and panic. The feelings of hurt that he kept hidden under mountains of work threatened to erupt to the surface. "I'm very busy, Eddie. I have several new projects—"

"I know, I know, you're doing your best to not think about things and pretend you haven't had your heart ripped out of your chest and stomped on. But look, I'm winding things up here, and I need you back here to sort some things out."

"No."

"Don't start having kittens over whether we'll see Chelsea. We run in very different circles to her. There's going to be no parties, no women, no mayhem. I'll be as sober as a judge; I swear on my dashing good looks and my expensive sports cars." Neil didn't say anything. "Neil, you can't just leave the country every time you get your heart broken. Besides, I promise you, coming here is going to be worthwhile. And the weather's nice."

"No," Neil said flatly. "Goodbye."

When he hung up the phone, his hands were shaking. It was going to be fine, he told himself. He just had to get over this, just like he got over having his heart broken by Florence, over and over again. There was nothing to it. Just had to keep busy.

In his next meeting, Neil thought about New Zealand

and Chelsea. When one of his executives asked him a question, Neil realised he hadn't been listening for almost twenty minutes. Abruptly, he ended the meeting.

"Marlene, cancel the rest of my meetings," he told his PA. "I'm going to go to the gym until I pass out."

33

———

It was two days later that Rachel invited him over for a late-night briefing. "One of the New Zealand projects has had some strange developments. I'm going to need you to go over it with me."

Neil looked out his window, shutting his eyes as his vision swam. Nearly sixteen hours a day of looking at spreadsheets was taking a toll on him. He had headaches. Not enough sleep? Not enough water? He almost looked forward to the day he collapsed.

"Eddie's taking care of the New Zealand business. Can't you go over it with him?" Neil said. His voice was as close to pleading as it got.

"I've gotten everything I can out of Eddie on this matter, and I need *your* expertise."

This wasn't going to go away without his intervention, Neil realised. That was how he came to be trudging up Rachel's front drive with a case full of papers and a notebook computer with a dead battery. *Crappy technology,* he thought angrily to himself as he stomped up her stairs to the house. How could the battery be dead? He had only turned it on... well, in the morning. How badly was he losing track of time, he wondered.

Rachel opened the door and ushered him in. In her most comfortable lounge, he smelled the aroma of freshly brewed coffee and was stopped dead at the sight of two extra faces sitting in the room.

"Eddie," Neil said, disbelievingly. Even more disbelievingly, he looked at the woman who accompanied him. "Delta," he said. "This is certainly a surprise."

"Don't be mad," Rachel told him as she took the notebook computer from his hands, along with the papers he'd been carting around. She gently piloted him to a seat.

"How on earth can you tell what he's feeling?" Neil heard Delta mutter to Eddie. Eddie waved his hands and shushed her. Delta gave him a poisonous look.

"What do you mean, don't be mad?" Neil started, rage seeping into his voice. "What conspiracy are the three of you cooking up?"

"Neil, look at me," Rachel said, crouching beside his seat to be eye level with him. He looked at her. "I'm your best friend, aren't I? Yes, that's right, I am. And part of that is sometimes lying to a friend if he's being too stubborn and self-destructive."

"She means you're being an asshole," Eddie added helpfully. Rachel shot him a look. "I'm his brother. It's part of *my* job to be brutally honest with him."

"Neil, we have some things you need to hear, sometime before you kill yourself with exhaustion or decide to go live in Iceland to get away from your romantic problems." She handed him a coffee. "Just trust me and Eddie. If, after you've heard what we have to say, you still think we're full of it, you can yell at us and storm out."

"You want to talk about her, don't you?" Neil said. The

inflection made it clear enough who he was talking about. His chest felt tight. His heart was doing that hammering thing it liked to do when he thought too hard about Chelsea and the hole she had left in his life. And the shame. The deep shame that Florence had told another woman what he was like, and she had sided with Florence.

"Yes," Rachel said, squeezing his hand briefly before resuming her seat next to Eddie. Neil was aware Delta was eyeing him warily. In between his own extreme discomfort, he could tell she was uncomfortable too, but her chin jutted out stubbornly, and she glanced at Eddie for her cues.

"I went back to live at your place when I went back to Auckland. I'd been there a few weeks when Delta turned up on my doorstep, looking for you. She had a bunch of papers." Eddie jerked his head at Delta.

"You could just say, 'Please give my brother the papers,' you know," Delta snapped at Eddie and passed a folder to Neil. Neil took it, with half an eye still on Delta and Eddie. Whatever this was, it must be important enough for them to put up with each other. They obviously didn't get along. Flicking the folder open, he saw a bunch of emails between himself and Helen Blake and some hefty financial payments.

"I don't understand. I didn't write these emails."

"You didn't?" Delta asked, leaning forwards intently. Neil was shaking his head as he skimmed them.

"This is insane," Neil said, looking up. "According to these, I'm paying Helen to promote Chelsea?" He flicked the pages. "Oh, and then to fire her? Where the hell did these come from?"

"Are you sure?" Delta asked. Her voice was dangerous. "Look at the payments from your bank account."

Neil bristled at her tone but looked at the other pages in

the folder. "That's my account, yes, but I don't keep track of everything that goes out of there. My accountant does." He looked between the three of them. "What are these?" he demanded.

"Remember when you messaged me asking if Chelsea had lost her job? Didn't tally up with what she said was in these documents. Or maybe I didn't want to think you were that much of a scumbag. So I went to talk to you. Got Eddie instead."

"Tell him who she got these from," Eddie interrupted.

"I'm getting to that. She got these from a woman called Florence. She said she was your wife. She gave these papers to Chelsea."

Neil felt the world stop around him. Delta's words echoed in his head.

"But she's not my wife," Neil said. "And these are a lie."

"That's exactly it. I'm glad you're catching on," Eddie said. "So, this is embarrassing but, as it turns out, incredibly useful. When you and Chelsea... well, when you told me about Chelsea, I hired a private investigator to follow her around."

"You did *what*?" Neil nearly shouted.

"I know, I know, but look on the bright side: as a lucky side effect of my brotherly meddling, I happen to have detailed documentation of the entire time you two were seeing each other." Eddie smiled brightly. "I talked to my man, and he categorically said there was no evidence she was seeing anyone else. None. He had all her movements documented." He passed a sheaf of papers to Neil. They appeared to be daily reports of Chelsea's movements. Neil flicked through them. He stopped at the report of the day they were on Rangitoto.

"This is how you knew we'd missed the ferry."

"Yep. See? Lucky thing. Anyway," Eddie rushed on, "after Delta comes to me with her bits of paper and we compare notes, I put the PI onto doing some research for me. Turns out Honey had been sold. They'd been in bad financial trouble for a while, and only became liquid again when the mystery payments from 'you' started turning up. But they were sold only a few days before Chelsea was fired."

"Who bought it?" Neil asked. He had the dreadful feeling he knew the answer already.

"A shell company that led back to one of the companies that you and Florence co-owned a while back. Your name was still on the accounts. So that's where 'your' payments came from. Then me, Delta, and my PI went to pay a visit to this harridan that was taking payments from 'you' to do things to Chelsea's job. She was clearing out her desk and quite drunk, so very talkative."

"She felt quite rotten about the whole thing, in a way," Delta interjected at this point. "Eddie and the PI showed her the emails, and she did believe they were from you. She thought it was because of how you two met. Helen was only in it for the money, which Florence seems to have plenty of."

"Thanks to Neil being a sap," Eddie added. Rachel and Delta both elbowed him. He looked aggrieved.

"Florence went to all this effort to wreck us?" Neil said. It seemed now like the inescapable truth, with Florence's fingerprints all over it. "But she hasn't even tried to get back together with me."

"Are you sure she's not your wife?" Delta asked, even as Eddie tried to hush her. "Stop it. This is important. This is really important."

"She's not my wife. We were together for so long, I suppose she considered herself that." Neil paused. Unwanted memories flashed through his mind. "I tried leaving her a few times, but she always found a way to get me to go back. I felt responsible for her pain. I told her a year ago it was over for good. I hadn't seen her since, except when she puts herself in my path. It's why I went to New Zealand. To get away from her. I didn't think she would follow me there."

"Chelsea was the first serious relationship you've considered since you split up with Florence," Rachel said gently. "I think she wanted to make you, and the woman with the audacity to go near what she still considers her territory, hurt."

"She lied to you about Chels." Delta leaned forwards again. "She doesn't have some string of rich ex-boyfriends. She didn't have men on the go from Honey. She was posting messages like that because 'you' promoted her to that job. She didn't get a giant cash injection from Florence. She got enough to fly home and abandon you. That's it. Eddie's PI confirmed that too."

Neil covered his face. His first proper relationship since the mess that was him and Florence, and Florence had destroyed it.

"We figured out how she even got wind of your involvement with Honey," Rachel jumped in. "It was your driver in New Zealand. Florence knew you'd hire a driver; after all, she knows your weaknesses pretty well. It was just a matter of finding out who it was. He was easily bought. Once she suspected Chelsea of being involved with you, she put a bunch of spyware on Chelsea's work computer."

"Ringside seats for your whole relationship, since Chelsea spent half her workday talking about you and all her angst to Delta on instant messenger," Eddie said.

The three of them looked at him, obviously waiting for

some kind of reaction to their well-intentioned detective work.

"What do you want me to say? That I'm an absolute idiot?" Neil asked them. "I promised myself this wouldn't happen, and it did. This is why I didn't want to fall in love. I can't do it. I have lost so many years of my life to Florence and her manipulation, and now I've fallen straight back into her trap and she's torn up a relationship where I was actually happy with someone who actually cared because she can't let go."

Neil could not share any more of his thoughts; his voice had grown too thick with unshed tears. Anger and helplessness raced through him as he thought of a grieving Chelsea, who thought he had betrayed her. Who believed that all her worst fears had been made real.

"Love is messy," Delta said. "Love is risk. Are you going to sort it out with Chels? Because I think you're an idiot if you don't."

"Is that all Florence told her?" Neil waved at the papers. "There was nothing else?"

Delta frowned at him. "That and that she was your wife. Why?"

Neil didn't answer; he just bowed his head. Relief and trepidation warred inside him. Relief that she hated him over lies. Fear that she would still hate him if she learned about the smoking wreckage of his relationship with Florence.

"Florence's hobby is to make Neil believe he's a jerk," Eddie explained to Delta. "She made him think he's responsible for the accident that hurt her spine."

"Why would she do that?"

"He was driving. But it was an accident. She then used it to make him stay with her for another three years."

"That's *enough*, Eddie," Neil ground out through clenched jaws.

"You need to tell Chelsea," Delta said. "She's the only one who can decide if she wants to be with you. Give her the truth. The whole truth. Florence can't destroy you if you have no fear."

"Could Chelsea forgive me for not warning her about Florence?"

"Can you forgive her for believing the worst about you?" Delta asked.

Neil bowed his head. "I can. I want us to start again. To try to trust each other."

"Don't let it get you down, Neil. You were conned by a master who has no life outside of figuring out how to screw you over. And she has almost a decade of experience in playing you like a fiddle." Eddie hastily shut up when he saw the look on Neil's face. "By which I mean that's a great idea, trust. Let's hear it for trust." He leapt to his feet and clapped his hands jovially. "Four tickets to Auckland, New Zealand, then?"

34

———

"I'm sorry, dear, there's nothing I can do at the moment," Marion Vines told Chelsea. "The dealer insists they have a very high-value tender and aren't looking at other offers at the moment. I just don't have the resources to find out who the high-value tender is from. I'm going to keep doing my best, but I'm sorry to say it looks like we may not find out who has purchased your mother's art."

Chelsea squeezed her eyes shut. Tears pricked at her lids.

"Thanks, Marian. Thanks a million. I can't tell you how much I appreciate you trying to help me."

"I only wish I had better news for you. Take care, dear."

Chelsea ended the call and leaned against the wall. It was a grey, miserable day, sticky with humidity. A regular Auckland summer's day. It made her think briefly of Rangitoto, but she pushed the thought away.

She'd had no luck finding out who was buying her mother's art, or even how much to counterbid—if she could have even found the money.

Which was why she was here, outside her aunt's bed

and breakfast. About to do what her aunt wanted and join the family business. It was her only chance to try and change Esme's course of action. Working at a bed and breakfast wasn't a terrible prospect by itself, no worse than reception work at Honey. But the constant fear of incurring Esme's wrath and endless guilt trips made the prospect difficult to stomach. Still, maybe her aunt's toxic behaviour would distract her from the aching wound left by Neil.

Squaring her shoulders, she walked into the air-conditioned front room where Mikaela was typing at the computer.

"Hi, Mikaela," Chelsea said, forcing a smile.

Mikaela looked up, surprised, fingers freezing over the keyboard. "What are you doing here?"

"Is Esme around? I'm here to join the family business at last."

Her phone rang unexpectedly. Chelsea flushed and fumbled in her pocket, pulling it out. It was Delta. She pressed the button to cancel the call and looked back at Mikaela.

Her cousin was shaking her head.

"What the hell are you doing that for?" Mikaela asked. "You *got out*. You got away from her. Don't walk right back in!" She walked out from behind the counter, strode over to Chelsea, and grabbed her upper arm. With her talon-like nails digging into Chelsea's arm, she began to wrangle her out the door.

"Ow, quit it, Mikaela. What's gotten into you?" Chelsea had no idea what mood had possessed her cousin this time.

"Saving your stupid butt from the biggest mistake you'll ever make."

"You're the reason I'm here in the first place. If you

hadn't told your mum that I ruined your life, she wouldn't have sold my mum's art!"

In her hand, her phone was chiming incessantly. Chelsea moved to mute it and caught sight of a slew of missed calls and messages from Delta.

Delta: Where are you????

Delta: You've moped at home for nearly a month and now that I need you to be home you're OUT??? Call me now

Delta: Call me noooooooowwwwwwwwww

Delta: CALL ME CALL ME CALL ME CALL ME CALL ME CALL ME

Just then the phone rang again, and Chelsea answered.

"Delta, leave me alone. I'm in the middle of something."

"Don't hang up! Chels, I've spent two twelve-hour flights sitting next to Eddie bloody O'Connell. I am jet-lagged eighteen ways to Sunday, so do not hang up. You have to hear this. She wasn't his wife. Those weren't his emails." Delta's voice blared over the phone. Mikaela watched Chelsea with the gaze of a hawk.

"What?"

"Neil. Florence wasn't his wife. Those weren't his emails. She's an ex, Chels, an ex with a world of letting-go issues. She went and told him that you were cruising for cash and she paid you off and all kinds of other garbage."

"He's not married?" Was this a dream? One of those dreams you got after something terrible happened, where you thought the bad thing wasn't real, only to be crushingly disappointed upon waking? The tantalising fantasy hung in front of her: Neil wasn't married. Neil wasn't lying. Neil loved her.

"No! Never has been! Me and Eddie and Rachel got to the bottom of it all. Chels, he loves you, and he's come back. He wants to see you."

"I don't know... When? Where?"

"Moneybags wants to see you on top of Mount bloody Ruapehu. He said you'd understand. Said he couldn't get White Island on short notice."

Mount Ruapehu. A reasonably active volcano in the centre of New Zealand's north island, most of the time a benign giant covered with snow and ski slopes. Once a decade, it threw ash, gas, and boiling water into the air. For most New Zealanders, it was no big deal.

"Is he mad? That's his worst nightmare."

"Nah, Chels, he said his worst nightmare wasn't being on the mountain. It was being on that mountain without you. Romantic, right?"

Mikaela ripped the phone from Chelsea's hand.

"When and where does she need to be?" Mikaela asked. "A helipad? How am I supposed to know where those are? We're just south of Warkworth. Okay. She'll be there." Mikaela ended the call and handed the phone back to Chelsea. "Come on, Chelsea. You've got a date."

Chelsea stared as Mikaela dug keys from her pocket and started heading towards a red station wagon.

"Are you coming?" she asked.

Chelsea hurried after her. "Esme is going to kill us," she said as they climbed into the station wagon.

"She's not going to be happy no matter what we do, so might as well do what we want, right? Isn't that your philosophy?" Mikaela sighed. "You shouldn't be here, Chelsea. Not because you've given up on life. Not because I screwed up big time. If you want to be around our family, I want you to be here because you want to be. If Mum keeps bullying you to be here, you'll just hate us more, and our family is too small for that to happen. You're like my sister, Chelsea."

Mikaela concentrated on a particularly tricky intersection before continuing. "You didn't sell me out to Mum when you could have to deflect her anger. You didn't tell her about Stacey or why I'm not dating men. You didn't even try to blackmail me. You said you'd help me find a wife. I didn't think anyone in my family would react like that. I've been doing a lot of work with my therapist, you know. I love my mum, but she's toxic sometimes. And I'm learning how to manage that. And it's my stupid fault Mum's selling Vicky's art. I'm trying to fix that, but right now, this is what I can do for you. I want you to get to this helipad and to this volcano and to this man, because you deserve this chance. For what it's worth," she added after a moment of consideration, "Mum would never turn you out. You're the only connection she has to her sister. And as rubbish as she is at showing it, she still misses Aunt Vicky something awful."

"Mikaela, I don't know what to say," Chelsea started. She didn't recognise her cousin. "I don't know how to thank you."

"I'm no good at being thanked. Super awkward." They pulled into the carpark at the helipad. A helicopter was revving up, and someone was running over to meet them. Mikaela looked at Chelsea and smiled, a wide self-deprecating smile that could have been Chelsea's own. "How about we try to be friends, as well as family?"

"You got it, cuz," Chelsea said, her eyes blurring slightly. "Thank you."

"Any time."

During the entire helicopter flight, Chelsea's heart hammered in her chest. She was flooded by adrenaline that had nothing to do with the helicopter or the rendezvous point, and everything to do with the pain she was risking in meeting with Neil.

She could not imagine how it could be true that what happened in San Francisco was a bizarre contrivance, but she wanted to know for sure.

Please, let this not be a mistake, she beseeched the universe as the helicopter landed on a plateau on the side of the mountain. She unbuckled her safety harness and pulled off her helmet, then all but tumbled out onto the grey ground covered in scoria. The crater of the mountain loomed some way away, looking for all the world like a desolate and barren stretch of rock. The mountain had been quiet for years. Here was the top of the road, a desolate semi-flat patch of barren grey land, utterly featureless except for the lone figure of Neil.

"You look like a wreck," Chelsea found herself saying. It was true. He was pale and sweating, and there were dark circles under his eyes. "The volcano's freaking you out. We should've just gotten coffee, honestly."

Behind them, the helicopter lifted off, heading to Taupo to refuel.

"It's not the volcano," Neil replied. "It's the thought that we might not fix this."

Chelsea's heart clenched at the pain in his voice. She wildly cast around for a less painful question to ask.

"Is it true you own Honey?"

"It turns out I technically do," Neil said with a faint smile. "It was a surprise to me too. I didn't buy it. I didn't write the emails. But I do co-own the corporation that bought Honey. Florence is the other owner." Neil took a deep breath and a step towards Chelsea. "I'm sorry I didn't tell you about Florence. I should have done so, so you could understand who she was and why she means me ill. Why she means you ill."

"Delta told me that Florence wasn't your wife. Is that true?"

"She is not my wife. She was never my wife. She was my partner for almost ten years, though the final three years—" He took a deep breath. "—were simply one of the worst times of my life."

"One of the worst times of your life? Is that what I am to you?"

Neil was interrupted by a woman's voice. Chelsea didn't need to recognise the voice to know who it was. The sudden stiffening of Neil's whole body was enough to tell her. They both turned to see Florence clambering out of an all-terrain vehicle. She breathed heavily, and there was something unstable in the way she gritted her teeth under a smile and limped towards them determinedly, leaning heavily on her crutch.

"What the hell are you doing here?" Neil demanded. "This doesn't concern you. Turn around and go home."

"You lied to me!" Chelsea shouted. She was so angry at the slight blonde woman she could hardly see straight.

Because suddenly it was clear. Neil's and Delta's words against this stranger's. Delta would not lie to her. And, she now understood, neither would Neil. The pain and humiliation fell away, and there was a fierce surge of rightness inside her. Neil had told her the truth. He loved her.

Chelsea covered the distance between her and Neil in a few seconds and looped her arm around his, squared her shoulders, and faced Florence.

Florence stopped ten metres away, swaying in the heavy wind. "I was trying to warn you, Chelsea. I was trying to save you from this fickle bastard."

"Florence, that's not true." Neil's voice cracked with emotion. "I stayed with you for years and years. Even after I shouldn't have. Even after I stopped loving you. I should have left sooner, but you refused to let me go."

"Did you tell her what you did to me? Did you tell her you ruined my life? That after what you did, the very least you could have done was love me and be with me?"

Neil dropped his arm from around Chelsea's and turned away. "Neil?" she whispered.

"He doesn't want to be reminded! That's why he left, because he's a gutless snake." Florence's voice was raw with rage and hurt. "He left me because he doesn't want to remember. He doesn't want to do what's right."

"For God's sake, Florence!" Neil shouted. He too sounded pained. "Haven't you punished me enough? I would do anything to undo the accident. *Anything.*"

"But you won't stay with me!" she sobbed.

Chelsea looked at Neil, who gazed at the rocky ground. His body language was ashamed and defensive. Chelsea's mind reeled with horror as she tried to imagine what could have happened.

"What did you do? What happened, Neil?" She gave his shoulder a gentle shake. "I want to hear it from you, not from her."

"There was a car accident," he whispered, eyes shut. "I was fine. It damaged her spine. We were arguing. We had a fight at a party. It was one fight of many. We were angry with each other. We were heading home. We were breaking up. In the car, I was telling her it was over, that I wasn't happy anymore. She didn't want me to go. She wanted to keep me. I was driving, but I was distracted. There was an accident."

"Speak up!" Florence shouted. "I want to make sure you're telling the truth! It was your fault we crashed. You weren't paying attention to the road. You were busy yelling at me. You were angry with me, weren't you, Neil? You know that deep down you wanted the crash. You wanted it to kill me or to hurt me. To be rid of me."

Neil ignored her and continued his own quiet narrative to Chelsea. "She was injured. I had bruises and a fracture. Her spine was hurt. She was in so much pain. I couldn't leave her. I stayed with her for years after, because every time I tried to bring up leaving, she would remind me she needed me. She'd remind me of what I'd done. She always wanted me to think it was deliberate. That I was trying to kill us both because I was unhappy. I used to worry she was right. That maybe subconsciously I was trying to hurt her."

Chelsea gripped both of Neil's hands in her own.

"I'd give anything for that accident to not have happened," Neil said. "I wish I had waited to start the argument at home. I wish we weren't angry with each other in the first place. I wish... I wish I had died and that she was unharmed."

"But it didn't happen that way," Florence interrupted. "And you won't stay with me. Your love will make everything all right, Neil. Leave this candy-haired harridan and come home with me." She had come over to them. Her free hand gripped his lower arm.

Neil looked between them.

"I just want you to let me go," he told Florence.

"It's you that needs to let go, Neil," Chelsea said, tears coming to her eyes. "You're letting her hold on to you with this lie she's fed you. You don't need her permission or her forgiveness to move on. But you need to forgive yourself." Chelsea dropped Neil's hands and walked away, giving him and Florence space. Whatever he needed to do to put the nail in the coffin of that relationship, he had to do it without her. She stood by a sheer drop, the beautiful vista marred by unshed tears.

Neil remained with Florence. He suddenly understood what Chelsea meant. What he had to do. He looked down into Florence's face. He was still a slave to its whims. He hadn't been free; he had been a prisoner on the run.

"Emotional extortion is not the same as love, Florence," Neil told her, taking her hand off his arm. "You can't make me love you. You can only make us both miserable."

Florence was shaking her head.

"No. If you do not come back, I will never let you be at peace. I found you here, didn't I? I can find you anywhere. If I am unhappy, you will be unhappy. It's as simple as that."

She turned and loped away with her uneven gait. There was something about her face that frightened Neil, and the purposeful way she marched across the scoria-strewn plateau. The way her eyes were fixed on...

"Chelsea!" he shouted.

When Chelsea heard footsteps behind her, she thought it was Neil, until his panicked shout rang out behind her. Turning, even through the blur of tears, she recognised Florence's figure rushing towards her. Before she could act, Florence's foot slid out from under her, sliding on the dozens of pieces of rock. Her bad leg twisted under her, and she fell heavily, her momentum sliding her with terrifying speed towards the sheer drop. Chelsea's arm shot out and grabbed Florence's arm just as she slid over the edge. Chelsea braced her legs and leaned backwards to prevent herself from toppling after her.

Thank God she's so tiny, Chelsea thought, gasping for air, *and that there's more of me to love.*

Neil was there a heartbeat later, helping her pull Florence back over the lip and then position her on solid ground away from the edge. The other woman's face was even paler than usual, and her eyelids drooped. There was blood on her forehead, and her crutch had disappeared down the cliff. Neil couldn't seem to find any words.

"Florence!" Chelsea cried. "Florence, are you all right?"

"Just a bump. Bumped my head." She blinked at Chelsea and Neil. "You didn't let me fall."

"Of course we didn't," Chelsea said. "What do you take me for? Neil, we need to get her to a hospital. She took a knock to the head." She looked around the barren mountaintop. "Do we have any way off here?"

"My phone's not connecting," Neil said, pulling it out of his pocket. "I can't call for help, and the chopper's not due back for another half an hour."

"No reception on mine either. What is wrong with the networks in this country?" She sighed. "We'll need to get a little bit down the mountain."

"There's her car," Neil said, nodding at Florence. They both looked at her nervously, but she showed no signs of doing more than blinking at them. "But can you drive?"

"No, no I can't. Can't you?" Chelsea asked. Neil shook his head, not looking at her. "Of course you can. You said you were driving..." Pain flashed across Neil's face at those words, and suddenly Chelsea understood.

Chelsea realised she had never seen him drive, not once. There were the drivers and the taxis, but never had she seen him behind the wheel. She'd always assumed it was simply the money, that he was so rich he didn't need to drive anywhere.

"That was the last time you drove, wasn't it? When you had the accident?"

"I don't trust myself behind the wheel anymore." Neil looked up at her. "She told me, the night she lied to you, that you left because she told you about the accident. That you recognised me for the monster I am."

"Oh, Neil, no. No, no."

"Do you still want to be with me, knowing all of this? That I might have subconsciously tried to cause an accident—"

"Neil, please, don't think like that. Look at me, please, Neil. Look at me."

Neil lifted his head and turned slowly to look at her, his blue eyes on hers.

"Neil, I trust you. I trust you to take me in a car and get us to safety. I trust you to get Florence to safety and not want to hurt her, even after all this." She reached out to touch his face. "I trust you that I am safe with you in your car. But I won't make you, or care any less about you if you can't."

"You wouldn't rather wait for the helicopter?" he questioned.

"Neil," Florence mumbled. From the look on Neil's face, Chelsea knew he too had forgotten she was there. "I trust you. Please drive. I know you wouldn't hurt me."

But Neil didn't look at her. His gaze was on Chelsea alone.

"I trust you," Chelsea repeated again.

Neil nodded. "All right. Let's go."

Chelsea and Neil helped Florence over to where her car was parked in a parking bay. The keys were still in the ignition. After Florence and Chelsea were safely installed in the back seat, Neil slid into the driver seat. Chelsea could see he was shaking

---

Neil felt sick. He felt tired, wrung out, and stretched beyond any resources he had. It was bad enough that Florence had revisited the awfulness of the car accident, the event that had filled him with guilt and had bound him to her for so many years. Then there was the fright: first that she might mean to harm Chelsea, then seeing her disappear over the ledge.

Now he had to drive. Chelsea had told him that she trusted him, but he wasn't sure that she understood what she was saying. After all, she hadn't been there the night he'd messed up and landed Florence a spinal injury. For years, he had heard how he couldn't be trusted. That he had subconsciously hurt her. Neil wondered at himself, wondered if it was true. He could never forgive himself, never trust himself not to put lives in danger by getting behind the wheel of a car.

And here was Chelsea, looking at him with such calm trust. It mattered more to him than Florence imploring him.

"I trust you, Neil," Chelsea said again. "You can get us down from here. All three of us."

"For you," he whispered and turned the key in the ignition. Shaking and feeling ill, he put the car into Reverse and felt the old patterns of driving come back to him.

"You're doing great. Keep it up."

As they inched down the treacherous volcanic road, Chelsea's voice kept him calm.

After an eternity, she said, "We have reception! You did it. We can call for help." Neil parked the car and shut his eyes and shook. Chelsea's warm hand found his, and he heard her voice call the emergency services for Florence.

Florence didn't speak a single word until the ambulance arrived, not even during Chelsea's endless chatter to try and keep her awake. When the paramedics arrived, she went with them without glancing at Neil, nor beseeching for help. Neil took Chelsea's hand.

"Do you think she's letting it go, or was she just rattled by the bump to the head?" Chelsea asked as they watched her being loaded into the ambulance.

"It doesn't matter," Neil said. "I'm letting it go."

EPILOGUE

Chelsea's little flat looked packed when she came home the next day after spending the night with Neil. In truth, there were barely more than half a dozen people waiting for them with cake and drinks, all looking genuinely happy to see them.

"What's all this?" Chelsea demanded.

"A party, obviously," Tony pointed out, handing her a fancy-coloured drink with a little umbrella.

"We're so happy nobody fell off a volcano, not even the evil ex, and that you are back together. We decided to throw you a party!" Kim announced. "You *are* back together, aren't you?"

"Yes," Chelsea said, looking up at Neil and grinning. He leaned down to kiss her. "We definitely are."

The room erupted in cheers again. Rachel appeared from the kitchen carrying a cake. Somehow in the chaos, everyone ended up with drinks and a slice of cake, perched on makeshift seats around the room.

"What's the verdict on Florence?" Rachel asked.

"A concussion. They're keeping her under observation, but they say she'll be fine."

"What is it with women hurting themselves around you, Neil?" Eddie asked. Neil looked unamused.

"Eddie, I will end you if you say another stupid word, so help me," Delta told him. Eddie gave her a withering look and helped himself to another slice of cake. "You have not grown on me at all."

"Feeling's mutual," Eddie mumbled, mouth full of cake.

"Florence talked to me today," Neil announced, and the room went quiet. "She's giving up all connection with me. Financial, business, everything. I told her to have her lawyer call me when her concussion was gone. She said nearly falling off a cliff put her life in perspective. I think she'll leave me alone now."

Everyone in the room scowled with disbelief. Chelsea squeezed Neil's hand and smiled at him. They might not believe it, but she did, and more importantly, she knew Neil was well on the road to finally putting it behind him.

"Thank God," Delta said, breaking the silence.

There was a knock at the door. Neil squeezed Chelsea's hand. "I invited another guest. I hope you don't mind." With that, he went to answer the door. Mikaela walked in.

Chelsea squeezed through the packed living room to envelop her in a big hug.

"Thanks for yesterday, Mikaela."

"I couldn't have you stealing my job," Mikaela said with a shadow of a smile. She cleared her throat. "Got good news too. Your mum's art is safe, Chelsea. Mum didn't put it up for sale. She doesn't want to sell it. She actually started crying when I confronted her. Said it's all she has left of Vicky. Guess she has a heart after all. We had a talk. She agreed it's probably best you don't come work at the bed and breakfast."

"Wow, Mikaela, she's turned over a new leaf." Chelsea felt strangely touched; the picture of Esme crying over her mum was oddly affecting. *Maybe we are a family, underneath all the emotional blackmail and mind games.*

Mikaela shrugged. "I wouldn't count on it. But hey, maybe she can do a bit of growing too."

"I guess I'm looking for a new job now."

"About that," Neil said.

Chelsea looked up at him. "No, Neil. I'm getting a job. That's that."

"I know. I wanted to offer you one. As it happens, little though I had to do with it, Honey now legally belongs to me. It's in total shambles at the moment, and I wondered if someone with experience in the field might be interested in taking over." He looked at Chelsea.

She burst out laughing. "You want me to go back and work at Honey?"

"No, I'm asking you to *run* Honey."

"Neil, I am the worst at it."

"On the contrary. You were the best they had." He smiled. "With your unorthodox touch, I think you could bring something special to that company. I saw how you ran that social event. You have a gift for being genuine and social and engendering trust."

"For God's sake, I'll insult the clientele. You know that better than anyone."

"Yes, I do. And it turns out, there's no better way to make a millionaire stick than to be brutally honest with him. And besides, you can make pink hair the new mandatory dress code." Neil smiled. "Just tell me you'll think about it?"

Chelsea responded by kissing him.

"Well, this calls for a toast," Eddie said. "Let's all raise our glasses to the brilliant and good-looking Eddie who got Neil to sign up for Honey in the first place."

"Uh, how about Chelsea's amazing trio of supporters who helped her through this courtship?" Tony countered.

"The marvellous best friend who stopped the brother from ruining it all," Rachel added.

"Me for getting to the bottom of this mystery and making everyone talk to each other," Delta chimed in.

"How do you manage living in this circus without going mad?" Mikaela asked Chelsea with exasperation. "To Chelsea and Neil, the actual couple."

As the guests chorused their agreement, Neil wrapped his arms around Chelsea. She wondered how she could have ever thought he was unreadable, stolid, a suit. Trusting each other had been the greatest risk, and yet...

"I can't wait for our next adventures," Chelsea told Neil. "I don't know why everything turns into such a hot mess when I'm around. It figures that when some guy wants to tell me he loves me, someone almost falls off a cliff."

Neil laughed out loud. "You're an adventure. And loving you is the greatest adventure."

THANK YOU FOR READING!

Thanks for reading *As Sweet As Honey*. I hope you enjoyed it!

It'd be awesome if you would take a few minutes to review the book, on Amazon or Goodreads, to share your thoughts with other readers.

If you'd like to hear about new releases, specials and other bonus content, be sure to subscribe my mailing list, and never miss a happily ever after:

https://www.subscribepage.com/annakleinwrites

ABOUT THE AUTHOR

Anna Klein completed a Masters degree in English in horror literature, but now writes about sweet, geeky and slightly awkward people finding love. She loves to escape reality through books, TV, movies and roleplaying games. She believes art is the closest thing to magic in the world.

She's handy with both a sewing machine and a sword, and she lives in Auckland, New Zealand with her husband.

"As Sweet As Honey" is her second book. Turn the page to find out more about her first book, "The Modern Woman's Guide to Finding a Knight"!

THE MODERN GIRL'S GUIDE TO FINDING A KNIGHT

BY ANNA KLEIN

Connie is a dressmaker who loves to attend the local renaissance faire. Fearing that the wealthy elite she seeks as clients would snub her if they were to learn of her unusual hobby, she keeps her professional life and renaissance faire life carefully separated. However, everything begins to change when she's saved from death by Sir Justin: a rising star in the jousting tournament, and actual knight in shining armour.

Completely smitten, Sir Justin seeks her out after the faire. But out of his armour, off the jousting field and confronted with a woman he has utterly fallen for, his courage fails him and to his own horror, finds himself accidentally pretending to be his own best friend.

As the elusive Sir Justin courts her over the internet and from afar at the renaissance faire, and her friendship with Sir Justin's 'best friend' deepens, Connie fears allowing her faire life and real life to mix. Sir Justin, in turn, is faced with the most frightening challenge he can imagine: extricating himself from his lie, and winning Connie's heart as himself.

When Sir Justin takes the lead in the jousting tournament, a series of increasingly sinister events make it clear that something rotten is afoot, something that threatens not just the future of the faire, but also Sir Justin's life. Can this damsel risk her professional life and team up with unlikely allies to defend her friends, save the faire and nab the knight?

Out now on Amazon!